PART ONE

Solitary Angels

Nights Too Short to Dance
Marie-Claire Blais
Translated by Katia Grubisic

Library and Archives Canada Cataloguing in Publication

Title: Nights too short to dance / Marie-Claire Blais ; translated by Katia
    Grubisic.
Other titles: Cœur habité de mille voix. English
Names: Blais, Marie-Claire, 1939-2021, author. | Grubisic, Katia, translator.
Description: Translation of: Un cœur habité de mille voix.
Identifiers: Canadiana (print) 20230445489 | Canadiana (ebook) 20230445519 |
    ISBN 9781772603507 (softcover) | ISBN 9781772603583 (EPUB)
Classification: LCC PS8503.L33 C6413 2023 | DDC C843/.54—dc23

Originally published in French, copyright © 2021 by Les Éditions du
Boréal, as *Un coeur habité de mille voix*

Printed and bound in Canada

*Second Story Press gratefully acknowledges the support of the Ontario Arts
Council and the Canada Council for the Arts for our publishing program. We
acknowledge the financial support of the Government of Canada through the
Canada Book Fund.*

Published by
Second Story Press
20 Maud Street, Suite 401
Toronto, ON
M5V 2M5
www.secondstorypress.ca

"Like Nan Goldin, Marie-Claire Blais invented her own grammar to
capture the public struggles and private intimacies of communities that,
while close to her heart, thrived at the margins of mainstream, normative
society. Revisiting characters first introduced in 1978, *Nights Too Short
to Dance* is an impassioned call for love, justice and collective action
that, in Katia Grubisic's vibrant translation, thrums with poignancy and
urgency—a work of vast empathy amid menacing times."

—**Pasha Malla**, author of *Kill the Mall* and *The Withdrawal Method*

NIGHTS TOO SHORT TO DANCE

Translated by Katia Grubisic

MARIE-CLAIRE BLAIS

Second Story Press

For Michel, who through his courage changes the world.

Don't move, I'll lift up your pillow so you can look out the window at the falling snow, let it come, René said, let the snow bury us all, his voice high, a distant squeak, Olga, Natasha, Tania, whatever your name is, let it snow, 'tis the season, I won't be around for much longer anyway, a few nights at most, my dear girl, could you help me take off these goddamn pajamas, if I have visitors today I want to look good, I want to be elegant like in the old days, I used to play piano in cabaret clubs, bars that were mostly for women, maybe a few men now and then, rarely, I used to play waltzes there in my fine clothes, I charmed them all, Tania, I'm telling you, is snowing like Moscow, the Russian nurse said, same as Moscow, never stops, children walk back from school reciting Pushkin, and take off my dressing gown too, René ordered, where's my shirt, the bright white one, and my black jacket, the blue tie, get them from the closet, I want to dress as if I were going out, I might well get a visit from my mistresses, they might come, Olga, what mistresses, Madame, what are you talking about, don't call me Madame, René said, don't forget that I'm a man, I look like a woman, especially to you who knows everything about me, too much perhaps, you've been looking after everything my body needs, I wish I could look after myself but my arms and my legs are so weak, I can't get used to this, if God created birth, a joyful act, how could he not soften the end for his creatures, explain that to me, Olga, why did he make me a woman when I'm actually a man, what do you think, I think you are a woman in *natoor*, Olga said, you're saying it wrong, René replied, it's *nature*, I should teach you to improve your pronunciation, the misfortune of the life of my parents, Olga said, was living under dictatorship where God does not reign, so jealous are the dictators, Olga said, do you feel more comfortable, Madame René, is it time to listen to your music, great music every morning, I know, I am bringing your phone, and you will listen while the snow is falling, you'll have to read what's written on the screen, René said, my eyes are going, I can't read anymore, just yesterday I was dancing with the girls, my soul was full of joy, what else is there if we lose joy, who are you telling, Madame René, when I go home in evening to prepare dinner for my husband, the Bulgarian, he beats me because he doesn't want me to stay with you, Madame, he says bad words, like you are not the best patient, I know, leave him, my dear girl, leave him, René said, come live with me, I'll treat you well, except I won't be around much longer, oh, don't cry, I know men have a steely heart, woe to them, I wasn't one of those, I've always treated women with respect because I understand them, your husband is an ignorant man, my dear Olga, how can you live with such a man, a sadist, really, come live with me, it's just that I'm on my way out, the path of no return, how ugly it is, how horrible, I'll give you my house and all the snow outside, is it cold in here or is it my health failing a little more every hour, it is little bit cold, Olga said, I will make fire in the fireplace, it will warm up your apartment, Madame René, the water maybe was cold when I washed your face, your neck, your breasts, I don't have breasts, René said, you know that, what are you talking about, Olga, I'm built like a man, I'm sturdy, I don't have breasts, please don't talk about me like that, all I'm missing is one thing, one body part, all it took was for me to be virile in my head and a strange, rather attractive man was born, there I was, women believed in my manhood, and, I must say, they loved me, though there were abuses, on the part of the women I dated, I mean, they suspected that the manly ornament was only in my head, sometimes life is just a game, you know, I'll explain it to you one day when you've left your brutal Bulgarian, it's no life at all to be beaten by a man, a real man, and not feel ashamed, you're still a child, René said, and I feel sorry for you, so what's going on with my party clothes, Olga, can you tell me, Olga, Tania, Natasha, why God made such pitiful conditions for humankind, he just didn't think about it, it's that simple, René said, if he had given it any thought, we wouldn't even be here. Neither you nor I, not the Bulgarian who beats you, no, there would nothing, not a stone, if you think about it, that's what we do, we bring forth calamities, I'm telling you, Olga, calamities. I suppose it could be, René thought, that my Russian nurse is not Russian at all, that she's lying, that she knows neither Moscow nor Pushkin, we have no choice, we have to lie, it's all games and pretenses, so often we are mere projections, lying just means you have more imagination than everybody else, it's a mantle of glory, René thought, turning his face toward the screen his nurse held out to him so he could listen to the music, tell me what it says on the screen, I recognize the composer, Italian, right, René said, as if dazzled by the sound, yes, Madame, it is Italian *compooser*, composer, René said, *composer*, don't mumble like that, it's grating, you know I don't like it, are you really from Russia, tell me about that some other time, read me the rest, it says he died at twenty-six in abject poverty, Madame, very sad, the story of all these musicians, it is young woman who conducts this orchestra in men's clothing, evening clothes, how you like them, Madame René, she could look like you in younger way, you were certainly irresistible, the nurse said, in suits from good tailors, I was, René said, but the life of a playboy is never very long, I've dragged it out enough and look where I am now, old and dying, basically alone in the world, oh that is not true, the nurse said, I am here, and the telephone is always ringing for you, you have many friends, Madame

René, and they come from everyplace to see you and hear you because you speak to them so beautifully of music, of love, especially of love, René said, the women I've been with, I've always made them dream, we can't live without dreams otherwise everything is trivial, it's banal, I'm telling you, come, slowly, bring the phone closer, as René listened to the sublime strains of the morning's music, her body was exhausted by a constant, vicious physical ache, her limbs were on fire, inside her nothing was at peace, except her ear, ever attentive, as she listened, the music wrapped her up in softness despite her pain, it came from heaven, though heaven didn't exist, she thought, those voices together, the countertenor and contralto, sweet imperfection, the very incompleteness of that union was what made it beautiful, the masculine and the feminine wrapped together in a surprising interleaving of sounds, cries of joy and sudden deep plaint, René thought, sometimes the man had the voice of a woman, sometimes the contralto borrowed a man's voice, those sustained, subterranean sounds, René listened and her soul was exalted, she had no body at all, Madame René is listening to religious music, Olga muttered, it was boring, couldn't they put something else on, but René could only hear the countertenor and his bewitching supplication to God, there was something so carnal about it somehow that it brought tears to her eyes, she told herself she was listening to the voices of her own beloved ones, the very voices of the irreconcilable loves of all the poor humans who misunderstand each other yet who are one, who form one whole like this Pergolesi duet, the single, unified chorus of infinite disparity that this man, this woman, these virtuoso voices were expressing in their splendor. Too often the choir was a supplicant, broken and castigated the moment its members claimed their individuality, that's what had happened that June night in New York, or in the early morning, rather, as the bars were opening, or closing, young gay men still hanging around at the door and on the street as the sun came up, there were lots of young Black men and very young

Hispanic men, several white men, a whole retinue of youth was out there and that morning, that day, that night the police raided everything, everywhere, René couldn't forget the Stonewall riots, she'd been there, yes, she thought, she was everywhere there was resistance, that was her struggle too, in the Village, the night of June 28, the police said it was just a routine raid but it was violence coming right at us, they put us up against the wall and beat us, they threw us out of the bar, and that sparked our revolution, a flame that would never go out, we were going to wipe it all clean, the stigma of that year, 1969, that night in June, the police were barricaded inside the bar and outside we were armed with bricks, with whatever we could find in the street, sticks and shovels, we waited for them and when we were all out in the street together it was their turn to be shaking there inside the building, the very place they had come to persecute us, yes, it was finally their turn, we were tired of being classified as mentally ill even by intelligent doctors and psychiatrists, and all the religious prejudice too, there was no one to defend us so we had to defend ourselves, alone, in San Francisco, in Los Angeles, there was a long history already of activism to stand up for our rights, and that day, June 28, we still mark it today, that was the beginning of our freedom, that night we learned to protect ourselves, it was the start of a revolution, René thought, since that iconic day there have been marches, constant demonstrations, the world is going to change, René thought through the great sweep of the morning music, I was with Lali in New York, we were always together, little brother and I, united in the struggle, Lali was my brother, but now we only talk to each other on the phone, those struggles aren't over, now that René was listening to his music, Olga, the Russian nurse, was cleaning up the room, there is so much mess around you, Madame René, Olga was saying, you can't get better in mess like this, there are books everywhere that you can't read, more and more with time, who told you I want to get better, René shouted, who told you that, instead of marching down in the street like I used to, I used to be an activist and now here I am nailed to a bed I can't get out of, this is how the monstrous god debases the human spirit, there were so many memorial marches, it made me so happy, René thought, and I was always up ahead with the transgender crowd, I had to be there, out front, leave the mess, dear child, René commanded, her voice as masculine as the countertenor droning on from the phone, but her own voice didn't carry as well, though René had been a good singer back then, in those days of silly, provocative songs or soft romantic tunes in the bars and the cabarets, when women would dance together to the rhythm of her voice. Little brother, when will Lali come visit me, René thought, I liked you, my foreign brother, your foreign tongue, but you were still my brother, beautiful androgynous thing, I liked you, my beautiful brother in arms, always standing so straight in your military coat, in winter you would go out in just your shoes, no gloves, no hat, the wind in your short hair, your hair was as short as mine back then, or you had that shock of hair over your ears, and bangs, you always had patients to visit, I remember, I've heard you still go out to the bars in that city where they speak English and it's as cold as it is here, near the river, soon we'll hear the waves rubbing up under the ice, Lali was retired but she still saw a few people at her office, mostly young AIDS patients from working-class neighborhoods, victims of their own naïveté, AIDS was the disease of other generations and they were seventeen or eighteen, they didn't want anything or anyone to curb their freedom and above all they didn't want to hear about the past, the emaciated men and women parading in San Francisco roused neither pity nor fear, they didn't care, they didn't wear condoms, they didn't want to hear anything about it, Lali said, and she rushed to their side when it was too late, they died of pneumonia, they went blind, they had been spreading the virus around for a while, René knew how kind Lali was, she was fierce and uncompromising, she derived some happiness from those charitable acts, she was so kind with René, and there was always a bit of madness, René thought.

That was how she had lost everything with Nathalie, she hadn't taken in the girl out of kindness, a little escort in tears, just a girl battered by the men she attracted, yes, it was out of love, of course, but that word often hides a sexual despotism, at the time, when René had been courting Nathalie, she had been a master of that kind of tyranny, and Lali would tell her, look for work instead of spoiling women, René, you will get very poor, my brother, René had given Nathalie everything, yet Lali and her malaprops had it right, René thought, Nathalie's sexual wiles, that ruthless charm René was never able to conquer, what we call passion is hard to resist and it would ruin René, but she had no regrets, not yet. You, brother, a little crazy with your stories, Lali would say, when René was so lonely in her post-Nathalie weariness, she wasn't getting out of bed, lying around in a pajama top and men's long johns, and Lali wanted to shake her, you're so glum that Wolfie, Billie, and Venus haven't eaten since the morning, do you hear, they're barking, you're a bad father, René, and René was up in a flash to feed her darling dogs, I was passing by, I'll wash your hair, Lali said brusquely, impatiently, pushing Rene's head down in the sink. Brother, don't exaggerate, René said, can't you see my heart is in pieces, I'm going to fix you with cold water, Lali said, brother, it is bad, very bad, you and your women. Nathalie loved luxury, and why not, René thought, I could compete with her lovers, I gave her what she expected from rich men even though I wasn't one, but sometimes that's how you show your love, without really knowing where you're going, I loved her swathed in furs, glittering in expensive necklaces, especially when we were in Paris, in Rome, it was like a fairy tale, yes, René thought, an expensive fairy tale, my pockets were getting emptier by the day, maybe risk made the passion that much greater, the gamble was the challenge. Lali had known how to drag René out of that indolence, out of the depression during those days after Nathalie, René said, Louise had saved René with her care and tenderness, but she studied too much, René thought, she spent all her time at the university, studying music, mathematics, philosophy, she was a doctor, a professor, a philosopher, she wrote books, it was too much trouble to live with an intellectual, someone that gifted, René told Lali, brother, she's so smart it kills me, how's the sex, Lali asked, it's fine, it's always okay, René sulked, she's only ever thinking about her books, that girl, believe me. But Louise loved René, she was hurt that René would call her a giraffe, her antelope, Louise said it was insulting to be part of René's emotional zoo, there were already too many people in there, too many animals, she deserved to be called Louise, she deserved to be treated with dignity, but René had imagination and explained to Louise that when she was in love she felt like she was living in a forest with so many tender beasts, the antelope and the bee, Lali the wolf, it was a comfort, and René had to get through the heartbreak of Nathalie going off with a man, someone rich and powerful probably, oh, Christ, René swore, as she used to, why is this happening to me, I'm a connoisseur, I do know women, don't I, Louise, why? Pull yourself together, put on some fancy clothes, I'm taking you out tonight, it's been months since we've seen you out in the bars. At the end of the day, when the Russian nurse had left to make her husband dinner, Louise came by, much to René's delight, he was still bedridden and just reading for hours, it was as lovely as the great morning music she listened to on her phone, Louise's voice was pure silk, my giraffe, René said, I should have loved you better before, I was an idiot, I couldn't think about anything except Nathalie, I was wrong, what will we read tonight? This new Louise pleased René, she wasn't a student anymore but a professor, distinguished, but why was she so suspicious of Olga, she's not Russian or anything, she barely has a nursing degree, Louise said authoritatively, you shouldn't keep that girl in your house, you should be careful with her. No, no, René said, I met her on a dating site, she seemed pretty, I called her and she came, don't worry, my antelope, she's good at looking after me. I'd rather you had someone more professional around, Louise said.

Louise had warned René that she'd be late, so René, putting her phone down on the bedspread, told Olga to start reading, I know you'll make some mistakes, big mistakes, but read anyway, it's the part about Combray, you can read, Olga, I hope, the sentence begins there even though there isn't exactly a sentence but a whole book to be grasped at once, Louise would say, it goes on like that, even while I was asleep I couldn't stop thinking about what I'd read, I can't find the page, Olga said, I don't know the book you talk about, there are so many books on your bed, and you see nothing, maybe I can't see anything, René said, but you're my witness that I can hear everything, oh Madame, I don't find page or book, Olga whined, and is very boring and long, can we change, Madame, don't forget that my parents lived under *dictatoor* and we had to run away in middle of night, all right, stop, be quiet, René said, I'm going to wait for Louise to come back from her conference, give me my phone so at least I can hear those heavenly voices calling to me, you told me that the conductor in the picture, the contralto, she's a woman, yes, woman in evening dress as you like them, you have so much taste in your clothes, she can conduct the orchestra and sing, Olga said, it's a miracle, René said, in my valorous youth, when I was courting a lot, women couldn't be chemists or conductors, they had to look after their families and that's it, you are a little old, Madame, in the time of my grandparents there was nothing like that either, no, nothing in Russia or elsewhere, there have always been innovative women, René said, you don't know anything about it, perhaps your grandmother was too and you don't know, I didn't know her very well, Olga said, we had to run away at night, I was wrapped in my mother's shawl, I was afraid, Olga said, through the sublime orchestration of the voices on her phone, René heard Olga's story, was it true or was it a lie, why did Louise distrust Olga, an old man like me can't get by on mistakes and misgivings, I have believed in the honesty of women, men, what else can I do, I'll tell Louise tonight, that's how the sentence starts, a sentence so soothing I can't stop thinking about what I was reading even in my sleep, I can't stop opening the book of the past and seeing all of them again, wondering what they've become, where are they, the first hours of passion are as virulent as poison while the final hours aspire only to calm, that's what Louise gives me with her hours of reading, the calm before the end, the calm of Combray and the music of Pergolesi, then René got angry, stop cleaning the room, she told Olga, what a dreary task when your life is hanging by a thread, well it's my life, René said, not yours, stop it, I'm putting your shoes away, Madame, Olga said, it's no use, René said, I'm not going to be putting them back on again, can't you see I'm bedridden, otherwise I'd be on my feet, getting ready to go out, I've always liked going out, Nathalie on my arm, or some other girl, especially at night, starlight gleaming on the snow, we would go out together, walking, lissome, the open cabarets and bars under neon arcades, oh, that charmed life of nights too short to dance, to sing, I'm sitting at the piano and they scramble up close, I can feel the warmth of their arms around my neck, in those days I wore colorful scarves and smoked a lot while I played, I drank whisky, neat, sometimes a cigar, I played all night long, Madame, are we going to put the piano up for sale, no, René shouted from the bed, never, do you hear me, never, don't be angry, Madame, I understand, Olga said, we'll keep it for a while, that piano doesn't leave here, René said, do you hear what I'm saying to you, no, Olga said stubbornly, there is too much of your music, I cannot hear anything, this is music for liturgy, can we change, René felt like the Russian nurse was staring at her accusingly, such guilt, shame, but how could she possibly know when with her half-open eyes René now saw only shadows, fleeting shadows in the room, and Olga's shadow weighed on her, not always, she thought, only sometimes, when her immobile limbs seemed unbearable, I was so active, militant, I was everywhere, I'm still there, I'm in New York that June night as the police jeer at us, people are out in the street, facing the hostility, it was like a siege, we were all together, rekindling the flame of our revolution, where are they, where did they all go, it was a fairy tale, they wanted to break our backs with the butts of their rifles, they wanted us deposed and defeated, and that night we rose up and the resistance was born, sweeping away all the prejudice, all the slights and slander, how much injustice we faced, the music gradually got the better of René's anger, that infrangible bigotry, René thought, Lali had to fight to become a doctor, Louise had been despised in those days, long ago but still too close for René, there were often priests among the professors at the university, today they were congratulatory, they admired their strength, Lali and Louise and so many others who were suddenly in the limelight, among her friends, stars of a long and secret but tenacious fight, don't get old like the others, Louise had said, don't give in, don't get lazy, get up and walk, René, we need you, you're as lethargic as you were after Nathalie, oh, René replied sadly, it's not that anymore now, it's not Nathalie drifting over my bed, it's called contemplating the afterlife, it's something else entirely, my dear Louise, no one knows what's on the other side of the river and surely that's a bit worrisome, no? Especially if you don't know how to swim, like me, well, get ready for a quick reincarnation, my dear René, things will be better for you, you'll finally be a man, you'll have the right body parts this time, and double the conquests, will I find you again, my good friend, René asked, of course, Louise said, her voice full of compassion, we've known each other for several reincarnations, so everything had been said, written, ordained, René thought, all that was left was to leap into the beyond and relax while you waited for the next go-round, but where would René go, she sometimes felt she had lived several lives already, each one more complicated than the last, when would that triumphant return come at last, a perfect birth in a body that fit perfectly, when would that be, René thought, bring me my dog Saturn, bring him to my bed, René ordered his nurse, he is too fat, Madame, and besides he is dead, he has been dead many years, you do not remember, I still miss him, René said, and Billie, Wolfie, all consigned to eternity, how sad, open the door when you hear Countess, when she scratches at the door, Countess is so fickle, she's been away for more than a week, Olga explained, don't you think, Madame, that she might never come back, I assure you that she will, René replied quickly, and maybe, who knows, like before, with a belly full of babies, Madame, that is impossible, she is spayed, what is certain is that my Countess will come back, René said, I hope it won't be too *leet*, Madame, too *late*, I told you, pronounce your words properly, René said sternly, and believe me, I'm sure I'll see Countess again, I can feel her yellow eyes on me like a caress, after this fatal leap over and into the great beyond, after fording the frigid waters of the river on foot, I will be taken to paradise with all my pets, René thought, not that I could share such a thing with a woman who has no notion of how much love you can feel for animals, that will be my first consolation, René thought, I don't even know if there will be others, seeing them again will make up for the nothingness to come, all the dead animals of the whole planet will be there too, I'll be their shepherd, that should keep me busy enough not to start dreaming of a perfect reincarnation in a perfect body, that will do, René thought, I can't tell her anything, this woman understands nothing, nothing at all, I could have kept Louise closer, René thought, or Lali, but Louise is still teaching at the university, Lali's often at the hospital, devoted to her young AIDS patients, those kids who still don't believe in the virus, whose lives are turned upside down, their stubborn refusal to understand what era it is we're living in, so, I can feel it, the pestilential virus will increase and we'll exclaim, as if we're surprised, what's going on in public health, has another version of AIDS come back, stronger than before, Lali is right when she says we're going to find ourselves in the middle of an epidemic that will decimate humanity by the thousands, yes, what Lali fears most could happen, it would catch us completely unprepared, René thought while listening to her great morning music, nothing was more beautiful than the sky where angels sang, embodied and alive, their voices woven together just so, to please our senses, to lift our spirits, René thought as she listened to the pure, haunting voices, the music felt like the opposite of the hate crimes on the rise everywhere, there was a creeping hatred encouraged by presidents and ministers and deputies, so much discrimination, and would discrimination become legitimate or even legal again after all the progress activists had made, would homophobic attacks be normalized, accepted, we always think everything happens some-where else, not at home, but that's not true, it's at your door, it's in your town that homophobia is being sanctioned, homophobic attacks are skyrocketing, horrible, monstrous attacks are going around on social media, in her terrified immobility René would have cried, but her nearly blind eyes were dry, the absence of tears was the scariest thing, wasn't it, that lethargy, not moving, not feeling, you became insensitive to everything, hardened, it was a living death, which René would always refuse, every sense that had quivered so incredibly for so long might have fallen asleep, that paralysis made her a man stricken, a woman unfulfilled as a man, it didn't matter, he was a fighter, always fighting, suddenly she was only that unnamable, unnamed person, he, René, and the proud identity everyone had persecuted, René, yes, was fading, the fire was going out, René heard the Russian nurse saying, we will wait to sell piano, Madame René, I understand why you are attached, it is the past, isn't it, I am attached too to my past in Russia, at twelve years old I could recite a poem by Pushkin, you know he was born like me in Moscow, but I should not bother you, Madame, you are listening to your music, it is snowing a lot, I hope Countess has taken shelter, she'll be hungry, René said, we'll have to feed her, my poor little Countess, but it was Lali René was thinking of, Lali leaving Germany for Canada as soon as she was done school, the vague past she didn't talk about, she sometimes mentioned that in her parents' house, so long ago, the chimney was crumbling slowly and Lali was afraid it would collapse on her and her younger brothers, Lali was afraid the chimney would fall on her, on her face, her back, was it because of that image of a fortress tumbling down on her back, her head, her face that Lali complained of back pain, had the chimney collapsed and crushed her bones, René wondered, although they had never been lovers, they had often slept together as brothers, huddled together, Lali covering herself with her military coat, Lali couldn't drive back to the country, René said, she'd had too much to drink, and where did she pack all that beer away, René asked, laughing, she was always thin as an arrow, even when she'd had too much to drink, but René sometimes saw another side of Lali, during the night when René turned on the lamp looking for a dog or cat, Countess maybe, he could see Lali's body where the military coat slipped off, there were marks, scars on Lali's back, what were they from, René wondered, Lali didn't talk much about herself, if she mentioned the past at all she would interrupt herself with stories about her parents, that chimney spewing its sulfurous smell across the city, the hole in that chimney about to collapse, her parents' property had been seized by German authorities in 1943, René was gathering snippets of Lali's life, her parents ruined, destroyed, *lost lives*, Lali shouted from her nightmares, lost lives, lost, Lali's golden gaze and her short hair, her whole being could be completely revived by a smile, I had a bad dream, she said, but you're close to me, René, my brother, René covered Lali with the military coat, sleep well, little brother, sleep well, it was just a dream, René said, thinking that 1943 was also when Germany ordered the final deportations of German Jews to Theresienstadt, Lali was born right after all those horrors, maybe that's where that sudden gleam of fear in her golden-brown eyes came from, and her strength, René thought, Lali could survive anything, born and reborn, there was something stern about her that could seem unapproachable, a merciless righteousness, but inside Lali was the fragile ghost of a survivor, a sphinx, René thought, and she was so androgynous that if she'd been born earlier she would have been tortured and killed, a victim among the many marked by pink triangles or black ones, the undesirables, she would have been called a criminal, a deviant to be condemned, even to death, and René felt emotional around Lali, Lali who was born late enough to escape the Reich's deportation of homosexuals, she wouldn't have been spared in the rosa Winkel detentions, no one knew exactly how many victims there had been, and so many were nameless still, for a long time no one would talk about the torture they'd experienced, René often thought of the men and women in the camps whose names had been erased in the deepest darkness of human history, that sacrifice would be avenged by generations to come, René thought, by her, by René, New York and the blows raining down, fighting for her rights, rights they still didn't have, how long would that take, no, it was for him, René, yes, René thought, until the very last breath, when would we be free of what we suffered that June night in New York, the fists and nightsticks, the raids, when would the violence end? When she came to see her for a medical exam, Lali told René, you have had a small heart failure and quickly hopped to bed but you must get up, René, I will show you exercises for the arms, your legs they are numb, you are lazy like before, so lazy, René, you would live a very long time if you want, your laziness is a vice, Lali said, it will kill you, no, René replied, she would never get up again, unless Countess came back, scratching at the door, what a miraculous day that would be, her beloved Countess, her little panther, unless Nathalie came back to her, in her fur coat, the necklaces René had given her laid against her throat, unless, listen, René said, Lali, you might be able to live with such draconian rules but I can't, I've got Latin blood, and indolence is the most delectable decline, I have my music, I have my books, my antelope Louise reads to me every night, my bed is my gateway to infinity, you can't understand, Lali, you're too materialistic, you see, Louise was just as severe, she was implacable, she would say to René, oh you and your euphoria, René, listening to a cantata or the same sentence I'm reading for the hundredth time, you think that's living, brief moments of ecstasy in which you're completely passive, ecstasy is the purview of those who are alone in bed facing death and God, René was offended, although she missed other, more sensual bliss, of which she was now deprived, in the arms of all the women she had courted since she was young, he had turned so many lives upside down, a little Don Juan incognito in a sailor suit, grooming a whole crop of unhappily married women to comfort, wasn't that what love was for, a lover was an angel of peace, of fulfillment, casting a spell over slumbering senses, there was young René walking along the terraces by the river, when sailors came to town no one noticed that she was a woman, she slipped among them gracefully in her white outfit, René was so young then, she enjoyed the company of men, sailors and deckhands, anonymous male company that shielded her from their solidarity, René thought, she went to the bars with the boys and the women would flock to her, to her piano, I will sing for you, ladies, she would say, chain-smoking as she played her tedious melodies, what Louise now called her depressing songs from the thirties, those were the days, René thought, and you've got to face facts, you can't go back again, but how can you really turn your back on the past, René thought, at that time insults targeted gay men, they were called fairies and faggots, René wasn't sure what clan she belonged to, but any insult to anyone else struck her straight in the heart, homophobia was official policy back then in every federal institution, the army had strict rules and however much René dreamed of becoming a lieutenant, a leader, a military hero, an air force pilot, or else to go to school, she knew that her wavering sexuality meant exclusion, in the UK they used to punish transvestites by hanging, anyone who was deemed to have committed unnatural acts under the Articles of War, obviously now no one was hanged anymore, there were no more castrations or lobotomies or electroshock, but still any real legitimacy was withheld, by silence or by contempt, little by little, conversion therapies were being abolished in North America but if some autocrat came to power, who knows, all those punishments might be brought back, René thought, the whole legal apparatus would leap back on the bandwagon, René had had a fairly free and frivolous youth, but only because she'd lived her loves in secret for a long time, caught up in marital machinations that amused her even today, she had distracted bourgeois women bored with their absent businessman husbands with attempts at seduction laid out like courtly tributes that ended up in bed, any bed, she was a sexual nomad, it was a feverish time, René thought, with shame and repression all around her, already at eighteen, parading around on the terraces by the river, the full, joyful expression of pride at being himself, René was preparing for the revolution, which for him would start that fateful night in New York, June 28, he thought, it was just the beginning, the younger generations seemed to know nothing about René's exploits in defense of their own, but Louise told René otherwise, we are all grateful to you, Louise said, we'll all gather around you, and you'll see, but first you have to listen to Lali, you have to get up, exercise, make an effort, René, I'll help you get dressed in your most elegant clothes and you'll sit in your red velvet armchair and greet us, just like you used to, with that triumphant lightness of yours, you've got to admit you took things so lightly, René, you really behaved like a man, abandoning your friends, your mistresses, and you, especially you, my dear, my friend, I abandoned you, I left you for Nathalie, how sad, how blind I was, and above all it was a lot of male vanity, Louise said, towering and imperious, but still as loving as ever, René thought, I made mistakes along the way, like many men, René replied wistfully, though right then, with Louise watching over her, over him, René, as attentive and delicate as ever, her doe, his antelope, Louise who was so faithful, René remembered going out at night in Paris with Nathalie on his arm, late, when everyone was headed out to the bars and private clubs, everything had to be chic, with a kind of smirking aestheticism, as

Nathalie wanted, the trans kids, girls in tuxes like boys, the garments of the night, men and women, and Nathalie shining among them in her fur coat, all those necklaces around her neck, in the heavy smoke of the bars and clubs Nathalie waltzed, she danced only with René as if she were chained to him, she clung to him, pressed against René's flat chest, his starched white shirt, his suit, they were inseparable, René thought, inseparable but worldly, a slightly snobbish couple, and with a kind of taunting superiority because René was older, that's how Louise described them, light, very light, intolerably snobbish, unbearable, yes, Louise could hear René complain, shipwrecked in her bed, the girls, all the girls, whatever became of them, Johnie, Gérard, Polydor, Doudouline, l'Abeille, there were gaps, disappearances among the recently married couples, it's thanks to me that you're finally allowed to marry, René said, while you were having fun, I was in the street fighting for your rights, I was protesting, we were in the streets too, but it was a bit after you, you don't go out anymore, you've decided to live in your bed, I got old, René said, I wanted to crawl into my den, like an old wolf, and leave honorably, it's too soon, Louise said, get up, the struggle has only just begun, Johnie, Gérard, Polydor, Doudouline, l'Abeille, what happened to them, René asked, pleading in the dark, Louise thought, they couldn't let that darkness close René's eyes for good, they had to dazzle René, bring her friends around as soon as possible so that she could feel the old happiness of seeing them again, despite what René called the gaps and disappearances, they were there, very much alive, or at least most of them, and Louise was the cantor of those bygone years for René, gathered in the living room at l'Abeille's, do you remember, we waited for her until four in the morning, her real name was Marie-Christine, Christie, but we called her l'Abeille, the Bee, she was a painter, we never quite understood the mystery of her paintings and drawings, all that symbolism about the pain of being alive, she went out a lot at night, she was always jittery when there was a full moon, she would go out in her short jacket, the cowboy boots that made her a little taller, with her headphones on, she hung out in the parks, looking for Gérard under the fluffy canopy of the trees in the snow, sniffing coke, always more, she waited for Gérard, I did lines as the night closed in on me, as black as a black coat, Gérard said later, married and content, nothing like how she had been, Gérard had taken their friend's name out of loyalty, out of devotion to a friend who had died, the other Gérard had died at twenty and this one would tell the girls that she was Gérard reincarnated, Gérard gone at twenty, twenty candles on her last cake, we remembered, twenty candles celebrating a life ended too soon, like a wildflower, Louise said, and the second Gérard bloomed in her stead, she liked a sniff now and then too, later everything would change, the two Gérards were one, the old Gérard and the one today, Louise told René, who was motionless against the pillows, attentive, a little distracted by the nurse near her room, we used to hang out in the living room at l'Abeille's place, with Christie, our painter, when's your first show, we'd ask her, admiring her paintings, the black lines, her black paintings, those arcane drawings on the walls, when are you going to have your first exhibit, the paintings were the night work of a young artist, but she had already drawn and painted a lot, and Johnie would say, girls, you can't just be idle forever, you've got to produce, you've got to live, make up your minds, I'm going to be an astrologer, that'll be my career, stop daydreaming and get a move on, girls, but you can't call yourself Johnie, I told her, Johnie was the smartest of them, the most reasonable, she was born with the enlightenment of all the others, she had insight I could only describe as celestial, sure I can call myself Johnie, Johnie said, I'm a devotee of Radclyffe Hall, we can't live here together much longer, not through the winter, this damp old building is going to be torn down, we're squatting, that's what we're doing, all of us together, Doudouline who would become a great actress like her mother but who didn't know it yet, sitting on Polydor's lap, Polydor already a little drunk, before nightfall, Doudouline tilted her blond head toward Polydor's shoulder, complaining that she would never shine as brightly as her mother, my mother had already acted in tons of plays when she was my age, but you write music too, rock songs against the dictatorship in Haiti, you are our actress-activist, and a songwriter, Polydor said, my sweet, no, don't ever say that, you don't know who you are yet, Polydor murmured, and Doudouline listened, her head on Polydor's shoulder, she loved how calm Doudouline was, her gentleness, like a round planet of sensuality, of desire, we're young, Polydor said, why are we getting all worked up, we have plenty of time, Polydor said, we were so wrong, Louise said, Louise pushed the pillows up under René's head, it was irritating, she thought, that the nurse Olga was always there watching her, you could come to my house, René, I would take care of you, Louise said in René's ear, why don't you tell me the story of the girls in those days, René replied curtly, did they grow up, or were you just lolling about being eighteen years old, I was already worlds ahead of you with my experience, I was already heading out on the high seas, I seduced and conquered, though that was when they wouldn't let me into the army, René said, suddenly so tired, they didn't tell me exactly why, but it was a short walk from that to the revolution, René said, this furniture is so shabby, Johnie said, we cannot sink to the level of the ugliness of the place we're squatting in, there's so much noise on the bridge, and you bought our beds on credit, we can't demean ourselves, Johnie said, Johnie was a well-bred girl, her father would have liked her to be an architect, she was studying psychology, Louise told René, but that night we were waiting for l'Abeille, Christie, the painter, to bring home the first Gérard, when she finally came home with l'Abeille in cowboy boots, Gérard pressed her long body against Johnie, leaning her bony frame against hers, just as long, skinny Johnie, and we were all reassured, Gérard said it's freezing in here, though she was more high than cold, don't move, l'Abeille said, I'll make you some soup to warm you up, Gérard looked like she had passed out against Johnie's back, Johnie said, I will read your future in the cards, each one of you, like I called the elections by spinning my little white ball, what troubles me, Gérard, is the dark aura around you, you've got to get off the slippery, deadly slope I see in the cards, otherwise, Gérard, Gérard, please listen to me, I'm begging you, Gérard wasn't listening to Johnie, Gérard was listening to the radio, repetitive songs, as if she were still at the bar, on the dance floor, swaying half asleep on her long legs, her curly hair spilling over ice-pale cheeks, everybody knew they were fake, those names, Louise said, Doudouline, l'Abeille, Gérard, Polydor, they were just protection against the outside world, against attacks from the outside, where we would suddenly be as naked as soldiers without armor, yes, we knew, the house was our retreat, our refuge against the enemy, against the hate, yes, we understood, between us everything was allowed, the kiss and the embrace, we loved Gérard's curly eyelashes and Johnie's silence, Doudouline's tantalizing opulence, though we were worried about Polydor, she was drunk a lot, she always seemed to be sipping from the same glass of wine, ice cubes tinkling, Doudouline, her voice like a caress, saying from the living room that her poor mother had almost given birth to her onstage, she had been in a Racine play, Mama still blames me, Doudouline said to l'Abeille, who was bringing Gérard a steaming bowl of soup, and you, l'Abeille, you will be the painter of our generation, Doudouline proclaimed in her soft voice, that is what you shall be, sometimes l'Abeille would go out with a man, she would head out with her headphones on, especially when the moon was full, she walked around in the park waiting for Gérard, if she met someone kind, someone considerate, that was enough, she told the girls, boys act like that so why shouldn't I if I'm tempted, you have to act as freely as boys do, as men do, l'Abeille would say, Louise had taken her under her wing so that she would stop going out to the parks, she was better than that, if you want to be the painter of your generation, first you have to work, at that time Louise was in her insane, tangled relationship with René, who was never faithful to her, I don't know how I survived that affair with you, Louise said suddenly as if she was still hurt, you were completely impossible, René, your obsession with married women was despicable, I was always alone, especially at night, how could I have loved someone as insignificant as you, because love is madness, it's a serious illness, René said, but love teaches us, I had to teach you something, sex, of course, Louise said, but I studied a lot, it was too distracting, I really don't know what it was I liked so much about you, René, I'm good company, René said, that's why you stayed with me, I was teaching you to live differently, not just in your books, I was introducing you to the range of what love can be, René said, wasn't that generous of me? In those days, Louise went on, Gérard was so addicted that when she went out with a woman, it was just to sleep with her, next to her, she would fall deeply asleep, hadn't she once fallen asleep standing up, right in front of us while we were talking, in the middle of a conversation, Gérard would come home shivering from nightly quests for cocaine and speed, are you going to be up all night writing again, Johnie, when are you going to finish your German degree, you can't always be so lazy, Johnie would say to Gérard, our goal in life is knowledge, not idleness, I remember Gérard in that red tux, coming into the hallway at l'Abeille's, her cheeks red from the cold, covered in a sheen of rain or snow, as dawn slipped through the windows, we gathered around Gérard as if we were afraid of losing her, which would happen, it was going to happen, Louise repeated, a second Gérard who was still Thérèse then was watching from the shadows, saying to herself, if she goes and disappears on us, I'll take her name so that she never dies, but for the time being we were still all together on our island, in the dead of winter, Gérard was with us, drifting, l'Abeille, the painter of her generation, had painted a stunning portrait of me, it was called *Louise dans le jardin*, Louise in the Garden, with Rosemonde, our ginger-spotted cat, it was the only painting where l'Abeille had used a bit of color, a green garden, a touch of orange on Rosemonde's nose, otherwise she only drew and painted in shades of brown or black, but the green garden in the painting seemed to glow, it sang out above our heads all night long and in the morning while we were eating our toast we were transported to the green grass of the painting, under the summer sun, Rosemonde on our knees, this is sweet, l'Abeille sighed, and Polydor, who was hungrier than the rest of us, licked the honey from her toast off her fingers, how sweet, l'Abeille repeated. René remembered the scars on Lali's back, the harsh awakenings at dawn when Lali would leave for the hospital in her military coat, how rigid my brother was, Lali was on an emergency call, *I will be there in a few minutes*, she said, *I'm coming*, and she slipped out into the storm, René thought, why was she wearing only shoes, it was winter, Lali's tracks in the snow, resting against the pillows, René thought of Lali, the nightmare of the collapsing chimney that haunted her nights, the chimney and the smell of fire, it never stopped, Lali said, she would never go back to Berlin, Lali said, and yet Berlin drew her, René thought, homosexuals had been persecuted in the camps, especially men, they were still being persecuted, René thought, it's true, as Louise said, that René should have gotten back up, he should take up the fight again against all those human rights violations, it was true, yes, but he no longer had the strength, his limbs were going numb, his feet, his legs, the fight belonged to the next generation, René thought, it belonged to Louise, to Lali, to Gérard the second, to l'Abeille, they refuse to see that I'm fragile, these girls, they still imagine me standing up in anger, my enraged protests, in men's clothes, when one of you is offended, I would say to them, so am I, I was still talking about how badly gays were treated in Niger, and transgender folks, massacred at puberty, the humiliating conditions, I would have been murdered, René thought, look at this, two men holding hands, two men are in love and they get three months in prison, or if they're not in jail they have to live in hiding, they're mixed up with AIDS patients, they can't even go out without putting their lives in danger, they get accused of indecent acts when all they want is to hold each other freely like any other couple, why is Louise so stubborn, my fight is over, I can't even get up without Olga's help, without her strong arms, I can't, René thought, when she heard Louise's voice pulling her out of her lethargy, listen, you can get up and have the girls over, you are the voice of our resistance, Louise said, placing her hand on René's head, was the gesture consoling or imperious, René wondered, I will see to it that we can all hear your voice, Louise said, I'll take care of everything, the wine, I'll organize everything, it'll be nice, Louise said, imagining René younger, with Nathalie on his arm, Nathalie or some other elegant woman, she picked them up in privileged circles, Louise thought, René's insolent smile was still a bruise, those naughty winks, it was so distressing, was there something of that same masculine flirtation in the way she winked at the nurse now, even if René's eyes were barely open against the too-bright light, okay, you rest a little, Louise told René, I'm going to keep telling my story, we were with Gérard, the glow of us, her long curly lashes, the pale cheeks shining in the shadows, it has to stop, Johnie said, the alcohol and the drugs, it has to stop, Johnie told Gérard, who didn't listen, when she went out at night in her red tux, we never knew when or whether she would come back, under the silk jacket she wore a Mickey Mouse T-shirt, well, I'm sick of your cigarettes and beer, Gérard said, I never drink or smoke, no, you snort lines in bar bathrooms, that's what you do, Johnie said, it has to stop, it has to, well, I'm sick of the neighbor's clothesline, of this dingy apartment we're rotting in, Gérard said in a voice that seemed to come from far away, was it the dramatic neutrality of that voice that bothered us, did we already know that Gérard was gone, and then of course there was Doudouline, she spoke so rapturously about her mother, she loved her so much, do you remember, Polydor, Doudouline said, we brought Mama a bouquet of flowers in Paris, we pressed our roses to her chest, the Great Sophie was still upset by that scene in the Strindberg she'd been in, she was wrapped up in the passion of her role, and when she saw us in her dressing room, she cried out, oh Lord, why did you give me children, Doudouline, can't you just go out with boys like everybody else, you always have to do something to upset me, Mama, we came to congratulate you, dear Mama, you see, I like Polydor better than boys, and those ridiculous names you have for each other, Doudouline, listen to me, have you considered my reputation, can I really afford to have a daughter like you, and especially the two of you in my dressing room, misfits, come on, get out, get out, girls, in tears, I said to Mama, you don't love me, you don't love us, finally she thanked us for the roses and hugged us, of course I love you, but don't come here to bleed my mother's heart, we'll talk about it later, see you later, girls, as we left the dressing room we saw Mama's many fans, the other actors were already invading her dressing room, one of them had a bottle of champagne, shouting, here's to you, beautiful Sophie, here's to you, we left Mama's dressing room, the decrepit and the damned were sleeping outside on the sidewalks of Paris and we felt like them because of Mama, she had chased us out of her dressing room, we were humiliated, rejected, Doudouline said, don't exaggerate, Doudouline, Polydor said, your mother wasn't expecting us, we surprised her, and she's a great lady, why would she wasted her time with us, right? Because I'm her daughter, Doudouline said, if she's a queen, I'm a princess, I'm an actress too, Doudouline said, though comedy is more my thing, whereas Mama.... Doudouline's breath hung suspended in the room, we could feel her joy and her sorrow at loving Sophie, all love is uncertain, Doudouline sighed, poor Mama, that winter she was living in what they called a *chambre de bonne*, a tiny, freezing rooming house, poor Mama, Doudouline murmured, she always said it was hard for an actress to start over at fifty in another country, the half-loving arguments between Doudouline and her famous mother only fueled Doudouline's adoration for the woman who had almost given birth to her onstage, every gesture of Doudouline was imbued with theatrical effect, she too would be spectacular onstage one day, she would make a difference, she told Sophie, she would make her mark, she would be known for rebelling against a society that was indifferent to the uniqueness of each individual, but during those winters, Doudouline was busy writing her songs against the dictatorship in Haiti, her words and her work were still raw, imperfect, she thought, against the belligerence of men, the girls knew, curled up in their armchairs or lying on the living room carpet with Rosemonde by their side, they could smell the stale beer smell in the close air thick with cigarette smoke, they watched horrifying images of war racing across on their television sets, they knew, didn't they, Doudouline asked, that the manipulation of violence was a man's game, it was generals who declared wars, they were the masters of our lives, of our destinies, and the silence of women was deafening, their voices had only even been heard at all for the past hundred years or so, and it took the struggle of many a martyred woman to get us the vote, for a long time the generals knew women would never have voted to keep the world in a constant state of war, the men were belligerent, but women would never have allowed the fratricidal wars that have become almost commonplace. Write it all down, Johnie told Doudouline, don't waste a thing, we have to defend our future or there won't be a future, even though the future is written in the stars, a catastrophic landscape where we see already whole worlds that will be decimated, some are still healthy but we can't afford to waste time, like Gérard does, and l'Abeille, who hasn't painted for days, I keep telling everyone that l'Abeille, our painter, Christie, she'll be the painter of our generation, the world belongs to us if we want it, even if we are women, just girls without much skill for now, but one day I'll be a university professor, no one is going to stop me, I tell them, it was strange, there I was showing off my hunger for knowledge when in those days, those winters, René, I was only thinking of you, your secret life with women, I'd been bewitched by a bad boy who was a woman too, you hardly loved me at all, you hardly kissed me, yes, you fluttered around me like a moth, René replied, you acted like a man with his wife, that's what it was, Louise said, there's nothing more shameful than male cruelty, why did you have to borrow their vices too, all their faults, and still you managed to seduce me, I liked you so much, it's possible to love with contradictions, René was nonchalant, and sadly now in my current frail state you are very dear to me, it's too late, René hadn't spoken as much as he tried to hold back the words, out of pride, but he did say, reaching out his hand to Louise, my antelope, don't keep reminding me of the past, what happened to Gérard, the first Gérard, that's the past too, Louise said, how did we lose Gérard, I don't know, wasn't she our responsibility, all of us, we should have stopped that slide into addiction, wasn't it, where did we go wrong, Johnie opened her notebooks, she was playing with her pencils, we can't let this happen, we can't, she would say to l'Abeille, what's happening to Gérard, we can't let that happen, those words seemed to erase all our worries, Johnie spoke in such a soothing voice, we liked her melodious reassurance, it took our fear away, she freed us from the impending shock of anything at all, the sudden outbreak of war, however distant, the shock rattled us to the bone, or Gérard going to jail, what Gérard is doing, I'm telling you, girls, it's not a good attitude, it's negative, it's such a bad choice, Johnie said, Gérard's dissolute existence, girls, do you hear me, it.... No, it can't go on like this, the clubs are going to close soon, l'Abeille announced, who's coming out with me, she said, putting her headphones back on, Thérèse said she would go climb the mountain before the sun came up, did you see that, yesterday, girls, at the Dernier Club, they close at five in the morning, the manager caught her lover cheating, she's a strong woman, the manager, she's got hands like a carpenter, did you see her throw her girlfriend down the stairs, you could hear her tumbling down, should we be acting like that, I'd rather go for a walk on the mountain, breathe the pure air of this endless winter, don't go wearing out your lungs until the wee hours at the Dernier, but it's nice to smoke one last cigarette with a friend, l'Abeille said with a cigarette in her mouth, just one last one, and a dance, then you see everyone out in the street, it's a little less cold even with the snow blowing in your face, that's why you keep coughing, Thérèse said, you'll regret it, no, no, I won't regret anything, l'Abeille said, regret is for old people, not for us, so then I had to worry about l'Abeille, too, as well as Gérard, she was coughing more and more even then, she'd go out without a hat or gloves, you should get some sleep, I told l'Abeille, at first, Doudouline was saying, dictators are mostly noticed for their insignificance, it's only when they're fully in power that their tyranny is seen for what it is, because if they're kept away from the masses, they're nothing, they puff up their image to make people think they're benefactors for the people at their feet, I come before you as a doctor, to heal you, they say, yes, I will heal whatever ails you, I stand with you to seek the end of social inequality, I stand for fraternity and humanity, here I am, at your service, a mere country doctor, or an ethnologist who bought his diploma, there he is, reigning over his people, dominating and crucifying them, getting thousands of innocent people arrested, condemning them to death, who would have thought that such corruption could spring from such insignificance, a great criminal, who would have thought, we're never suspicious enough of mediocrity, of trivial assassins, never enough, Doudouline was saying to Polydor, who listened attentively, her eyes aflame, was all of this when you went to stay with your mother in Haiti, Polydor asked, my parents are actors with an acute sense of justice, Doudouline said, and when I traveled with them they taught me how to live, even though Mama was often distracted by work, Doudouline always spoke of her parents with pride, they were actors, an artistic family, all she was afraid of was standing out among them, she said, it's more like you're too unique, Polydor said, don't worry about what they think, Polydor sipped her wine, we're your family, isn't that enough, Polydor said, she kissed Doudouline on the forehead, you know we love you, right, and she left with l'Abeille to head out to the Dernier, staggering a little, be careful, l'Abeille said, the manager might throw you down the stairs, bam, I don't think she likes young people, it's because there are too many of us who go to the bar for last call, everything else is closed, and when the cops come by around four to check, we're piled on top of each other so they don't see us, it's well over the one-hundred maximum capacity in there, but that woman hits hard, I don't trust her, Polydor said, she chucked her girlfriend down the stairs, the love of her life, it was brutal, Lali had to take her to the hospital, I bet she's in with the police and the mafia, I just bet she is, Polydor said, our own bars aren't worthy of us, Johnie said, we shouldn't be going there, to underground clubs, there's almost no light at all, or they're so high up, tucked away, all the lies and secrecy, it's not right, Johnie said, the police lurking in the shadows, no, it's not fair, but I predict that it won't be like that in the future, the law will protect us, there is social uprising in the cards, it will be good for us, and nights went by like that in the smoky air of the living room, with Johnie's calm voice, trading on vague hopes, some nights Gérard wore jeans with suspenders and stood at the door and said nothing, half listening, don't go out again, Thérèse told her, we never know when you're going to come home, take off your sheepskin coat and stay with us, can you hear me, Gérard, I'll warm up some soup, you're not eating, you'll be nothing but a ghost before too long, look at what's going on, Gérard said suddenly, wars are breaking out, fierce and desperate, on TV, epidemics and famines, don't you see what's happening, don't you see what I see? It's the apocalypse, Gérard said, and you don't see it, you don't feel anything, music chirped out of l'Abeille's headphones, *Beat it, beat it*, one more drink and that's it, she said, girls don't like the lonely end of the night, you have to stop dancing, you go home alone and they call over to each other, hey, can I come with, can I get in your car, can I come warm up at your place for an hour? The cars pull away on the snowy roads, dancers pull away from each other, couples unravel in the dull light of dawn, why can't I come in your car with you, can't you see it's snowing and I'm alone, one of them cries, but the cars disappear into a world of snow and the abandoned girl walks alone in the street, there's always someone we don't love enough, l'Abeille told Polydor, when I walk home through the park no one follows me, Polydor said, I'm lucky, maybe a man now and then, under the trees, just like that, there he is, some guy walking by your side and you let him kiss you, hold you, a stranger, aren't you ashamed, they're probably men waiting in the park for another man, l'Abeille says, we talk a little, I ask him who he's waiting for and he says I don't know yet, but it's too cold for anything so he leaves and heads toward the mountain, though I tell him it won't be much warmer up there, a man like me can't spend a night without sex, he says, good-bye, beautiful, he'll say and he runs off, blowing on his cold fingers, standing at the door, Gérard took a few pills to lessen the weight of the world, Johnie heard Gérard's rapid breathing as she wrote in her notebook, *From Sappho to Radclyffe Hall*, the words suspended on the blank page, that'll be the title of my thesis, she told me, what do you think, Louise, Gérard eventually collapsed from exhaustion on the sofa, snuggled up to the cat, we could hear Gérard's quickening breath, this can't go on, Johnie said, she seemed to be watching over Gérard as she slept, was she asleep, was she in withdrawal, what's going on, Johnie pulled the blanket back over Gérard's shoulders, l'Abeille could hear Stevie Wonder on the dance floor or in the kitchen, Ray Charles, Michael Jackson in her headphones, l'Abeille was always dancing, Doudouline said, what's my destiny, l'Abeille asked Johnie, what is the mystery of my fate, you would be the painter of our generation, Polydor answered from the next room, if you didn't go out every night, if you were more disciplined, real artists don't go out every night for one last drink, Polydor said. That's where Gérard is buying dope, I'm positive, Polydor said, at the Dernier, there's cheaper hash from South America, Polydor said, stay away from that, the quality is no good, Polydor said, who consumed nothing but wine, stretching that languor out all day long, we all knew, Louise told René, that for all her wrenching despair what Gérard was looking for was her mother, her adoptive parents were kind, they'd been spoiling Gérard since the day they adopted her when she was ten months old, but her parents underestimated the extent of Gérard's obsession, she searched everywhere for the woman who had given birth to her only to abandon her in an orphanage, she could have been a hooker or just a girl, a teenager, if she were a prostitute Gérard would greet her reverently if they met in the street, having a hooker for a mother would be a badge of divine honor, according to Gérard, while being born of a fifteen-year-old girl would be a mark of innocence, where had Gérard's mother come from, she would have liked to meet her and tell her, with the endless respect that was her due, Mama, I am your daughter, Gérard, it's me, and to ask, without anger, Mama, why did you abandon me, it would be nice to have a fifteen-year-old mother who would always be young even as Gérard got older, you wouldn't know who was the mother and who was the daughter, they would love each other so much, they would never leave each other, Gérard's fantasies expanded as her addiction did, Gérard would tell the girls that she remembered everything, from the bars of the crib in the orphanage that she shared with two Black babies whose diapers never got changed, sometimes they dropped the bars so that the three of them could play on the floor and eventually learn to walk, she remembered the smell of urine and the bottomless loneliness in the dark, she cried and cried, they could tell it was winter outside because the orphanage walls were cold, the cold was everywhere, especially when human hands touched the children, supposedly to wash them, those hands, those arms, that contact had to be avoided at all costs, the cold ran through everything, Gérard said, why had she been adopted and not the two others, she still felt like the separation had been an assault on her rights as a child, they should all have come together in the same family, the Black babies and Gérard, but we couldn't afford to adopt three children, Gérard's parents told her, disconcerted, and we liked you, so long and so pretty, a little skinny, yes, and not very clean, you were so alone in that bed, behind those bars, I wasn't alone, the two of them were with me, why did you split us up, it seemed impossible to heal the wounds in those childhood memories, Louise said, fragments exploded like a mine in that little head, and we all thought it was still like that today and that we couldn't do anything about it, except Johnie, who kept repeating, it has to stop, it has to stop whenever Louise brought up Gérard and the past. She was shocked that Olga the Russian nurse had ironed René's shirts, which were piled up on the bedside table, Olga had also taken René's clean men's clothes out of the closet, she had shined her shoes, all this overly clean ceremony reeked of preemptive mourning, Louise shuddered with horror, her friend René was alive and well and all this funereal preparation around him was disturbing, while René, calm in bed, listened to Louise's stories graciously, attentively, we all need to know where we come from, René said, since we know for sure where we're going, and there's no turning back, Gérard was right to rebel, who knows, maybe she had been placed in a bunch of foster homes before she was adopted, maybe she had experienced multiple rejections, maybe she had been abandoned over and over again, Louise listened to René's musings, Olga had buttoned up René's shirts and hung the scarves and ties on a hanger, she was even more irritated by the fact that René's shirts had been buttoned by the hand that controlled his confinement, the buttons were done up all the way up to the neck, the shirts were a sign of René's incarceration under his Russian nurse, she never opened the windows, she never got René out of bed, when the girls come to visit, yes, all together, Louise said, I'll dress you up in your white dressing gown or in your most elegant clothes, won't I, René, it'll be a celebration, René didn't answer, just asked again impatiently, what happened to Gérard, will you tell me already, Louise said that it was hard to talk about the past sometimes, she felt like her throat was closing up, it was just us, l'Abeille's house was an enclave, so we thought we were avoiding harm, but harm came to us and it slammed into us even harder, Louise said, I can see Gérard withering away in l'Abeille's velvet chair, I can still see her just wasting away in her red tuxedo, this all happened just a few days before we lit twenty candles on the last funeral cake for Gérard's birthday, the birthday party she didn't come to, she would have been twenty years old, we thought, well, maybe she'll wise up, or would she, we didn't know, we could hear Doudouline's punk tunes playing in the room, Doudouline was a punk, running her revolutions in her chosen art, singing, and Polydor was gazing admiringly at Doudouline, love in her eyes, you're as lovely as your mother, the Great Sophie, Polydor said, no, Doudouline snapped, no way, she's thin, she's exquisite and I'm—but Polydor jumped in to fill Doudouline's silence, adding, even more beautiful, I'd say, you're only saying that because I'm on such a draconian diet, and I'm hungry, I am always hungry, Doudouline said, I've had enough of soup and broth, that's all good for Gérard, who lives on invisibility and air, Doudouline said, I grew up backstage in theaters with a sandwich in my hand, Mama didn't have time to cook or even to be with us at home, it was our father who looked after us, even though he was an actor too, but it's from my mother that I got my voice, the best of me is all from my mama, Doudouline said, a bit too humbly, I remember that we didn't really like that excessive humility of Doudouline's, we were so happy to go see her sing, we loved her and told her so but she thought we were just being nice, Doudouline boasted that she had learned to read on her father's knee, not at school, and that was why she was so independent, she said, her family was a family of actors, passed down from father to son, from mother to daughter, yet I had to go to school where I learned nothing, there's nothing sadder than coming home from school at four in the afternoon when it's already dark in the city and you can't see where you're going in the snow, but you hear the snowplows scraping by and you're scared they might grind you up, Polydor said, sipping her morning wine, or her dawn wine, you're constantly drinking, Johnie grumbled, I'm just sucking on an ice cube, Polydor said, can't you leave me alone, no, Polydor said, Doudouline went over to the piano and sang a few variations, everyone listened, and sometimes we sang with her, Gérard was half passed out in l'Abeille's velvet armchair, watching us without really being there, we couldn't tell what was going on behind her eyes, Gérard was increasingly hanging out with a group of girls and boys we didn't know, she was only half living with us and staying somewhere else, she was spending whole nights away from home, and l'Abeille had resigned herself, she didn't wait for her in the parks anymore, this new group of Gérard's lived in a shithole, they lived only for coke, heroin, we didn't even know where they were hiding, many of them were panhandling, we couldn't leave our Gérard to such sketchy, dangerous company, l'Abeille said, she told herself she would eventually find Gérard's hiding spots and that she would be saved, yes, if we got her to detox in time, we hadn't seen Gérard for days and nights, despite l'Abeille walking and watching in the streets at night, through the fog of winter, Gérard had run away and that was what hurt most, where was she, who was she with, and we waited, when we finally found out, it was too late, Polydor wondered if Gérard was wearing those plastic shoes, the streets were an ice rink, the sidewalks, I remember the twenty candles on the cake, Louise said, it looked like a nice party to celebrate Gérard's twentieth birthday, she wouldn't be coming home again, she had disappeared, escaped, where was she then, we could still see her in l'Abeille's smoky house, we couldn't forget her hair, her curly lashes, her eyes sparkling in the night full of shadows, we could hear Gérard's laughter, she used to laugh a lot with l'Abeille, a sarcastic laugh, what she wanted was to become an actress with Doudouline, she wanted to be a comedian, a great comedian like the Great Sophie had been, though she had a preference for grand tragedies, Doudouline said of her mother, l'Abeille said she could hear Gérard's footsteps in the kitchen, was she feeding Rosemonde, whispering sweet nothings to the cat, don't go out at night, naughty girl, stay with us, stay close to me, aren't you afraid of the biting cold, we could lose you under mountains of snow, darling little cat, we don't want to lose you, we want you with us, by the time we found out, it was too late, Louise told René, tears running down her cheeks, a space heater had exploded in one of the slums where those junkies lived, those hoodlums, Gérard's dealers, the others were able to get down by the stairs by holding on to the iron railing, but they forgot Gérard upstairs, we don't know if she was already unconscious because of the smoke, nobody thought of Gérard, we don't know if she had died of an overdose before or after the explosion and the roar of the flames, but those cowards forgot about Gérard, they didn't wake her up or take her with them, they could have dragged her down the stairs to the street, it was still snowing, what a terrible thing, it's unimaginable, each one of us left our youth there, in that abyss with Gérard, that pit of indifference from which she couldn't be brought back alive, hardly breathing, we could have taken her to the hospital, Lali would have looked after her, she would have cured her of everything, it was too late, her body was blackened and burned when the police found her, and when we saw her after that, the clothes from her night's escapades flaking off her skin, I can't talk about this anymore, Louise said to René, that's how it is, René said, Lali, whose knowledge and skill was so much bigger than all of you, she could have saved Gérard, what a horrible thing, René said, what a thing, is there some sliver of light somewhere, I mean, is Gérard sending you messages, the dead are messengers too, René said with certainty, maybe, I don't know anymore, Louise said, wiping her eyes with a tissue, how come you think the dead can speak to us? I know they can, René said, there are signs, there are messages if you pay attention, I'll send lots, René said, laughing, and especially to you, Louise, I'll try to explain my behavior better, how my seducing married women was meant to free them from their husbands' oppression, to show them pleasures they didn't know, and sometimes I loved the husbands out of some twisted male complicity, I would tell them how to get their wives back, there were a few threesomes, that's awful, Louise said, I had no idea how many times you cheated on me, how gullible I was, I never knew the measure of your faithlessness, Louise said, troubled by René's confessions, don't cry for an old lover, all I know is that I did those women a lot of good, I brought them out of their ignorance of themselves and their beauty, though that didn't stop Nathalie from leaving with one of those men, unaware of how much better I was than them, what can I say, my dear Louise, that's how it is, you can't win them all, no one can, just don't think about it, you behaved very badly, Louise said, you're a very bad boy, but you're smiling through your tears all the same, René said, I'm probably not as terrible as you think I am, tell me again what happened to Gérard after that, what happened to Gérard, our youth shattered against the rocks of that first tragedy, Louise said, her voice still shaken by the dreadful memories of that winter night, the Great Sophie told Doudouline, you shouldn't have let her go out, daughter, she seemed to be as sad as we were, and you, Polydor, why didn't you do anything, that girl was so good at acting, for her to die like that, it's too awful, Doudouline's mother said, she couldn't comfort Doudouline because she was so angry with all of us, it was as if we had murdered Gérard ourselves rather than taking care of her, though in the end, on the day of the funeral, the Great Sophie took pity on us, she called us her poor little ones, she would rescue us, she said, it was snowing that day, still, and always the same winter of snow and ice, on the sidewalks and in the streets, Polydor noticed a woman that day, could that be her, Gérard's birth mother, who had left her, we still didn't know why, the lady looked like she might be African, Polydor said, and she was weeping quietly, dark glasses covering her eyes, Polydor said, you don't think it could be her, do you, girls, Gérard's mother, the long shadow of her during the prayers for the dead, she seemed as slender as Gérard, they were both thin, with a long neck, curly hair, we had never met that woman, what was she doing there in the procession, she never came over to us, no, she kept to herself, dressed all in black, she threw white flowers on Gérard's grave and we saw her leave without looking at us, could that be her, Polydor asked Doudouline, could that have been Gérard's mother, she seemed very young, perhaps she had been the fifteen-year-old mother Gérard dreamed of, the Great Sophie spent the whole time sobbing noisily, as if she had been onstage, and Doudouline said to her mother, Mama, please, this grief is mine, not yours, please, Mama, Thérèse on her knees had said to Gérard, I'll take your name so that you'll always be with us, my beautiful Gérard, and she had been quick to ask that we call her Gérard the second, the continuation of the first Gérard, so that the chain wouldn't be broken by the accident, it was only an accident after all, a horrible accident, though what did that change when you were twenty years old and you had your whole life ahead of you, Polydor said to Gérard the second, it's true, she's only changing bodies, our Gérard, the presence of Gérard's mother, if that actually was her, which was doubtful, had erased the presence of Gérard's real parents, those who had adopted her, they had been so discreet that they were all but forgotten on that dark day, in that dark procession, that morning the wind was cold up there at the cemetery, Polydor said, we were insensitive, we barely said hello to Gérard's parents, everything is so bad, all of a sudden, so bad, Polydor repeated, even our hearts are freezing, we don't know anything anymore, Gérard the second had watched Gérard fall apart in l'Abeille's velvet chair and now she was dressed in Gérard's clothes, jeans with suspenders, a Mickey Mouse shirt, the red tux was burned and had to be thrown out, and the red plastic shoes too, but the sheepskin winter coat, which had been a gift from Gérard's parents to their daughter so that she wouldn't catch cold, they were so considerate, so kind, they were so fond of their daughter, the coat was still on Johnie's bed, it kept her warm at night as if Gérard had still been there by her side, although these days she went out almost every night, Johnie said to Polydor, we always just slept together, it was cool, Gérard hadn't even thought about sex for a long time, I liked that everything was cool between us, Johnie's word, cool, she was busy with school, with astrology too, in the end she had chosen psychology, the human drama that inhabits us all, she said, that word cool was like a way of life, well, Johnie said, this household undone shall be ruled by reason, and the unbearable hollowness Gérard left behind, Johnie said, though she was too moved to truly express how she felt, as if the foundations of her very being had been laid waste, what's the point of sleeping here, I'll rent a place somewhere, I'll make it my astrology office, that's it, that's what I'll do, Johnie said, and as she listened to Johnie, Polydor thought that this separation would be the start of every other one, because of Gérard they would all be torn apart like a hundred-year-old tree broken by winter winds, the dull thud of falling branches, one after the other, dropping far away from each other, but Polydor responded bluntly that she would never leave Doudouline, even when she was as famous as the Great Sophie, we will live together at least forty years, Polydor thought and said as much out loud to the girls in l'Abeille's increasingly smoky living room, listen to me, she said, Doudouline and me, that's for life, you heard me right, for life, and what's more, mark my words, one day Doudouline and I are going to get married, and I promise you it's going to be the sexiest wedding ever, dressed in Gérard's sheepskin coat, that coat was a gift from her real parents to their daughter, and jeans with suspenders, the Mickey Mouse shirt, those big boots Gérard the second wore, only yesterday her name had been Thérèse, Gérard the second had gone skiing on the mountain, summer and winter, Gérard's final resting place would never be a

tomb, a grave, but a garden lined with chrysanthemums, a beautiful
garden that Gérard the second would tend and visit all year round,
by bike, on foot, or on skis, so deep was Thérèse's loyalty to Gérard,
an ardent devotion, an undying affection, and if winter brought a
lull for Gérard, Thérèse, now called Gérard the second, would put
twice as much energy into the act of remembrance, energy coursing
through her body, she went to the snowy mountain, the forest of firs
and pines rimed by the cold, morning and night, coming back down
with red cheeks as if she were revitalized, breathing new air, her
cheeks rosy like the first Gérard's had been, she'd been so pale for so
long, even if Gérard had had light brown skin, perhaps she had been
the child of that mysterious Black woman at the funeral after all,
Polydor said, why didn't we have the courage to talk to her, Polydor
asked, why are we all so spineless? But the other girls thought the
mother-daughter similarity didn't seem likely, or was it maybe too
likely, Thérèse asked, and bringing up the memory of Gérard
abandoned by her mother was heartbreaking, so much that they
would rather not think about it at all. Now we spent our nights in
silence, l'Abeille was tiny in those headphones, and smoking
constantly, it was stifling and so smoky it felt like the house would
catch on fire, the smoke was thicker and thicker, Johnie had left,
renting a place in town, like all of us she often worked in bars at
night and went to school during the day, we had been so close and
now we were all splitting up, each in our separate loneliness, and
Polydor promised l'Abeille that she wouldn't leave her, l'Abeille,
Doudouline and I aren't going to leave like Johnie, no, we're with
you for good, you and Rosemonde, together for life, Polydor said, I'll
cook, you can go back to painting in peace, even as she pulled away,
Johnie was nostalgic for their happy unity, Louise told René, it
wasn't much fun to find yourself without love or money, to have to
work evenings drowning in smoke until late at night, shivering alone
in bed, Johnie said, but what she didn't say was that she missed
Gérard, who was so tender, Gérard who always seemed so detached

from everything, she missed her so much it was ripping her heart out, Johnie had told herself she would remain unflustered in the face of pain, but since Gérard had slipped away in the night, she could hear cracks forming in the wall she had put up inside herself, and it was slowly giving way. She started studying harder, telling Polydor one bright morning that she was going to go into business as an astrologer, she'd had enough of bars where people smoked and drank too much every night, she would keep going to school for psychology so she could be independent, though who would come see such a young astrologer, she asked Polydor, who replied, I'll be your first client, I want to know what the Capricorn moon will bring this Friday, Johnie said that was exactly what she should worry about, the moon in Capricorn, and it would be a bad idea if Polydor made plans that day, I wanted to surprise Doudouline, but I think that'll have to wait, Polydor added, in this wretched winter the moon is in Capricorn all over the world, how can we ever shake this sorrow loose, will we ever be as happy as we were, Polydor said, and that's how it was, Louise told René, we were gradually coming out of our coddled shell, our group of friends had been held when we wanted to be held, warm and numb, a sort of dreamy oblivion, floating on our cigarette smoke, on alcohol fumes, snuggled up with Rosemonde in the big red velvet armchair, the time has come, l'Abeille was saying, to stop it with the parks at night, all the foolishness, it was so transitory, friends heading up the mountain looking for ways to fill the night, to satisfy their hunger, comely wolves between them among the trees on the snowy mountain, how bold, despite the cold that distorts every gesture, their hands freezing, their bodies statues, the time has come to put an end to all that, quick encounters at night in the car with girls, the caresses and furtive kisses, the time has come because, as Johnie says, maybe it's just hormones gone berserk, if we're all running around, hopped up on desire, nothing but hormones, is all the fuss really worth it, girls, look what's happening to Gérard now, while l'Abeille was talking, day was dawning in the smoky living room and we could watch the houses being torn down on the street through the window, soon this place would be uninhabitable, the old house where we lived with l'Abeille, our days of squatting in some handsome old dump were over, we'll have to move, l'Abeille said, but it can wait a few more months, we'll wait until the wrecking ball comes knocking, can you hear the noise of the demolition crews? René wasn't listening to Louise anymore, the story of Gérard's disappearance had upset her, and she said to Louise, sometimes it's contempt that kills fragile people like Gérard, it's society, René was thinking of himself now, of the hatred he had suffered from people, even though he shot them down, those who despised people like them, those who despised him, a slanderous word or disdainful laughter, all those moments clawed their way back into his mind, the foundation of human beings, René suddenly said to Louise, is their miserable cowardice, humans are too cruel to allow for any solidarity with those they deem to be different, I'm going to be leaving a world that's evolving as slowly as a turtle, René told Louise, no, no, come on, Louise said, don't be so pessimistic, you're a misogynist and a pessimist, you're part of the world of men too, even though you know how to defend us as if you were a woman, or maybe because you're a woman in a man's frail shell, yet you lack the one organ that would give you that virility, that would make you that much more impressive, imposing, implacable even, don't you go drowning in dark thoughts, my dear René, now Louise was thinking of René's body, under the housecoat she could see the edge of René's shirt, René wore wool or sometimes cotton shirts, always covering the chest. Even when she dressed in couture, Louise thought, René's chest was taboo, forbidden, fiercely, she never showed that part of her body, even when making love, the act that most undresses us, which lays us bare, which makes any thought of modesty an impossibility, René had always refused to show her breasts, in the male role she assumed with women, he was forever the master, wasn't he, Louise thought, she knew so little of

René's body, all she knew of that body was the pleasure it had given her, there were no breasts at all in the way René pulled away almost imperceptibly, her fiery, unbridled body, master of desire, Louise thought of how René used to say that women who wanted to become men were butchered by inept homophobes, the surgeons who sliced off their breasts were butchers, those women were scorned and tortured, when René talked about that cruelty, it was never about him specifically, but Louise was moved by René's words, she had told René then to keep her breasts, don't ever have surgery, René hadn't listened then, to Louise and so many other girls, what bad luck, Louise thought, to wake up one morning with breast cancer, her body had to be disfigured, her full breasts deformed, destroyed, the decay of living matter, while René would voluntarily put herself through the ordeal of surgery, her body disfigured too, such proud indifference, glorification through metamorphosis, even if it was a dismal failure, the body ruined, Louise remembered Lali driving her to her treatments, Louise had been so weak, she lost all her hair, the radiation, she didn't recognize herself anymore, how many women go through a scare like that, the weakness, they feel toxic, the sudden brush with death, those days seemed so out of joint, how had she ever gone through that, Louise wondered now, what might have helped soften the shock of having a breast taken, that life torn from her, Louise told René, was that she had written about those months, the chemical torture, running her hands over her bald head, that had been the worst thing, she felt like she would never be loved again, no one would ever look at her admiringly, she had managed to finish her dissertation, which was on the future of technological communications, she told herself that by writing the future she would land on some tomorrow in a constellation where anything can be invented, new beginnings would line up for her, scientific discoveries, and so the blaze of cancer inched back like a startled insect, would it lodge in her liver, in her sparkling brain, her young woman's heart still new, what would happen to Louise, tonight, tomorrow, later, and in the meantime women were dying, disappearing by the thousands, would Louise be one of them in a few months? Death sometimes came slowly, would Louise be that lucky, many of them were doomed, waiting in the hospital during their treatments, I have three children, they moaned, look at me, look how I am, so thin, Louise was writing day and night, the future of communications, the future, a future the seeds of which she contained, the nascent nucleus was within her, a symbol beyond immolated flesh, the left breast of which only a morbid shadow remained, a hollow in healthy flesh, you finish the dissertation, Lali said, you heal, yes, Lali's words would come true, and suddenly the treatments eased up, Louise's hair grew back in tight strands, Louise braided her hair, her beautiful, ornamented head, Louise's dissertation was a success, it was accepted for publication, Louise could say to Lali, I'm better, I'm out of the woods, you won't have to be driving me to the hospital all winter, no, it's over Lali, the girls gathered around Louise like in the cool shade of a tree in springtime, Polydor would say, let's drive down to P-town, we can go as early as June, it would be an escape from l'Abeille's smoky living room, those few weeks of respite for Louise on the New England beaches, they couldn't hear the grinding of the wreckers edging up to their door anymore, that was when Gérard, the first Gérard, started pulling away from us, Louise went on, on those nude beaches, for men, for women, but René was lost in thought, his head drooped though always he could feel Olga's eyes on him, he wasn't sure how to define her gaze, yes, on the beach, we were so happy, and Gérard ran away to another, more experienced group than we were, less innocent, and the drugs, she tried coke for the first time with those girls, we had no idea, she would come back to the hotel late at night, we stopped waiting up for her, when she traipsed in she would rest her head on Johnie's shoulder, sweet bliss, other nights she would go to Polydor and Doudouline, she slept between them, Polydor would whisper in her ear, you're hanging out with girls you don't even know, where have you been Gérard, and Gérard would beg us to let her sleep until noon, she would say, girls, you don't know how happy I am at last, you can't imagine the joy, and she fell asleep almost instantaneously in her Mickey Mouse shirt, you can't imagine what it means to me, and we would hear her sighing in the night, our windows open on the ocean, its haze of fog and seagulls mewing, that's how it started for Gérard, Louise continued emotionally, the first encounter with cocaine, heroin came later, another beach vacation, Gérard had gotten a job, that was all she could think about, waitressing in a bar with the sea lapping at her feet, surrounded by happy revelers, day and night, almost naked in her white shorts, her skin browned by the sun. That was how we lost Gérard, during those holidays when I was healing, getting my strength back, in the middle of the ocean l'Abeille told me she was so small that I could have carried her on my back, swimming toward the lighthouse, you're beautiful, Louise, our beloved giantess, I envy that, I wish I were as big as you, and I remember telling her, you have to start painting again, Christie, the painter of our generation, you have to, and as the waves rocked us I no longer felt ashamed of the breast I'd lost, I told myself that maybe René had suffered some incredible indignity to her body, even if she hadn't said anything about it, some unbelievable mutilation she couldn't even talk about, René turned to Louise suddenly, you know me too well, my dear, like a wife knows her husband, you know me too well and so little, so little, she was sitting up in bed, her elbows propped up on pillows, you know me too little, Louise, René said, a poet once wrote that we go to the grave with gladness, trembling with pleasure, but I can assure you, Louise, it's not true, alas, everything goes numb and stale, there's nothing more unpleasant than the sensual, happy memories slowly going numb, everything fades away like a chalk drawing on a blackboard, what do you think, Louise, the drawing is our life, a dot in space, though I must say I've lived a good life, I haven't wasted a single second, Louise listened, imagining René's childhood, the little boy already imposing his manly image, René had told her, laughing, as if René were laughing at the child he had been, I would punch the other kids, René had told her, I demanded respect, the way my parents taught me, they bled, those morons, we were all sealed up in our snowsuits, there's nothing less attractive, I would hide in snow forts behind the house after school and try to show the little girls my fake dick, I was a boy and I knew it, René said, I would push my finger through the zipper of my snow pants, it took forever to take everything off, and the girls were startled, you don't have a real dick, they said, it's only your finger, the little girls got tired of my games pretty quickly, you remember everything, Louise said, yes, especially hiding down in the ditch in the summer, the smell of new growth, in a dugout beneath the cherry trees, the juicy, overripe cherries, I smeared juice on the girls' faces, we played like that, they liked it, I remember that smell, the smell of leaves at the end of summer, the sultry heat, the smell of sweat and bursting cherries, and I made myself a penis, which they thought was even more fun, it was exciting, I ended up getting kicked out of the girls' school, René said, calm now and cheerful, Louise thought as she listened, René was always so proud of herself, of her childhood rebellions, the challenges she took up, he was René and no one else, he always had been, long before the surfeit of conquest, all that foolishness, Louise thought, once more Gérard's silhouette stood out against the blue sky of the New England beaches, she went back alone in winter when the seaside towns and villages were foggy and cold, Gérard would go off alone in her red plastic shoes, I've been offered a small comic role in a local theater, she said, I can't refuse, though it was her dealers who were waiting for her, Louise told René, and her first taste of dope, which would turn out to be fatal the day of the fire, heroin was already in the air there under the frozen sky, Gérard's silhouette was sliding into the silence of places unknown, there was no more sunshine and summer on Gérard's browning skin but a winter like ours, with winds and ice storms, snowstorms, Gérard's long, scrawny silhouette wandered through the streets shrouded in fog rolling in off the Atlantic, we could hear the melancholy call of a lighthouse, was Gérard's absence a sign, lost in the rising mists, was that the first sign of her disappearance? All at once we could hear the wreckers at the door, our old house was going to come down, we would have to go squat elsewhere, l'Abeille said, let's get out of here, and Rosemonde too, before the roof caves in on us, I saw another old house on the rich side of town, still handsome, with a front lawn, in the summer we'll be on the mountain until the city comes to chase us away, but we needed a tenant, that's how it went, and Christie, the painter of our generation, suggested that we look for another home, this time on the mountain, l'Abeille, who went to concerts all the time, came home with a musician who was going to live with us, a Polish pianist, see, girls, we're moving up the ladder, the snowy mountain is taking us under its wing, l'Abeille could see how unhappy Louise was with René running around, would she come home more often, and would Louise finally stop putting up with a cheating husband like René, my life with you then, René, was so uncomfortable that I didn't even know who I was, between convalescence and hope, I didn't know, even though my hair had grown back, and you, you used to pounce on me with your love, with embraces I didn't want, you used to say that only love cures everything and when I didn't believe it, you would almost attack me, I was under siege, I would rush to l'Abeille's house as if it were heaven, Chopin in the living room, Manfred at the piano, and Polydor, Doudouline, and Gérard the second sitting cross-legged next to him, they looked like well-bred little children glum like that, thinking about Gérard, was she cold out there in the ground, they would go visit her, ski out before the end of the day, bring her flowers, winter flowers white as snow, everything was so white everywhere, the streets, the houses, the cemetery, which was full of flowers in summer, covered with snow, l'Abeille's house was crumbling, it was on the verge of collapse, l'Abeille would set up her studio in the huge rooms, she said, the house had been condemned because a tiny earthquake had fissured the walls, l'Abeille said, you can see the cracks, you can hear the mice in the walls, if the power gets cut off we have a fireplace and wood, we have beautiful chairs, we're as bourgeois as your friend René, who's too old for you anyway, l'Abeille told Louise, when are you going to leave him, l'Abeille asked her, come live with us, you'll be better off here, I was telling the girls that if they kept squatting in uninhabitable houses, they'd end up on the street, and then all at once l'Abeille had started painting again, with radiant optimism, she had started with a canvas on her easel and when that ran out she kept going, she painted a fresco on the walls from her bedroom to the living room, through the bathroom and the kitchen, she painted compulsively to the sound of Manfred's music, his piano, or to Michael Jackson's simpering voice in her headphones, no one could stop her, she was painting only in black and white, lashing at the walls with her brushes, and if they asked her what her endless painting was called she replied, *Les pas de Gérard dans la neige*, Gérard's Footsteps in the Snow, I can hear and see her footsteps when I paint them, l'Abeille said, and it's also named *La joie dans l'éphémère*, about finding joy in what is fleeting, the wreckers are getting close and soon these walls will crumble, they'll mash us all up with it, l'Abeille said, laughing. Here was a home where happiness would be born, and Johnie came too, for Manfred's recitals, for l'Abeille's soups, Doudouline's rehearsals, soon she would be up on stage with the Great Sophie, Doudouline's mother had told her daughter not to go by Doudouline, it was a ridiculous name, her birth name wasn't Doudouline, it was ridiculous, Polydor, Johnie, what did any of their names mean, the Great Sophie asked Doudouline, who replied, my dear mother, there can't be two Sophies in the same family, Papa named me Anne-Sophie to avoid confusing the two of us, Doudouline is what Polydor calls me, it's the name of our love, Anne-Sophie told her mother with assurance, it will pass, it has to pass in the end, Sophie said, this love affair between the two of you, have you thought about me at all, about my reputation? Sophie saw that she had upset her daughter and regretted it immediately, she took her in her arms, Doudouline, my child, I've said too much, you know I love you as you are, I'm a mother first and an actress after, isn't that right, my treasure? That said, you could stand to lose a bit of weight, and you, Polydor, with the wine all day long, all that sugar, it's too much, Sophie said, Doudouline looked at her mother thinking she didn't even have to get up on stage to play her role with her mother, every moment was theater, a perpetual drama, almost a farce, with her two-faced, beloved mother, Doudouline didn't know how to defend herself and she felt sorry for Sophie, Mama, I know it's a bit hard for you, but love is love, you see, love alights like a bird on a branch, I know, I know, no one knows that better than I do, the Great Sophie replied, except your father, don't you know how many lovers I've had, that was a few years ago, I must say, when I was young and beautiful, you're still beautiful, Polydor listened to the dialogue between mother and daughter as she opened a bottle of Spanish wine she liked, the smell made her nostrils tingle, there was nothing as delicious as pouring wine into a glass filled with ice cubes, it was like celebrating summer in winter every single day, until Doudouline came to Polydor and took away her glass, no, not another one, that's enough, Doudouline said sternly, I'll hide the bottles, I'll throw them all away, I'm not going to share my life with a drunk, do you want to end up like Gérard, my dear Polydor, wake up, you can't talk to me like that, Doudouline, Polydor said, suddenly upset, not you, no, you can't, it's your mother's influence, this isn't you, Polydor was about to cry, there in her new room, their room, where a mattress had been rolled out on a rug, Rosemonde slept on the rug, and Polydor would wake up the cat with her noise and her crying, Rosemonde, darling, Rosemonde, you see how they treat me here, she said I'm just a drunk, she's my love and that's what she thinks of me, Rosemonde opened her sleepy eyes, meowing a little, if that's how it's is, I'm leaving, I'll leave this house, we're never going to get married, I'm telling you, Rosemonde, and Rosemonde listened politely, resting her front paws on the carpet, she didn't like arguments, the clatter of voices, the shouting and tears, but she didn't mind being disturbed to help find a peaceful solution, her bright green eyes looked at Polydor so gently, she seemed to say, come, no, you can't leave, don't be afraid, you can't leave, aren't you happy here with us, we're not out on the street anymore, we're not cold, I dine on new potatoes every day and you too, Polydor, who wasn't convinced by Rosemonde's mute comfort, lay down on the mattress crying, it's because of her, the Great Sophie, from the theater, my Doudouline isn't the same anymore, Rosemonde, with her piercing gaze, watched Polydor sitting on the carpet, you're so beautiful, Polydor said suddenly, distracted from her grief, the orange in your fur, l'Abeille should be able to paint you like that, I'm going to tell her tonight, where did she get to now, we haven't seen her since this morning, do you think I'm drunk like they say I am, it's so unfair what they say about me in this house, Rosemonde, I'm going to go away, at least for a few days.... Rosemonde seemed to be saying don't go, where would you go, do you want to live on the street like I did for years before l'Abeille took me in, abandonment, hunger, nights prowling the dumpsters, is that what you want, Polydor got up suddenly, put on her navy peacoat, it was very thin, it was her spring coat, but she couldn't bear how long the winter was anymore and she left the house through the door behind the living room, Doudouline didn't see her go, as night fell she headed out to the bars where she used to go with Gérard, though Gérard cruised on coke and only drank water, danced all night, often without even looking at who she was dancing with, and at the Dernier, the last of the last call downtown, Polydor got scared that the hard-ass manager would toss her down the stairs like she did with her drunken customers, but the boss lady, as they called her, said to Polydor, you're already tipsy, you, my pretty, you'll only get one last drink, not two, just one, you understand? Dancing and staggering, Polydor looked for Gérard among the girls on the dance floor, but she didn't see Gérard, she didn't see any friends at all, these girls were older, no, it wasn't like when she used to come here with Gérard, should she be worried that the cops would come count how many people were in the bar, were there so many that Gérard would have sat on Polydor's lap, saying, it's so they won't see me, Polydor, Polydor was sure that Gérard was so tall they'd see her first, and as she danced Polydor thought she should be going, the bar, the vibe was flat now, without Gérard, she should get a cab, her thoughts were all over the place, dripping in her head like ooze, that was how she felt, and anyway the manager shouted last call, girls and it was time to leave, first consider how to get down the stairs without falling, Polydor was unsteady on her feet, and then outside the street was covered with snow and ice, where am I, Polydor thought, where are the taxis, no, she shouldn't have smoked that hash cigarette the girl in the bathroom gave her, shouldn't have, she wasn't used to it, first she had to remember where she was, why was it so cold, the wind cut through the thin fabric of her coat, it was so hard to walk, one foot in front of the other on the icy sidewalk, since there were no taxis she huddled out of the snow against a building to wait, a bank, she would wait, she had to rest, catch her breath, she slid down the stone wall of the stately building, a bank, that was it, Polydor had fallen asleep, she saw some homeless people nearby, she wasn't really asleep, she was inside a nightmare and couldn't get out, her feet were so cold in her boots, and a woman in a fur coat over bare breasts woke her up and saved her, she took Polydor back to her car, come on little one, what are you doing here with these guys, they rape girls like you, you've had too much to drink, haven't you, come on, come with me, I'm working but I can't just leave you out here in the street with everybody, the car was spacious and smelled like fake pine, the woman lowered the windows in case she came across a man out alone, she said, prostitution is my job, you see, I like to work in my car so I don't need to deal with my husband as much, he's my boss, I'm Henriette, Madame Henriette to clients, but you're not a client, what's your name, little girl, Polydor was going to say Polydor but she said Ariane, my name is Ariane, I have a job in a bookstore on weekends, I have—I.... She was holding back tears, she was sobbing, she couldn't remember anymore why she had left l'Abeille's house, the living room warmed by the fireplace, she couldn't remember that her thoughts were as gloomy as the bottom of a well, where do you live, Henriette asked, I'll take you home, you know we need a union and laws to protect us, the women in my line of work, girls your age have to help us, the government doesn't respect us, Henriette said, come on, I'm not about to lose a client because of you, girl, tell me where you live, and when she thought later of that unfortunate, drunken night outside the bar, Polydor would wonder if maybe that had been her, if Henriette was the prostitute mother Gérard had been dreaming of, she was probably delirious, like everything else that night, she wouldn't tell anyone about it, not even Doudouline, but it would have been a comfort for Gérard to know that Polydor might have found her mother in the woman who had saved her from her humiliation that night, Gérard's mother, breasts bare under the fur coat, maybe she would have laughed, good-humored and smiling again, yes, Polydor thought, maybe. As Louise finished her story about Polydor, Olga was dusting René's piano, this will have to be sold soon, Madame René, won't it, this piano so big in your dining room, but this time it was Louise who answered Olga, please leave the piano alone, we will never sell it, and Olga, offended, lowered her head without answering, these friends of René's were invading her domain, she seemed to think, Madame René was unquestionably Olga's property, Olga, born in Moscow like the poet Pushkin, it was embarrassing that Madame René had so many visitors, the intimacy between Madame René and Olga had cooled, we all made mistakes when we were young, René said suddenly, more than just mistakes, we made a lot of mistakes, Louise said as she put her hand on René's arm, with that gesture that connected her to René, Louise wanted to push away the presence of Olga, her shadow, Polydor became a serious bookseller, she started reading all the books, Louise said, that's how time transforms us, though our dissolute urges and our rebellion might have been the best thing about us, the most sublime, yes, Louise said, René still felt that rebellious instinct when he thought back to being kicked out of schools, the girls' and the boys' schools, and though he so wanted to be a pilot in the army, a male pilot, that had been trampled in accusations of perversity, being transgender was still unnamed and unnamable then, so you see how things are changing, Louise said, the army is gender equal now, you'd be welcome there now, René nodded his head, it's too late, I think of all those who have been rejected like me, who suffer the worst prejudice, I think, René said, and then she said nothing, Louise admired the fact that René still looked so distinguished in his elegant dressing gown, the only thing missing was a scarf, he always wore scarves, or ties in the exquisite colors that had been in fashion then, but Louise couldn't revive that old aestheticism for René, right here in the apartment with Olga lurking, how could she get rid of that woman, Louise thought, Lali would have to come back, yes, she had to, she lives so far away, and she's still seeing patients, especially those new AIDS patients, they're so young, they never thought to protect themselves, they flaunt all the rules, Lali says they need to be educated, lives are being lost, Lali says, teenagers, for them sexuality is freedom, a wilderness playground, working-class girls and boys, Louise thought, René took Louise's hand in his, he felt like he was being held in the safety of a harbor on a sunny day, tethered, Louise had always been such a comfort to him, even when René was unfaithful, for all the forgotten men and women, that progress you're talking about has a pretty bitter taste, René said to Louise, René thought of all the heroic women pilots whose bravery was only now being recognized, the women who had fought in dark wartime skies, René thought, they were still fighting, yes, and what did we know about them, the women who'd flown in World War II had long since been forgotten, Soviet women who'd been fresh young volunteers, their helmets and the medals pinned on their military uniforms, later their faces grew hardened, their eyes were dull, the ravaged old women of the female squadron, what was left after heroism for those women, no one noticed them, they went from flying planes to lives that were suddenly so common, confined to marriage or motherhood, they had lost that exhilaration, the sky whose furrows they had creased, the night's beauty crested with stars, the sky weighed on them now, oppressing them with exploits they could no longer accomplish, they were no more than mothers raising their children, the sky, so captivating, moving, and inconstant had fled in every possible way and they were chained to their role as women and mothers, that was the fall from grace for so many women, from heroism, that oblivion, that silence, we're going to throw a big party for you and you'll get to see all the people you love and everyone who loves you, who are following in your footsteps, keeping up the struggle, protesting, fighting for their rights, l'Abeille, Polydor, Johnie, Louise said, you'll see how much your fight has marked us all, to you it seemed lonely, though in saying this, by aligning herself with René, Louise was chastising René for being so profligate, though not in so many words, for her dissolute passions, her parents had been careful and generous and René had blown her inheritance seducing women, shabby women like Nathalie, all those first-class flights, expensive hotels in Paris and Rome, what an arrogant couple they'd been, René and Nathalie, and all the baubles, offerings to a capricious woman, it still pained her, she was still shocked, Louise went back to l'Abeille's to finish her thesis, she told herself she had to write about women and cancer, it seemed urgent, why were so many women victims of cancer and what was left after mutilating the female body, at l'Abeille's house flames crackled in the fireplace and they could see mountains of snow through the windows, were the cracks in the ceiling getting longer and wider as the winter winds raged on, l'Abeille with her headphones on had gotten a message from Manfred, my dear Marie-Christine, Christie, l'Abeille, my dear friend, I had to leave very quickly for a tour, Toronto and Vancouver, all my love, your friend Manfred, just a little note, would you agree to marry me, I would be so grateful, I would be very grateful to you, I could become a citizen of your cherished, lovely country, for some years now my papers as a touring concert pianist have not been in order, and we could divorce soon after and you could marry whoever you wanted, someday, that is, I don't want to make demands upon your sentimental life, far from it, all my love and kisses, my dear friend, your devoted tenant, Manfred, l'Abeille had replied that it would be an honor to be the wife of a great pianist with a humble heart, she liked his long uncombed hair, his romantic air, his feline step like Rosemonde's as he skirted the walls, his green eyes like Rosemonde's, a feline man, there was nothing more charming than that in a house, he was self-effacing, they never heard him come or go even when he left for months on end, might he leave her a note on the closed lid of the piano when he left next time so that she wouldn't go looking for him all over town and never find him, in her home she was responsible for every soul, the lost as well as the salvageable, she reigned like a benevolent fairy over the order and chaos of her people, I will be your wife for a few months, she wrote to Manfred, as long as it takes for you to become a responsible citizen, dear Manfred, you would be doing me an honor in this marriage and divorce, I've just signed a petition which we delivered to the mayor with the girls, demanding that we girls should also have the right to marry, men or women or bigender people, I will not marry until I meet my true love, which seems far away even though Johnie said that the mess of my planets predicted that I will marry a woman before thirty, that's a long time, which means I'll make a lot of stupid mistakes between now and then, a few days ago I spent the night with a defrocked nun and I cannot tell you what that was like, but each time I come out of it and I'm not jaded, I start believing again that there's a truly great love waiting for me just like Johnie sees it in the stars, under the bright sign of Cancer, with a Taurus, a professional, a good woman, so my dear Manfred you have lots of time to keep me as a wife, especially since you're still paying the rent every month, Polydor is studying philosophy now and she's been promoted at the bookstore, her preference now is for coffee with a drop of cognac so she can study late at night, Doudouline and Polydor still love each other, the Great Sophie had a bed delivered for them, she said it would be more decent than sleeping on a mattress on the floor, Doudouline was mad because the bed was too small, she said, once again Mama doesn't want me to share my bed with Polydor so she sends me a bed for a single person, that's just like her, and dear repentant Mama had a much bigger bed delivered, with pink sheets and warm blankets, the household was sheer happiness, it's still snowing hard and every day I scatter breadcrumbs on the snow for the birds, they're cold, I noticed that you liked that, Rosemonde likes it too, she looks at them from the window, moving her mouth, her jaw makes a little noise in the quiet, I would have liked to marry Louise under the Cape Cod sky last summer, I thought about it when we were swimming together, she's a big, beautiful girl, I like her a lot, but she has René, what a fickle husband, swimming in the Atlantic waters I felt it for the first time, a great love could come to me, let's hope for the future, according to Johnie's predictions, which all seem to come true, though not always exactly as we'd like, my dear Manfred, all my love and kisses to you too, I can't wait to hear you again at your piano, all of us sitting cross-legged next to you, l'Abeille, Christie, Marie-Christine, your future wife of a few months, so it was winter, Louise said, continuing the story for René, l'Abeille was drawing and painting, she had finally bought some canvases, a gift from Manfred she said, she wasn't painting on the walls anymore, they were already covered with her black marks, graffiti,

Polydor was earning a little money, as if Gérard was sending her some from her resting place, which was probably not that restful with worms gnawing at her bones, the cemetery director, seeing her so diligent with Gérard, offered to tend the plot for them, cleaning the snow in winter and planting flowers on the grave in the summer, Polydor shouting with joy because she would always be close to Gérard, she would wear the sheepskin coat, her high boots, the Mickey Mouse shirt, our relentless winters were turning her cheeks pink, Polydor was alive again as if Gérard's blood had flooded her veins with a rush of energy, incredible strength heightened by the coffee and cognac she'd become accustomed to. René was still thinking about the pilots whose hopes had been dashed, what use was the heroism of women, she asked Louise, I might even ask what use is individual struggle, and yet when I was young I never backed down from a fight, I never hesitated, there was the protest against homophobia in New York that crushing June where everyone risked their lives, René said, they threw stones and bricks at us, there was a man among the homophobes in the crowd carrying a child on his shoulders shouting, wicked lust, wicked sex, wicked love, wicked, wicked, René could still hear the screams in the crowd, they were everywhere, in every city, Montreal, Paris, in Ontario, during a peaceful protest, all we were asking was the right to live without being harassed, as he talked with Louise René felt the old resistance rise up again, the indignation, and I'm not even talking about the astounding cruelty in countries like Pakistan, Iran, China, where gays are incarcerated, tortured, hanged, when will this end? Louise listened, she was watching Olga, what was the woman doing here, why had René hired her, she called herself a nurse but was she even, of course you wouldn't kill a fly, Louise was about to say to René, it's hearts you break, but Louise said nothing and kept on with her story, as I was saying, René, Polydor was zealous about keeping up the cemetery plot even in winter, Gérard the second had started helping too, they were shoveling snow and they saw a patch of grass appear, all shriveled up under the snow, soon there will be tulips, Gérard the second cried, and shovels in hand, standing beneath the still icy sky, they marveled, emboldened by the promise of the first spring flowers even though it was still February, it would be an early spring, what a thrilling thought, soon they would be breathing in the scent of lilacs hanging off heavy branches bowing in the wind, it's so good to be alive, said Gérard the second whose given name was Thérèse, just then the loveliest of birds landed on Gérard's grave, how had the bird survived the winter, Polydor asked, it was a cardinal, scarlet, a miraculous bird, Polydor said, it was so rarely seen in winter, the bird appearing like that, motionless, gently resting its feet on the snow and not moving, was it a heavenly affirmation that Gérard's soul was free from strife at last, from sorrow, later Johnie said that Gérard had undoubtedly been reborn elsewhere, in a warmer reincarnation, but that as a bearer of demands and rebellion Gérard would always be a disruptive element, wherever her flight might take her, would it be India, no, not India, Gérard said, she would be a newborn abandoned by her mother on the tracks, not even swaddled, crying and screaming for days and nights before a police officer took her to an orphanage, no, that wouldn't do, and the worst would be in China where her mother, crying, would have no choice but to wrap her up in newspaper and hope for the charity of some good Samaritan who would adopt a girl child, the mother would return to the countryside, crushed, a modest peasant woman, her baby's cries still ringing in her ears, her belly, her womb aching, and as her tears fell on the dry earth she would say, my child, my little girl, where are you, could that be the next life for our Gérard, Polydor asked Gérard the second, no, Gérard the second replied, hardly able to believe the cardinal's appearance on such a harsh day, so close to her, on the snow, no, I see her flying away, our Gérard, toward a great destiny as a liberator, yes, I can see her, Gérard the second said, I see her flying away toward a summer sky, singing, I am finally free, she whose mother might have been

African, that striking, grieving lady at the funeral, or else her mother was that high-class prostitute who sheltered me in her coat, Polydor said, and saved me from the dangers of the street at night, any woman who offered kindness and protection became Gérard's mother, Polydor thought, any woman who takes you into her car at night and holds you to her heart, cooing, now, now, what's the matter, she asks, and you feel like she's always been with you, that she's part of your life, past and present, Polydor said, Gérard the second listened without understanding, what woman are you talking about, who held you to her heart when you were in danger, when did that happen, you never told me about that before, Polydor fell silent, suddenly she didn't want to confide in her, in the spring, when the lilacs start to bloom, Polydor said, l'Abeille and Manfred will be married, a phony marriage, Polydor said laughing, we'll be there, all the girls together to celebrate in the courtyard, then the handsome musician will leave again, he'll leave a note on the piano, good-bye my dear, beautiful friends, I am leaving on tour to Mexico, love and kisses, your Manfred, brother and friend, l'Abeille's husband, at least until the summer, that's how it will be, Polydor said, as springtime nears Rosemonde will sharpen her claws and l'Abeille will hone her senses, getting ready to go out at night again, even if l'Abeille kept telling them that she was more mature now, no more flings and affairs, believe me, girls, but the surge of hormones Johnie talked about was inevitable, Polydor said, sensuality was the purview of the young, not the old, they were getting tired of it, l'Abeille said she wanted to live fully and experience everything before it was too late, but where was the violent, fiery vibration of true love in all of it, the girls were talking in the cemetery as the superb bird, the scarlet cardinal, listened to them and shivered and suddenly it spread its crimson wings and flew away, the four o'clock light fading in the winter sky. Is that Venus scratching at the door, René asked the Russian nurse, Olga, go open the door, it is wind, Olga replied, only wind, Madame René, no doubt we will have another storm, that little cat died a long time ago, Madame René, no, René said authoritatively, you don't know anything about it, she just goes out hunting around the neighbors' houses, I can feel it and I'm not wrong, she'll be back soon, yes, she'll be back soon, Louise repeated, we know that, Venus always leaves and comes back, doesn't she, René, a photo of Nathalie on René's bedside table caught Louise's eye, so, Louise thought, René hadn't gotten rid of it, even though the frame stood among photos of René's pets, all the cats and all the dogs, Nathalie's face, her blond hair, that sexy air she had seemed to spill out of the frame as if she were about to step into René's richly decorated apartment and lie down on the velvet sofa with a drink in her hand, I'm nothing like that cumbersome doll, Louise thought, no, not at all, Nathalie was blond while Louise's eyes were dark, her hair was black, her skin was nothing like Nathalie's pink, alluring skin, was she even attractive, Louise wondered if she was even desirable, it was stupid to compare herself to the other woman, Louise faced the photo the other way without René noticing and continued her story, it was a time of sexual revolution, at least l'Abeille said it was, and although Gérard was missing from their mayhem, every day the girls were bursting with life, with overflowing joy of every kind, l'Abeille said that even if religion were parading stark naked in the street, even if there were slight advances in the revolution, in liberation, women always got left behind, it was as if they had never existed, as for the women of l'Abeille's motley group, it was honestly like they didn't exist at all, unnamed because of some narrow-minded modesty, people talk about men, about their rights, but never about women, that tacit taboo, a silence unbroken, it would be a dishonor, or if we lived some barely visible existence, it was better not to be seen, it would only lead to condemnation, angry and shrill, she was so angry, l'Abeille denounced all social apathy, all the hurtful judgment, every unkind word spoken against difference, it occurred to l'Abeille that Gérard had been the spark of freedom that leads to an explosive awakening, she had discovered a small town and villages by the sea when she went down to work in the bars of P-town that summer, seaside havens for those who were shunned or attacked because of their sex, Louise told René, you had to see it, the splendor of that tiny Rome on the water, or some ancient Greece where boys loved boys, or the city of Lesbos transplanted to New England and chasing its puritanism far away, you had to see it, l'Abeille said, to understand that sexual freedom and sexual preferences can never be censored because only the bloom of sexual freedom leads to a harmony of bodies, and to justice. It was a revelation for Gérard that there on the shore she could unabashedly come into what l'Abeille called the right to be herself, the intense freedom Gérard had experienced might have seemed outsized, excessive, because now everyone who was like her or near her shared the same freedom, they believed it had been theirs for a long time, a transcendence, an urge to take risks, how wonderful it was, l'Abeille said, everything was crystal clear, gleaming in its excess, everywhere on the beach there were couples, boys together, girls together, there were hotels and houses for them only, what more magnificent lightness was there than the freedom to live without anger, authentic candor, then it happened, Louise went on, a sinister shadow, the dark side of sex, and once again it brought condemnation against some but not others, it brought exclusion, the little pink and green wooden houses along the sea closed down, the hotels that had been welcoming closed too, the houses slammed their shutters and all that was left was a small town, deserted villages, empty beaches, that's all, Louise said. In a widespread plague we were the lepers, the rejects, Louise said to René, there was a governor in Indiana who refused to give clean needles to addicts in the name of his faith, of piety, he refused to bow to the national medical experts, and so the epidemic flared and two hundred and forty people died because of his negligence, his answer to the AIDS crisis was to say he would pray and look what his damn faith did, it killed men and women who didn't have to die, Louise said, that's how the government can be utterly guilty and yet still somehow they're not held accountable, out of fear of disobeying we submit to the rules of cowardice, of bigotry, Louise told René, but you, René, I know you, you would say that the beauty of life outweighs this ugliness, yes, I do say that, René said, in spite of his suffering, how uncomfortable he was in his body, yes, I always do, my dear Louise, whatever we think, the beauty of life always prevails, think of the courage of the men, women, and children who survived, think of our beaches, where we used to go, in New England or elsewhere, the houses and hotels lined up on the shore are open again, swimmers' skin is warm in the sun, those who left have been replaced by healthy kids, one wave ebbs and another surges in its wake, René said, your pessimism has always been disheartening, you're so serious, why not just enjoy life like I do, I think I hear Venus scratching at the door, Louise took a few steps toward the door and said to René, no, she's not back yet, tomorrow perhaps, or the day after, I'm sure she'll be back, René said abruptly, I know you didn't like the songs I used to sing at the bar, my thirties' tunes, but I did best in girl bars, I was slim and handsome then, they were all drawn to me, life was easy, of course that was before I met you, my giantess, before I discovered your brilliant mind, your many qualities, Louise smiled at René but she was still thinking of Nathalie, her hideous blond hair in that photo on the bedside table, it was for her that René had spent a whole inheritance and now she was starting up again with the Russian nurse who was probably only an escort picked up online, one of those Russian beauties who were always available, do you need me, I'm here, she reeked of opportunism, it was disgraceful, and René's eyes lit up at her shamelessness, Louise remembered the committee René had founded to help the young women working in factories, they were exploited, they were getting fired because of their sexual orientation and ended up on the street, René had helped them, discreetly, one by one, René had gotten lawyers who supported the cause, it had to be said, Louise thought, that René was a complex man, or was that self-effacing compassion a feminine quality, when the two genders merged, René became the attractive creature that Louise had loved, neither woman nor man, or both at the same time, at once harmonious and halting, René was complex and the most complete being Louise had ever met, René's voice broke into Louise's thoughts, what happened to Polydor that night, did she remember, René asked Louise, Polydor's memory came back in jolts, Louise said, what had she done that night, what hadn't she done, it was like she was turning the pages of a photo album where each picture showed a painful transgression, crazy, risky behavior, she remembered a café where she had stopped, through the window she could see the snow falling outside, and a musician who was blasting away on an electric guitar asked the audience, mostly ordinary couples, men and women dancing in each other's arms, my friends, he mocked, how many of you have done drugs, and everyone raised their hand except Polydor, who was trying to sober up with a hot coffee and who was nauseated to find herself there, she was so apart from their normalcy, they were dancing so comfortably and drinking heavily, their coarse complicity, was it when she left that club and its stench of beer that she had crossed the snowy street to the bank, the stone wall was so tall, and the beggars crawled into nooks and gaps for the night under overhangs and stone porches, pulling her navy blue coat closed around her Polydor had fallen asleep against the wall, she remembered with a start that her boots were full of snow and opened her eyes to the winter mist, wondering where she was, there were two men next to her who stank of alcohol and vomitous wine, she recalled, and one of them had laid his big paw on her and asked, what are you doing here, are you new here, the second man had come closer, unbuttoning his coat, was that when the headlights of a car had flashed over her hiding place, shining also on the two men who were attacking her so slowly and awkwardly that it was hard to say if it was happening at all, or was it a scene out of a nightmare quickly dissolved and of which Polydor had been an indifferent witness, yes, that was her, Henriette, walking down the street looking for a trick, Henriette heard footsteps, a man running away through the snow, and she shouted after him, you don't have to run away, I'm ravenous but I'm not going to eat you, her laughter echoed in the night, they're running away from me, it's because I'm getting old, she whispered, they used to run at me, not away, just then Henriette had seen Polydor and the two men, she ran over in her long fur coat, I was so ashamed, Polydor remembered, so ashamed, but Henriette, even while she was taking care of me, was mostly worried about her clients, it was a shame, Henriette had said, that at sixty her chances were dwindling, she would have liked to be independent and not have a pimp, who was her husband, she was thinking of getting a divorce, she had explained to Polydor, will you behave yourself from now on, Henriette had asked Polydor, don't get mixed up with guys like that, they're no good, still, I wish they had a roof over their heads, it's too bad, living in the street in the winter, but don't come here anymore, don't run around with them, Henriette had said, I had hoped for a customer this evening, but nothing, just one man, he looked at me and ran off, you'll remember what I said, right, little girl, Polydor was immobile with shame, but her feet warmed up in Henriette's car and she felt stronger, she felt almost loved by this stranger, from then on Polydor was speechless with deference before the prostitutes she crossed in the street at night, her respect for each one was absolute, without Henriette's random intervention as she looked for a client, out after midnight, Polydor would have been raped by those two men, who had inspired only a dull disgust but no fear, she didn't feel much of anything anymore with the cold and in her strange coma, Polydor was the seventh child of a working-class family, she'd gone to work in a factory at a very young age, and she looked up to René, who had stood up for young women who were being mistreated by their bosses, whether through their vile words or otherwise, and then when they were forbidden from coming to work, it was time, René said, to unite to denounce discrimination in the factories, we have to march together in the street, all together, every man and woman has the right to work, young men had also been victims of discrimination, we all have to denounce the miserable wages the girls are getting in the factories, they're taken advantage of because they're young, the working hours are horrible, that was how René used to be, the bosses were corrupt, it's abuse, they're taking advantage of the poor, René said during those days of massive protest, René had started the strike, the mutiny, Polydor and Gérard the second remembered the punishing working conditions, the march at dawn, the cold, the factories with their infernal din, they made ice skates from morning to night, the pace was frantic, because we have to remember, Polydor said, never forget, the scar of having been a cog in the machine was seared into the flesh and it is an eternal humiliation, Polydor remembered warming her bare thighs on a broken heater, she remembered the boss saying to her in his office, we know things about you, we know everything, we know, his words stabbed at her, what did he mean, she didn't know except that she had refused the man's advances, though others, more fragile perhaps, would give in, but she said no, come on, come closer, don't be afraid, I'm just trying to get to know you better, what was he saying, how did he know everything when there was nothing to know, was he talking about her relationship with Gérard the second who had been called Thérèse, what was he implying, you seem very close, you and your friend Thérèse, I've been watching you for a long time, why had Polydor dressed so lightly in winter, just a skirt and thigh-high stockings, the navy coat was too light, she was only poor like so many others around her, she hadn't yet known the human warmth of the girls in the group, she only had Thérèse, who was chained to the factory just like her, the heater was barely warm at all, was it cruelty or neglect, Polydor and Gérard the second brought their starvation wages back to their families, and then there was the riot, all the workers in the street with their placards refusing to work, Polydor and Gérard the second marched and René joined in, when the army and the firefighters were sent to put down the protest, all of them huddled under the spray of icy water, bent over, afraid they would shoot, and René said to Polydor don't be discouraged, girls, we'll win in the end, can I take you out for dinner in the meantime, that's how René was in those days, Louise said, so sensual in her private life, so shamelessly selfish in seeking her pleasure with married women she said were more satisfied with her than with their husbands, wasn't it odd that women who were unfulfilled at home found some solace with René, though often they didn't even know her, they'd barely met her, just an evening, René, away from a worldly and chivalrous life, was fighting his battle, in all things he was a hypocrite, Louise thought, and that made him aloof, it was the end of winter that year, Louise went on, straightening the silk pillows under René's head, Gérard the second and Polydor were biking down to tend to the garden on Gérard's grave, and in her smoky studio l'Abeille was chain-smoking and painting, huge canvases, now her colors were red and white, a dot of red paint on a desert of snow, and we knew that blaze of color meant hope for the future, at least ours, but l'Abeille heard a cracking sound, the plaster wall of her studio was crumbling around her, the old house in all its opulence was falling apart, they would have to move, they would have to leave, the girls would have to find somewhere else if the house fell apart, Manfred was playing a Chopin adagio and didn't seem to have heard anything, and l'Abeille thought, with the first flowers of March, the red sun in her painting, and Manfred's adagio on the piano, the world would soon be alive again.

PART TWO

Day

PART TWO

Where are your evening clothes, Louise asked René, your scarves, the Italian shoes, we're getting ready for the party, Louise told René, but René was indifferent, what's the point of a party, Louise, you can see I can't get up, I can't have anyone over if I'm like this, you can see that, Louise, Olga locked everything up in the big wardrobe, that's all in the past, Louise, forget about the party, Louise, René wrapped himself up in his housecoat as he watched Olga, who was listening to Louise suspiciously, I gave Madame her bath this morning, said Olga, the Russian nurse, I take care of Madame as soon as she is awake, it's true, René said, Olga is beyond reproach, she's so patient with me, I'm a grumpy old man, no, you are charming lady, Olga said, you remind me of my old mother, always alone in Russia, women should be pitied very much, Olga sighed, Louise almost felt a twinge of sympathy for Olga but she changed her mind, where are René's silk shirts, Louise demanded, why did you lock everything up, it's absurd, I dressed Madame in man's underwear like she asked me, she is clean and fresh, but do not ask her to get up to see your friends, she is incapable, Madame is invalid, none of that is true today, Louise said, irritated, René will get up and walk, she will greet her friends with dignity, Louise said, noticing that René was listening to her with that same subtle old twinkle, that rebellious smile, isn't that right, René, today is a celebration, isn't it René, but René didn't answer, she missed Lali so much, little brother, Lali only seemed to think about her patients now, the new AIDS patients, she wanted to help soften their fate, she wanted to teach them to be careful, René would have liked Lali to come sleep near him again like she used to after a night out at the bar, Lali's body curled up modestly in the military coat, anxious to salvage a few hours of sleep before dawn, her short, boyish hair, that head so sensual and austere, René loved placing his hand against it, you can talk to me about Berlin, you know I'm your friend, little brother, tell me about yourself, brother, you know I get it, I understand everything, I will sleep, Lali answered softly, I will be at the hospital very early tomorrow, I will talk to you another night, good night, René, good night, Lali, cold conqueror, René thought, as if she had never known love nor tenderness, or had not known how to express it, she abandoned her lovers after a night of pleasure, the gift of herself taken sharply back, René wondered if Lali was that cold with her patients, was she rough like that with them, with some glimmer of kindness, and how did they feel about her, did they hope for a cure, did they feel the coldness of a mother toward children she didn't love? Lali was proud, and René knew not to cross the threshold beyond which she hid the pain of the past. She ran her hand through that boyish hair of Lali's, over her winter-cold cheeks, teasing her, tell me, Lali, brother, is sex just a sport for you, is it just to keep you in shape, is that all sex is for you, Lali, Lali answered, with her usual dour irony, yes, the sex is very good for health, when Lali was still living out in the country, René thought, she would drive slowly on the icy roads at night, holding a girlfriend's hand in one hand, dreaming of the hours that would follow in the warmth of the embrace, already feeling relaxed after a day's work with her patients, and she would say to the friend whose hand she was holding, it will be warm, and soft, very soft, in the dark stillness of her car, it was a bit battered because she took her dogs out in it on Sundays, when

everything was dark inside and out, in rain or snow, Lali seemed to
hold her one-night stand near, one evening, one night, and for the
woman who felt the touch of Lali's hand in hers as snow or rain fell
on the roof of the car and the windows glistened with light frost,
what a haven, she would think, for a few hours she was the chosen
one at this banquet of love deep in the country, it would be delicious
to kiss those lips, to catch Lali for an instant before she flew off
elsewhere, how could Lali's hard body be broken, her rigidity, what
soft caresses would it take, was there a breach through which you
could get to her heart to wake it up for a moment to the language of
love, you're always the most beautiful girl at the bar, you're so
remote in your military coat, why don't you wear boots in winter,
and Lali would say, shut up darling, you all talk a lot in this country,
I like silence, do you understand, my darling? Soon Lali would
loosen up her arms and her legs and take her lover in her arms, she
was slow and meditative in the other woman's arms, she smoked
when they were done, her sharp European cigarettes, very soft,
she would say, I like quiet, softness, you understand, my darling, do
you want to read comic books with me in bed, we have one more
hour and then I have to leave, hard times, hard life, my love, René
thought of Lali, how she read comic books, she avoided reading
anything that upset her, except books about science and medical
research, René found Lali's simplicity disarming, don't you ever read
poetry, René asked, no, I don't like what makes people suffer, and
poets suffer too much, Lali, I'm going to teach you to read poetry,
René said, sometimes words heal, you know, you are child of late
Romanticism, Lali told René, you are really a bit crazy, René, you're
too old to understand young people, Lali was a common soldier in
her military coat, René told her once, you're so dull sometimes, little
brother, but I love you, I love you, do you understand, Lali, you're so
stubborn. Lali was often surprised or scandalized even, René
thought, when René accepted invitations to those bourgeois orgies,
it was shocking, Lali said, you possess many women you don't even

know, just for fun, you debauched boy, Lali said, offended, bad boy, acting like a man in a brothel, no, René said, that was when I was much younger, and it was only a game, wasn't it, don't you think, you who put so little stock in sex? Sex is sex and that's all, don't make a big deal of it, whoever said I was a paragon of virtue? Lali, in life, we have to experiment, we try to understand and learn, and especially we never want to be bored, didn't you tell me, Lali, that life without sex is boring, Lali listened to René, you very shocking bad boy, she concluded, you are not like anyone else, Lali shrugged, she was getting tired of the carnal nights, it is enough, I like to be alone, I like solitude, too much agitation otherwise with the girls, what Lali meant was that she didn't want to be possessed by anyone, she didn't trust couples, and most of all she hated being deprived of her freedom, she had learned early on to manage alone in life, she had always been able to get by, to get ahead alone, that was how girls lived in Berlin, Lali said, they had seen their mothers come out of war and strife alone, unwavering, Lali shook her head, her pride was hurt, alone but with a few friends, René answered, right, Lali, I know you're going out every night with someone from the bar, René said, I can't look the other way, little brother, and René thought about Louise, who had written an essay on women and cancer, how could he be living in luxury, traveling around with Nathalie, while Louise was healing, while she was writing about all that, how could he, there he was squandering money on Nathalie in Europe while Louise was interviewing women with cancer, how do you feel, can I write about it, I'm your sister, I'm the same, I know how sharp a loss it is, the phantom breast, I know the overwhelming instinct to pull away, to retreat into the depths of emptiness, I know that vertigo when you don't know how to use your body anymore, am I still alive after the treatments or not, and the exhaustion that lingers on, not only in the spirit but in the body, so tired the body just goes cold, it's like your senses are paralyzed, René should have reassured Louise, he thought, he should have been more present, he'd been thinking only of passion and now he felt guilty, he was vain, he had no conscience, and here Louise was saying there would be a party for him tonight, she wasn't accusing him of anything except being lazy, which in any case was innate, he said, he was lazy, René allowed Louise to dress him, she wasn't as bossy as Olga, she knew how to draw him out as she put his clothes on, she had done this so often before, dress her old husband for a party, some unexpected outing, they would go out together like a real couple, it was what Louise dreamed of, going to the movies or to the theater to see the Great Sophie, the mismatched duo of Doudouline, who was known onstage by her birth name, Anne-Sophie, and Sophie, the mother, together on the stage like the clash of two opposing planets, René's mind was elsewhere, he was thinking back to his activist days, he had sometimes played the hero but there were lots of heroes and heroines, René thought, and they were quickly forgotten, whatever had become of all those people lying down in the street in Washington, demanding AIDS drugs from the government, they had come in droves, the sick and the dying even maybe among them, at the end of their rope, all lying down close together in front of the White House demanding financial and medical help, René remembered the angry cries no one seemed to hear, a little while later those who had come to beg one last time would be lying in the ground, perfect symmetry, just as they had been in the streets of Washington, with their hand-drawn signs and banners, their names draped in exquisite works of art in watercolor and oil, *I won't forget you Pierre my love, I love you Louis dear child, I love you*, the lyricism of their words, their poetry would be a homage, a monument, written and painted like bright red sheets, like blood spilled, these moveable monuments crossing from one city to the next and as far as the ocean, huge flags waving in the wind, the names too numerous to count, ten thousand, a hundred thousand, we could die far beyond any number, the counting was oppressive and we didn't want to know how many there were anymore, the figures, the governments would keep quiet about them and about their own part in it and under the ground all those protestors at the end of their lives, they were invisible, and the police wove in among the defenseless protestors, on foot or on horses, someone shouted, I remember, René thought, if you don't help us, you will be guilty of our death, another time, during one of the protests, someone was wounded, his head, and I remember the noise when he fell, we were stumbling over each other as we ran away, we had pepper spray in our eyes, I remember, René thought, he was hurt, he couldn't get back up, who still praises those heroes and heroines, who, René thought, as the memories flooded back, harsh memories, René felt uneasy, where was this coming from all of a sudden, his chest felt too small for his body, his ribs heaving, and he felt at last that this body was his, this man's chest beneath a man's undergarments, even if the operation had gone so badly, why was he breathing so hard, was that his own breathing he heard, what was that new sound, his breath catching in his throat, a rattle, a harbinger of the agony to come, Louise was focused on getting him dressed and combing his unruly hair and didn't notice anything and she said, just like she used to when she brushed his hair, before, you and Lali, your boys' haircuts, you and Lali, I won't forget to part it the way you like, I know you both so well, my darling, don't move so much, René, all I want is to make you beautiful for the party, René murmured that it was pointless, he felt so tired, and as if to amuse himself, he whispered in Louise's ear, you know, Olga was born in Moscow like the poet Pushkin, René could hear his labored breathing as he spoke to Louise, how come Louise couldn't hear it, from the living room Olga asked if Madame was all right, very well, René replied quickly, when will you stop asking me that, Olga? I'm almost ready to go out, aren't I, Louise, Louise smiled at René, yes, you used to go out on my arm, we used to go to the theater together, or out to dinner, with your expensive tastes, always the best restaurants, always on my arm, when we went out together, you're so big, my

antelope, yet you were still my little wife, René said, his breath
steadier now, he thought of how Louise had always comforted him,
how she comforted him still in spite of himself, but Louise said,
annoyed, not a little wife, a mistress constantly deceived, listen,
René replied kindly, my dear, it happens to everybody in the world,
in life, even for just a few hours, one day you become a monster, you
step into the nature of a monster, and that's what I was for a few
hours for you, but reason always ends up saving us from our
wickedness, reason and love, you brought me back to reason and to
love too, my love, while René was praising Louise, mollifying her,
how grateful he was to be at home and not in one of those care
homes where he'd had to stay for a time against his will while he
was healing, there was nothing as disturbing as those prisons for
the old or the very sick, where ghostly nurses pretended to look
after you even as you were held captive, René thought, no, it was
better not to have to be there, places of such desperate solitude
where among the other patients he'd been not a man but a woman,
no longer young, there was nowhere to hide, no way to lie, she was
betrayed by her body and her feminine name and René was just
another body among the mistreated masses, often it was brutal,
there was nothing but scorn for every individual's uniqueness,
especially sick women, old women, they were nothing, René
thought, what a painful discovery, to go through all of that only to
find out that women were nothing in those institutions where
inmates were held, they would leave those prisons blunted, reduced
to childhood. René stood up out of the wheelchair, was that when
she had called Olga to come rescue her, or maybe it had been more
like the fabrications of online seduction, or was it Olga who'd been
playing games, a beautiful young Russian woman who was available
and looking for work, what was it that had been his deliverance,
René could never be confined, he was a free man, hadn't he even
gotten up out of the wheelchair and taken a few steps toward the
door, had he run away, or was it Lali who had taken him in, yes, it

was probably Lali, telling him, I've come from far away to look after you, you will be better soon, you fell, nothing serious, and René told her, go back to your patients, you can't neglect them for me, little brother, I'll take care of you first, Lali had said and René saw her face again, looking at his left leg, his sore foot, he kept forgetting that she was Dr. Lali, his little brother from Berlin, thank you Lali, he sighed, his heart filled with an almost rapturous gratitude, thank you little brother, now go back to your patients, yes, go back, Lali, before I get too attached to having you around, I'm an old man now and I like to be alone, do you think Venus will come back soon, Lali? Whenever a dog wanders away when we are walking in the woods they always come back, Lali said, pragmatically, they always come back, you sleep now. Lali left quickly, back to Toronto usually, she didn't want to miss her flight, there might be a doctors' conference tonight, or Boston, Lali was always flying here and there, she was called everywhere urgently, Lali, who liked the pensive slowness and the silence of the countryside, and slow love too, René thought, no, the pace of her life didn't suit her, René could hear Lali telling him, the way she spoke in images, her abridged language, that she would have liked to work in research, especially during the global AIDS crisis, she would have been essential, she said there weren't enough women in research. She'd wasted a lot of time deciding where to live, first in the States, then in Canada, a dizzying exodus, she seemed to say, but what was she running away from, René wondered, what devastating past? René thought that Lali's disappointment or dissatisfaction was inherent in the character of many women she had known or loved, she wasn't thinking of Nathalie or Louise but of one-night stands with strangers, married women complaining about their chronic dissatisfaction, forever unfulfilled, idle and anxious, what was their purpose, was it merely to serve a husband and family, servitude wore them out early. For those who were highly educated, what use were their skills and their knowledge if they were just staying at home with children? Others worked in some field or other but felt that their talents and experience weren't properly recognized. Whatever the profession, men invariably seemed superior, crushing them without a second thought. It was incredible, René thought, that after a single sensual night, women could confide in him like that, their confessions were like pleas or prayers, as if each one were asking, tell us, René, you're nearly a man, how we can survive our condition? They gave him too much power, René thought, but it was reassuring that even brief flings could offer some solace, allow these women to stop beating themselves up, boost what little confidence or faith they had in themselves, as for Lali, the uprooting had been so deep and she was so disillusioned that René could only answer with silence and tenderness. When are we going to go skiing out in the country, René asked Lali, when, Lali, you have to be a bit lazy in life, without that you're dead, hey, little brother, when are we going to go for a walk together on the mountain, Lali, what's the point of working all the time like you do, you're not going to save humanity if it decides it won't save itself, right? Lali's golden eyes blazed under her baseball cap, which was as plain as her long, plain coat, incensed, listen, René, no laziness, I want to save humanity, Lali said as they skied together in the last snow of spring or on icy slopes in winter. What are you doing alone in the country, Lali, René asked as they skied across snowy slopes glistening in the sun, the snow an immaculate white and the first glint of the sun in the morning, how healthy it felt out there, those moments with René lit up Lali's eyes, she huddled under the blankets at night when the coyotes howled under the moon, where would the pack go in the fall, to what other forests, the hunters would hear them, where would the deer go, the doe and her fawn, where would they feed among the apple trees, Lali's cherry trees in summer, where would her fox go, where would they all go if they couldn't outrun the rifles, especially in the fall when evening came and the half-light fell on the fields and the woods, she shook with fear for the beasts, alert and quick, but in the daylight and especially when she was skiing with René, joking between peals of laughter that René couldn't ski, he always fumbled with the skis, one foot in front of the other like an astronaut, René was so funny, how restful and relaxed she seemed then, René thought, like Lali was almost happy. But if she heard a shot it was as if she had been shot herself, the moans of the animal were her own, she couldn't shake the gunshot's echo, it brought her back to other bullets, other shootings, a clamor of distressed cries that left her panting from the pain sunk so far in her restless past, would the chimney in the family house collapse today, would they all be killed, even her little brother, was today the day that disaster would strike, Lali was the animal fleeing, undone, blood frothing at her nostrils, she was dying the same death. But when she was skiing with her bumbling friend René, Lali could forget everything, René thought, and wasn't it his duty to free her from whatever it was that weighed her down, what was that, René wondered, he was overwhelmed by her silence, more and more closed in, sometimes painful. Was Lali that keenly sensitive with her patients, too, or did she act that much colder so she wouldn't feel anything anymore, a kind of patronizing commiseration, neutral and cold? What about your nice shirts, where are your nice shirts, Louise asked René, who was lost in thought as Louise dressed him, Olga opened the antique wardrobe and explained to Louise that René's clothes were all cleaned and pressed, everything in order, Olga said, and, remembering Olga's claim that women were to be pitied, talking about her old mother alone in Russia in her apartment in Moscow, Louise thought, so why isn't Olga with her mother, what is she doing here with René, and why didn't René ask me to take care of her, we've always been so close, it's insulting that she would choose a stranger, or was René keeping her friends away because she was too proud, René laughed and said that death was a foreign country anyway, and on the threshold of even stranger lands, death was an anomaly for everyone, the indescribable terror of a demonic stranger, so we might as well take all suspicious strangeness head-on, she said, that day Olga's round face had popped up on her computer screen as if to say I am yours, she was looking for work, I'm yours, yes, take me, it was so easy to pluck that sudden love, help or love or an out-of-work nurse seeking companionship and there was René, noble warrior, a fighter felled by a bone disease, was that it or was it laziness, the slow creep of the disease, Louise thought, René would never go to a residence or to the women's senior center, that antechamber of death, the decision was categorical, never again, René said, no, it had only been a fall, a broken leg, almost nothing, all women had to be saved, René said, we had to save all the women from the generalized abuse that society accepted, society was dead to others, we must, René said, and from one day to the next, no one quite knew how, Olga was sharing the house, René's apartment, with its antique furniture, the library, the bedroom, even if the bed was only the site of basic care, for washing, trying to heal René's body, Olga carried out her primitive reign with stubborn charm, gradually pushing away René's family and friends so that the two of them were sequestered, dangerously alone, and René, immobile and harried, was no longer the master. And the piano, Louise thought, she keeps talking about having to sell the piano, money, profit, was that all she thought about, that girl from who knew where? Was Louise being too harsh, maybe Olga was only a pitiful, exiled immigrant girl René had rescued from despair, without René maybe she would have been deported, without a roof over her head or without a country like so many others, why was Louise being so hostile toward an innocent woman, she wondered. Women were often like that, their latent enmity, the cloud of suspicion, yes. Louise felt badly for being suspicious, for the ill will she'd harbored about Nathalie for so long, for everything in us that can be so low, she thought, even the childish way Olga did her hair annoyed her, how slowly she walked even though she was young. What about Gérard, René asked, do you ever dream about her? The image of Olga faded, though she was always there, an intruding housekeeper in René's house, Gérard, Louise murmured, poor Gérard, we see her only in our dreams now, in fragments torn apart, she says to me, her voice high and clear, I live behind a wooden door painted blue, all you have to do is knock and I will answer, I run very fast, my feet skim the leafy ground and as I get to the blue door, it lifts into the air, the sky is blue and through the window of a red barn I see Gérard as if she were on a swing, I shout, be careful Gérard, it's too high, don't swing like that, and I can hear Gérard's bright, mocking laughter, from where I am I can't fall anymore, I have wings now, but I'm hungry, where are l'Abeille's soups, she asks me and suddenly a whole pack of little black dogs are rushing down the hill toward the street but there are cars everywhere, don't be afraid, Gérard tells me, they have wings too, will you come over, Louise, I'm sitting quietly behind the blue door and when I go through it opens easily but I can't find Gérard, I know she isn't far, I can hear her breathing, behind the door I see the desert and the barn suspended above and Gérard swings from a window open on a starless night, I recognize her long legs, the sound of her voice, she's singing like a bird, I'm here, I'm here, Louise's voice swelled with pain, Louise, René said abruptly, will you do me the pleasure of dreaming about me, will you, I'll come kiss you awkwardly so you'll recognize me, Gérard is quite right to hide behind her blue door, she's still in her coked-up clouds and maybe she feels good like that, it's better not to know too much, not to disturb her, René said, sadly now, what are we going to do about it, but I'll come back to tease you, my dear, that's for sure, I'll have to keep myself busy with my little fantasies, as in life, don't you think? Gérard seemed to have stopped time for an instant in René's room, swirling her butterfly wings around Louise and René, as if she had said, girls, do you think we really die, well let me tell you, it's not true. René and Louise fell silent, René let Louise dress him limply, René told Louise that he often thought of the suffragettes, the first women who fought for the right to vote, they were ridiculed in 1903, no one could imagine they would become heroines of emancipation, future saints, oh, René said, we owe them what we are today, even if they didn't think about trans people like me, it was too early, we had to get out of the rut of servitude first, all those women had known servitude, especially the poorest, in the factories, they were even more forsaken than Polydor and Gérard the second, suffragettes, what a reductive term, wasn't it, they had written that they had broken with the decorum of their time, isn't that right, Louise, that was their most glorious achievement, to break with propriety, under their propriety and corsets women were exhausted, they were dying in pernicious slavery. The suffocating British respectability of that era, the notion of decency predicated on the domination of men over women that was accepted for so long. Once that iron corset was broken, women were going to vote, they would claim the right to vote by provocation, indignant words, they would finally have the right to speak, they would finally have a voice. What an injustice those early rights were, too, they couldn't vote before the age of thirty whereas men could vote at twenty-one, how strange that that's our history, a humiliating history, and we know so little about it. Louise listened to René, telling herself that in his passion for justice and equality René was experiencing the vulnerability of women without knowing it, though she said that she was a man, she said *we*, she didn't separate herself from the feminine condition, the path of women was hers too even if he had the overbearing character of a man, Louise thought, what contradiction, what ambiguity, even if René's domineering side was a man's, the protest in her was a woman's, above all a woman who refused domination, any attempt to smother her vitality, wasn't that what had always attracted Louise, when she had thought, as a young woman, that René was above all a being, regardless of gender, an innovative being who, like Socrates and Plato to their disciples, would teach her the boldest lesson in freedom she was able to accept. Louise thought about her essay about women and cancer and the women's testimonies, she found them so upsetting, for a long time the word AIDS couldn't even be spoken, Louise thought, the shame was so strong, and it was the same thing when it came to women, the word cancer was silenced, as if we couldn't name or admit that the womb or the breasts, a source of life, were ailing, tired, worn out, it was unacceptable that a woman's body could tire of giving life after having borne it for centuries. That was what Louise had gleaned from the cancer survivors, their complaints, their secular weariness, Louise thought of l'Abeille, of her mother, l'Abeille had said she'd died in agony in a pool of blood, little Marie-Christine had seen everything, it was like a shipwreck, birth interrupted by death, a drowning man caught in his own rigging, neither mother nor child had survived, what a tragic shock, l'Abeille lost her mother and her sister at once, all that blood in her mother's bed, the day before her mother had been alive, her mother, who was a musician and a composer, it was so rare and so untoward that a woman was a composer at a time when all women were oppressed, her mother had given l'Abeille her first sketchbook, she had encouraged her drawings and her watercolors, during those years, during those years of such a singular connection between mother and daughter, l'Abeille had drawn and painted only in color, in joyful triumph, they were united by an unshakeable bond that strengthened their love of art and then suddenly her mother's room was closed, her music studio closed, the husband, her father, crying uncontrollably as he took his little daughter on his lap, what a tragedy, he kept saying, a tragedy, and l'Abeille had put aside the watercolor sketchbooks with their shimmering colors, her hope, her joy, from now on she only wanted to draw and paint in black, thick black ink, she no longer breathed, she no longer slept, she waited long nights against the door of her mother's room for her mother to come back. She called out to her, Mama, come back, come back, Mama, but there was no answer. Her father said, listen, my darling, you can't be waiting at the door every night, she's not coming back, but I'm here and I love you. But it was the artist mother that l'Abeille needed, she had taught her so much, l'Abeille resented her father for the birth of a second child who wouldn't survive, the mother who wouldn't survive, the two lives, mother and daughter, were inextricable, as if they had been stitched together, the father explained to l'Abeille that it was just bad luck, there was no making sense of it, you could only suffer through. L'Abeille had long made it a habit to follow her mother to church, where she had seen her mother conduct the church choir, surrounded by the exalted music of the organ, the adult and the children's choirs, the music she had composed while she was raising her children, on Sundays and holidays l'Abeille had heard that music, those songs, standing close to her mother, it was as if she had been projected into a cathedral where the voices of the children's choir mingled with her own. Elena, her mother, was the lost love she would never find again, Louise thought. L'Abeille was guilty of everything, guilty of living on after Elena's death, guilty even as a five-year-old if a child got hit by a truck crossing the same street l'Abeille had crossed earlier, the small deaths and the big ones piling up like rags in the attic of l'Abeille's stunned con-sciousness, Louise thought, until the endless black lines overflowed, spiders racing across white paper, and until she could draw that bottomlessness, all the layers of blackness that lived inside her. When Manfred appeared one day when l'Abeille's house was about to be torn down, he played a Chopin adagio between the cold walls of the house that would be wrecked soon before he left for another tour, leaving a note to l'Abeille on the closed piano, my dear Christie, Marie-Christine, dear Abeille, I must leave again, this time to Spain, lots of kisses, my dear little wife, my friend, when I get back I'll tell you all about my new fiancée, she's from China, I've often played there, be good, my dear, tenderly, your Manfred, in that arrival l'Abeille could almost already see a departure, he was like a flying cat, wasn't he, l'Abeille said of Manfred, she had a premonition that her mother, her dear Elena, was visiting her at last through the allegory of music that Manfred represented, at last she could draw and paint in color, banishing the drabness of the black. In those days, Louise thought, Polydor, who was working in a bookstore during the day and no longer in a factory, at night she was taking classes at the university, she argued with her philosophy teachers, who were often defrocked priests, the oppressive Catholic church having been swept away by the strong winds of the revolution, those priests, who were married or had mistresses, had little tolerance for Polydor's arguments and her intellectual prowess, which they considered to have been manifested too late, she was just a little factory worker who had delusions of philosophy and intelligence, all the philosophers were men and so philosophy, in its elite sophistication, could only be the domain of men, and they asked Polydor, where were the female philosophers? But Polydor, with her ingenuity, her youth long deprived of knowledge, could name and defend them, those women philosophers, their right to speak and to exist, even if they had to join the Christianity of men, even if they had to write their sacred music, as Vivaldi had, it was better to transcend their earthly selves through that sanctity, to live in a convent as prisoners of God, like Hildegard of Bingen, Polydor said, she could only express herself and all her genius in Christian seclusion, in a convent where she would have peace. Perhaps she'd only been recognized very late, almost into the twenty-first century, because for so long she'd been a divine sacrifice, with no homage expected, Polydor said. Precocious philosopher, at least for her time, hadn't she praised the light of God, like John of the Cross, rather than the less merciful and partial sectarian light of religion, wasn't her philosophical poetry esoteric in its glorification of God? God served as a pedestal and a rock from which a canticle of love poured forth, Polydor told the priests, who didn't listen. In those days, before l'Abeille's house was demolished by the city, Polydor would talk about philosophy, about her struggle to be admitted to university, we were squatting in l'Abeille's living room, smoking and smoking, falling over one by one like the wilting petals of tired flowers, l'Abeille would tumble onto her back with Rosemonde around her neck or tangled in her hair, on the couch, under the plaid blanket that only yesterday Gérard had wrapped around herself during a rare night at home, young doctors were often called to work in the emergency room and Lali had to leave suddenly, before dawn, above the couch the lamp's dim light shone on l'Abeille's sleeping face, Lali stopped for a second before running to the stairs and into the cold night, the chill in the trees and the damp cold of her car, she'd have to shovel it out, she stopped in front of l'Abeille, how lucky she was that she could sleep, Lali thought, standing next to l'Abeille, Lali felt like she was looking at a child, although she was only a few years older than l'Abeille, her friends, the girls in the group, except René, they all seemed very young to her, they weren't maturing from within like she was, Lali was already too old for her years, that was how Lali thought of herself, her past in a Europe that was growing older with every blow, beset and darkened by too many massacres, she couldn't quite name it but watching l'Abeille sleep deepened her understanding that she wasn't part of this new America, nor of l'Abeille's innocence, was Lali going to awaken that innocence, she hated hunters, those who killed innocent animals in the fall, but Lali was a quiet hunter herself, a young wolf gazing at the sleeping child, under the curve of the eyebrows, the eyelashes, where the look of greed was hidden away, and beneath the plaid blanket there was a body, an offering almost, asking for pleasure, at least soft caresses that would rouse her to quivering and contentment, she'd been called in on an emergency but would Lali have time, quickly, she leaned toward the sleeping Abeille, Rosemonde didn't approve and refused to move, mewling, Lali leaned in closer, the long military coat draped over her shoulders, no one would have noticed the speed and skill with which she undid l'Abeille's pajamas, without waking her, as if she had come to her in a dream, she was that good, with her tongue she could push open l'Abeille's lips, warm with the sweet taste of cigarettes, her kisses were quick, but no, she wouldn't have time, Rosemonde didn't approve, her yellow eyes darkened with black streaks, who was this person who dared disturb their sleep, though she was familiar and often came over, this was Rosemonde's holy hour and she didn't like to share with anyone, no, Lali had to be pushed away, but she was still there, she lifted l'Abeille's neck gently as if she were trying to settle one of her patients, as if she'd said, I have to give you an injection but you won't feel a thing, later l'Abeille would recall that she had dreamed of Lali, the military coat covering her, and it was more than a dream because everything was so pleasant, without moving or even quite waking she had achieved such a state of complete relaxation, a tremor more restful than rest and l'Abeille thought that it had been good but that Lali would soon forget her, she would have the same gentle coldness tomorrow, that distance she had about her, though not without affection, the young wolf would go elsewhere to hunt, not devouring her prey, or hardly, l'Abeille thought, life was all about expecting the unexpected, l'Abeille would tell Louise afterwards, but for l'Abeille, who had watched the approach of death with her mother when she had been torn from her, the brief moments of sensuality Lali stole here and there, among her friends or elsewhere, when she went out alone to every bar in the city, wasn't that just some entertaining prelude to what was to come in the emergency room, tending to the dying or patching up the injured, l'Abeille thought, Lali embodied that contradiction to which we have to adjust, that life and death mingle, always joined together, without our knowledge, lest the very thought be intolerable. Joy and pleasure, if not always happiness, softened the sinister aspect of the confirmation that death was always nearby with its sickle, its cynical skeletal smile, an evil fairy letting us believe sometimes that we are happy. Wasn't love the most beautiful consolation for the paradox that our lives would end, l'Abeille asked Louise, and Louise replied that she loved René, his complexity and

uniqueness, she didn't know that soon transgender people would be
front and center, demanding their rights be respected, proclaiming
their equality, René among them like a soldier, a captain at the helm
of the ship. L'Abeille told Louise that even though her mother had
been a great musician, she had probably always known that there
was little hope, at the age of fifteen, Vivaldi was studying to become
a priest but as soon as he was ordained he thought only of
composing, while l'Abeille's mother had married early and had
several children, she had composed music only for the church choir,
for organ, piano, voice, she had never been able to grow, with
teachers and public performances, which the young virtuoso
violinist Vivaldi had, while her world had gradually closed in,
l'Abeille said. But did male composers have an easier life, no,
l'Abeille said, she could still hear her mother's voice, Elena telling
her about the failure of her musician and composer friends, the war,
exile, the alcoholism that ended so many lives, Elena said to her
daughter, a little Mozart could die on the battlefields of the mind,
even if for a time he was a comet in the sky, the sun over rain-
soaked fields, the very light that brightens the day. L'Abeille had
heard the stories many times, it was better that l'Abeille was a
painter, that she learned to draw, Elena would tell her that there was
little future for a woman composer. But, l'Abeille thought, what had
seemed true in her mother's youth wasn't any longer, and without
knowing it, Elena had trained another generation to resist. But
l'Abeille could never forget her mother's bitter words, this country,
Elena said, people were ingrates or they were ignorant, they had no
taste for beauty, our country can't welcome prodigious musicians,
they wouldn't survive the oblivion here, our cruel indifference, a
little Mozart might be born, a little Rachmaninov, his parents
themselves are musicians who teach their child early and like his
father the little prodigy would compose his first études at the age of
eleven, the parents of the little Mozart or the little Rachmaninov
exclaiming in wonder upon hearing their child's first composition at

the piano one night, he's only five years old, those notes in the night, a winter night long and crowded with nightmares of the looming World War for the parents, but the little one at the piano doesn't know anything about all that, that's how they'll show him in the newspapers, pencil in hand, writing, composing his first pieces, a phenomenal child, but cursed already, Elena told l'Abeille, listening to the luminous improvisations, the parents of the little prodigy are moved, at the age of five the young musician gives his first public concert, he dazzles and mesmerizes, he is praised, he will become a great soloist, he is sent to study in Paris, he studies harmony and composition with the masters, the child is stunning, a miracle, a marvelous musician, when they compare him to Mozart at his age he says, Mozart is greater than I will ever be, because, little one, only he knows the desert of his solitude, he is already wary of what the future will bring, the happiness of being in Paris is interrupted by a war that breaks out beneath an increasingly dark sky, he has to leave, return to his country, he knows that from now on no one will understand him, the child evolves from prodigy to performer, upon his return, the child tries to continue his career as a concert pianist, at fourteen the teenager composes a concerto for piano and orchestra, the critics never stop lauding him but then, bad luck, the audience gets tired of him, he's not going to be the next Mozart or Rachmaninov, no, after a triumph in Europe as a soloist, here comes the fall, the pianist and composer is neglected by the critics and by audiences, in despair the pianist tries to win back his audiences with superhuman performances that last forever, they think he is prostituting himself, they punish him with silence, oblivion, he will die forgotten, that was the story Elena told her daughter, the little Mozarts and the little Rachmaninovs died, and they were men, what would have happened to her, Elena, a woman composer, wasn't it better to resign herself to marriage, and I was born of that disappointment, l'Abeille said, but a disappointment that was made up of a hope of success, she told Louise, I didn't lose my mother for

nothing, she will be me and I will be her, l'Abeille said, Louise
thought that it wasn't like l'Abeille to accept bitterness, let alone
resignation. There would be a rebirth, an outpouring of new strength.
And Clara Schumann, l'Abeille said, when she found herself
widowed with seven children, she was still writing and composing,
she directed the Frankfurt conservatory, she didn't stop, and she
entered the pantheon of women who revolutionized the art of
composition, l'Abeille said, for a long time there had been a revival,
new voices, but why was there never any mention of them, those
women, there was never any mention of their creations, their
exploits, l'Abeille asked, why had they been forgotten whereas
Clara's husband was so well remembered, his suicidal despair
already surging in his sublime works, perhaps he was an angel who
had come down to earth only to suffer, that was the angelic man
Clara had loved, he was the beauty of music exhausting itself to the
point of excess, the excesses of an aching romanticism that triggered
all manner of mental disorders, a devastating delirium, her husband
was institutionalized early on, imprisoned in his mental torment,
Clara had known that she had to understand the ardent genius and
the solitude, there it was in her many compositions, which often
overlapped with her family duties, and Clara had said, had sighed,
listen to me, I exist too, this is the music I have made, this is my
performance, I am a virtuoso pianist, a composer, a teacher, I am, I
exist, don't ignore me. Clara had composed a piano concerto in that
whirlwind of children's cries, of dirty, degrading work, the shadows
in which her husband's insanity kept her constantly close, although
she refused to be the handmaid of madness, as much as she loved
her husband, she didn't need to do that, no, l'Abeille said, so my
mother Elena composed a piano concerto with her children by her
side, crying, screaming, no one heard the concerto, she didn't have
time to finish it, she got pregnant again quickly, with a child who
was going to die with her, what grief, l'Abeille said, and what
followed was sadder still, my father, who had always been good to

us, sank into unexpected violence, he seemed passive at first, he stopped leaving the house, he stopped going to work, he was a violinist in an orchestra and he got fired, we lived in fear that he would direct that formidable violence toward us, when we went to bed at night we were afraid, we've seen it before, how apparently normal parents who love their children, after a mental or emotional shock so deep that it's beyond understanding, turn against their children and cut them down as they would a tree, in an unspeakable rage, they forget that they are their children, vengeful parents driven by an extreme violence, a primitive intensity, and I shuddered as I went to bed at night, I shuddered for myself and my brothers and sisters, that we would wake up with a gun to our heads, or my father bursting into our room with an axe, none of that happened, my father was hospitalized and the depression killed him, I think my mother Elena was always with us, holding back the sword over our heads, back to a realm where there was no violence, there was only her music and what she was to me, only sweetness remained, l'Abeille said to Louise, and it seemed so true, Louise thought, l'Abeille was a joyful being, she loved life in a way that seemed unwavering. Polydor and l'Abeille would talk, always late at night, there were philosophical women, Polydor said, even if her teachers stood in her way, an obstacle to her knowledge, to her identity, it was terrible, Polydor told l'Abeille, to feel so unloved and unappreciated, she sobbed over her cognac and coffee, slowly Doudouline would pry the cup of coffee out of Polydor's hand, no, don't touch that anymore, it's too strong and you'll keep me awake all night, but it's almost dawn, Polydor said, and I still have to study, come to bed with me, Doudouline said, I'm going on tour in a week with my mother, I'll miss you, Doudouline said, pulling Polydor onto her lap, my dear, don't cry, that's how it is for an actress, I have to go away, but you've been on tour with your mother for a while, Polydor complained, and I've been sleeping on my own, when are you coming back this time? Doudouline wrapped her arms around

Polydor's shoulders and pulled her toward the bedroom, Polydor, you know I love you, Mama trusts me for now but it won't last long, you know how the Great Sophie is, she's capricious, one day she likes me and the next she's making me doubt myself, it's so hard, Doudouline said as if she were in the theater, her voice shaking, you're the same, Polydor said, you and your mother, except that you're more talented, you're creative and funny, the Great Sophie is too classical, Polydor's jealous muttering dragged on until morning, when was Manfred coming back, l'Abeille wondered, sitting cross-legged next to Manfred's piano in her pajamas, when will I hear Chopin's adagios again, when, l'Abeille smiled, thinking of Lali's visit, l'Abeille had seen Lali again a few days after the dream dalliance, she stopped by to say hello to the girls and introduce her new conquest to her friends, a double conquest, really, Lali came to the house with a young woman, recently divorced, and her little boy, Lali was carrying him, wasn't it funny, l'Abeille thought with a smile, how perfectly bewitching Lali was as the second mother, l'Abeille's mood turned sad, Lali would inevitably leave this charming woman, like all the others, she was only playing again at being a wolf among sheep, a few nights would go by and she wouldn't be there anymore. The young, divorced mother seemed happy, she wasn't alone anymore, maybe she even believed that Lali was her soulmate, everything was an illusion, just bait, l'Abeille thought. Though maybe Lali did fulfill some essential role, she was the revelation of sensuality and pleasure in so many tedious lives, l'Abeille thought, what mattered was that she was there, suddenly leaning toward you, reminding you that you had a body, like the vision of a landscape that soothes you, like quenching your thirst at the river, l'Abeille thought, we have to drink from the wellspring of all consenting flesh, to be moved by the vindication of the animal in us, more than anything, we are animals, l'Abeille thought, though we have nothing of their nobility, and we aren't benevolent either, as they can be, l'Abeille held on to that moment with Lali, even if sometimes she thought she had dreamed it, repeating to herself, remember, don't forget anything, like when she was very young and her parents forced her to take a nap, she was absolutely convinced even without closing her eyes that she had known many other lives before this one and she regretted not being able to remember them, only diffuse, disjointed images, she'd had other parents who didn't fight, other brothers and sisters, they lived somewhere else, in Scotland, it was cozier than this house, they had fields where horses ran free, servants in the house, and before the nap, before closing her eyes, l'Abeille would think, don't forget, remember where you are now because you might forget, and almost immediately the past lives would fade away, and the image that came back to her often, of a bluebird with its head turned upside down at the top of a Christmas tree, where was that, when had she seen that? Elena, her mother, would wake her in this life, not another one, her mother would dress her in her winter wool and say, come into my arms, we'll go sing in the church choir together, it's Christmas today, do you want to hear my cantata, do you want me to sing for you, and l'Abeille thought as she listened to her mother's voice, I must remember, I must not forget, and now, after remembering the dream with Lali, l'Abeille thought she could hear her mother's voice when she used to sing to wake her up from her nap, those long winter naps, and again she said to herself, I mustn't forget anything, I must not forget anything. Neither Lali or Doudouline or Polydor or Louise or Gérard the second, or the first Gérard, no, I can't forget. All the other useless flotsam rose to the surface of memory's river too like planks on the water and Gemma's face came back to her, Gemma running behind her as they played, such a dangerous game, they would dart across the street, across the boulevard, between the trucks, they would cross, run, they weren't afraid, it was as bad as playing on the train tracks to see who could run longest on the rails before the smoke of the locomotive appeared, the trains bearing down on them, it was a terrifying game, gloriously frightening for the reckless Abeille, her name then was Marie-Christine, or Christie, she had just started to write at school and she drew so well, she had learned to speak and write almost as soon as she was born, she had more time than the other students to draw, after school she strolled along the boulevard with Gemma, she took Gemma with her everywhere, what if we cut across the line, Gemma, what if we're brave enough to break the rules, what do you think, give me your hand, Gemma, let's go, there are big trucks coming, Gemma said, she was a docile, slightly fearful child, give me your hand, let's go, they're not going to run us over, Gemma, right, no way, they can see us, Gemma knew that night came early, it was almost dark, the bright lights of the nighttime were already lurking in the late-afternoon twilight, did the sun set at five or at four, they couldn't tell, you can hear the noise of the big trucks, Gemma said to Christie who wasn't l'Abeille yet, obviously Gemma could hear the noise, give me your hand, I'm telling you, we'll cross together, but Gemma didn't want to, Mama told me, Gemma was saying, but Mama told me, let's go, hold my hand, Christie said, she was the reckless one, the most daring one for these kinds of games, and then they were off, just a few seconds, Christie was almost out of breath she was running so hard, across the street or was it a boulevard, there were people everywhere, in their cars and walking, Christie's feet in her little white boots on the ground as if she were dancing above the street, Gemma was wearing white boots too, and her socks were white, everything was going to be very white that day, suddenly Christie wondered why Gemma wasn't holding her hand anymore, as soon as she was across, so close to the sidewalk, Christie, who one day would go by l'Abeille, she called her name, shouting Gemma, Gemma, she could only hear the horrible noise of the trucks on the road, or was it a boulevard, a street of some kind, what time was it, Christie's mother had students at home for her piano lessons that day and maybe from the street they could hear the piano lesson, every single note, everything was very white, the sky, the street, the cars' pale headlights, maybe there was a bit of fog, a thin mist where Christie wanted to look for Gemma who wasn't holding her hand anymore, she hadn't even screamed when—no, it was better to forget everything, l'Abeille thought, it had been an all-white day, and Gemma, that inert shape, the stain of white boots in the street, l'Abeille's recklessness, yes, the white day, the all-white drama, Gemma's socks and boots under the wheels of the trucks, it was because l'Abeille was guilty, guilty of recklessness, guilty of everything, no, it's better to forget everything sometimes, l'Abeille would tell Louise, because otherwise you can't breathe, and what would Louise say, caressing her cheek, no, nothing, you're not guilty of anything, not Gemma, not Elena, nothing, Louise would say. There had been days and nights of bleak whiteness, Louise thought of Johnie who, before meeting the girls and starting to write about Sappho, had been named Vanessa, Vanessa Laflamme, her older sister Émilie called her *petite flamme*, my little flame, Johnie's engineer parents, Johnie and Émilie's engineer parents, they only had two daughters, they liked to travel with their children in the summer, it was during a stay in Greece, a summer of sun and white marble, Johnie had told Louise, we were so happy and free, my sister and I, she was already eighteen but I wasn't yet, my sister rented a room in another hotel than where we were staying with our parents and she would meet boys there, men sometimes, Émilie told me, you have to learn to make love with boys, it feels so good, when you come it's like your body is exploding in gigantic liquid waves, you have to learn, and Johnie, Vanessa, said to her sister, I'm not interested, Émilie, I don't want to, Émilie, and Émilie, who was the sexiest girl Johnie ever knew, said, you'll understand later, you don't want to now but later you won't be able to resist, because women know, that moment is eternal, it's ecstasy and you won't be able to resist, little sister, Émilie was telling Johnie how she had made love in a cave with an archaeology student, the memory had stayed with Johnie, making love flat under a stone or in a granite cave, how grim, in icy underground tunnels, even in summer, Johnie said, oh, I'd be scared, Johnie had said to Émilie, and Émilie who was eighteen was gnashing impatiently, all she wanted was to escape her parents, listen, she told Johnie, you're all going home, you and Mom and Dad, but I want to celebrate my freedom, no limits, nothing's going to stop me from living how I want, I'm going to go traveling alone all summer, I'll hitchhike, I'm not going to come home until the fall, don't forget me, I'll write to you, I'm not going home with the family at the end of the summer, not this time, Émilie told Johnie, I'll tell you about my adventures when I'm back, I'm going to have so many adventures, one after the other, I'll tell you all about it, when they got home they got brief news of Émilie, she was in the Jura, hitchhiking, it was so beautiful, the Black Forest at night, she slept just about everywhere except never in a hotel, no, never that, she was free, she was an adult, she had met a Moroccan student, was she already in Morocco, she had crossed by boat, by cargo ship, there were only men in the cargo ship to Casablanca where she arrived alone in the middle of the night, the Swabian Jura, the sun melting on her shoulders, she was always in a bikini under her skirt, in sandals, she swam naked on all the beaches, she'd lost weight but it was nothing, the dark woods, the dark woods in the Jura, the forest at night, she'd arrived alone in Morocco and had given the last of her money to a little beggar in the streets of Tangier, could Daddy send her some more, could he, soon she would send them a more stable address, then silence, she didn't write anything else, she was supposed to leave for Marseille but nothing, no address, total freedom, nothing more, Johnie only had her memories of the white room in Greece, they were so close to the beach, the white marble, the heat, the beauty of the Greek art, her sister said I want to become an archaeologist so I can travel better, Émilie told Johnie, my little Vanessa, my little flame, my love, you'll see, with men, you will see, I'm telling you, it's like a moment of eternity imprinted in the flesh, you won't be able to resist, after that kind of ecstatic feeling, it's incredible what we can feel, tell me, maybe it's better to know that there's nothing else, after that, Émilie didn't write anymore, the silence stretched all around Johnie, there was not a word, nothing, only the memory of a white gloom that would never fade, the room, the white hotel, the blue sky, they were all in Greece, that summer would be endless, wordless, after Émilie hitchhiked away, alone, alone, Émilie would go around the world, she would exist and she would experience, Émilie would never be seen again, despite the many attempts by their parents she was never found, where was she, Johnie asked Louise, she was still somewhere else, still alive, still eighteen and sexy, dancing with the devil, where was Émilie, Johnie asked Louise, was that one of the mysteries of eternal silence, forever silent and deaf to our pleas, our repeated entreaties, Johnie's parents, Johnie was Vanessa back then, her parents demanded an investigation but nothing, just silence, Émilie and Johnie's mother had been waiting for her daughter for months, years, Émilie's room was waiting for her, her old clothes, the same radio next to her bed, and even her dolls from when she was a child, her teddy bear, they were all waiting, those objects, but there was no word, nothing, Johnie said, and the family didn't talk about Émilie, of course she would come home, but when, she was a free woman, her parents had raised her right, she was so reasonable, she would come back but it was better not to talk about it anymore, they just had to wait, you have to be patient with children who rebel, Johnie's father said, but why rebel when you have everything, he asked, why, what had she lacked, several times he had written to Émilie, whatever happens or has happened, come back, dear Émilie, but there had never been an answer, we love you, dear Émilie, no matter what happens, what happened, but the words languished powerless in their hearts, Johnie said to Louise, no one talked about Émilie's sexuality, how excessive she was, since Johnie's parents didn't know anything about it, they thought she was still a virgin, rape was the worst that could happen, all they saw was a girl, a little nervous, giddy, and above all very beautiful, did she still have those same eyes, that same face, you could see the restlessness in her eyes, Johnie's father had said, we didn't pay attention, what was going on that we couldn't sense, Johnie didn't think of her sister murdered in a forest, in the woods in the Jura or elsewhere, no, she thought of her alive everywhere, breaking the law maybe, who knows, maybe she was even in jail for having resisted a police officer, for disturbing the peace, ethereal and illicit, always running ahead, untouched, untouchable, when she got into astrology, Johnie started looking for her, there was still that taciturn, stubborn Capricorn hanging over Émilie's birth date, why, was it a divergence, maybe, the stars seemed to be at odds with her, as if they were out of place, pieces of an unlikely puzzle, what did that mean, Émilie came to Johnie in her dreams, you don't have to look for me, I'm always near you, my little flame, I loved you like you were my own baby, when you fell off your bike I would bandage your knees, do you remember, Johnie in these dreams would tell her sister, no, she didn't remember, but our stay in Greece I do remember, what were you doing with those boys, you left me alone on the beach to lock yourself up with them, Mom told you to look after me, Émilie was disappearing in the dream just as she had in life, suddenly she was out of reach, inaccessible, the words remained for Johnie, hadn't she said, in the dream, I have gone beyond the edge of the earth and I am wandering toward heaven, or maybe she had said that the road was so long and she'd lost her way but Johnie shouldn't forget her because whatever anyone thought she'd already been back for a long time, Johnie had stopped confiding in Louise about Émilie, perhaps in an effort to keep her intact, she would talk about her later, she didn't know when, poring over her star charts, would the stars reveal to Johnie where on earth Émilie was hiding, in what corner of the universe, it seemed to Johnie that when Gérard died it was a second disappearance, like Émilie, Gérard had run away without going too far, she missed Gérard's long, lean body as if a connection with her own body had come undone, l'Abeille said, when are you girls going to stop growing so tall and I'm still so small, it was true, Louise thought, they were both so tall, and so close, they used to go everywhere together before Gérard got into drugs and pulled away, Johnie missed Gérard's physical body and her soul too, the secret of her soul would not be discovered and her soul went everywhere with Johnie. Émilie and Gérard traipsed around in Johnie's dreams, both in her daydreams and in the depth of night, either Johnie had the gift of communicating with the dead, they were alive for her, or else death did not exist, it was only a gateway, an oasis, a passage to the land of transformation, metamorphosis, ongoing rebirth, to all beginnings. Émilie might have decided to live in India, in a monastery, after her life as a bohemian sinner; as for Gérard, having escaped from the cemetery into the mountains, was she still jogging, as she did every morning, in her red plastic shoes? Johnie's astrology work was progressing, she had clients coming to her office, they were increasingly loyal, devoted, but Johnie was cool, she didn't like to be invaded, Louise thought, and before too long a profession would take shape, she was studying psychology, following advice Émilie seemed to have offered her in a dream, so that one day she would be a doctor to cure troubled minds, Émilie had said, nothing was more troubling than living. That was the mission Émilie gave her sister, she always called her my flame, little flame. Johnie wasn't living with the girls anymore, she found the heap of rubble the girls squatted in hard to take, so she lived in her fortress, a modest apartment with several staircases behind the shelter of a brick wall, on which Johnie hung some of l'Abeille's darkest drawings, as well as her bicycle, hooked on a big nail. Like Émilie, she was free, solitary. Johnie knew intuitively as soon as someone came into the apartment whether the vibes were good or bad, and if she didn't like a customer's energy, she opened the apartment windows wide, even in winter. In those hedonistic days, when nothing was happening, as l'Abeille said, she drew, she painted huge canvases, she told herself that a great love would come to her like rain in the parched desert. It couldn't be Louise, who couldn't get enough of her old husband René, although it was sweet to think of Louise, she must be so warm, like a caress wrapped around you, she was agile despite her height, and probably passionate, and she'd had enough of Lali's detached coldness, there had to be passion, sensuality, she wanted an audacious lover, the perfect harmony of bodies. L'Abeille thought about those days, already past, I can't forget anything, no, I must not forget that serenity, swimming in the Atlantic, the sky so blue, not a cloud above the sea, in that small town, they were so tolerant, it was a place for outcasts to find each other, girls who liked girls and boys who liked boys, beneath the enduring blue of the sky we melted into the deep blue sky as we swam, she had swum with Louise, so close to her majestic body moving through the green water, only a memory now, l'Abeille thought, and after swimming we played tennis, in the evenings we gathered around that bar with the straw roof where Gérard worked as a cocktail waitress, her white cut-offs, her breasts like peas under her low-cut camisole, the whole season was fun, pleasure, Gérard was tan, it was the most beautiful of seasons, l'Abeille thought, when Gérard came to you, mellowed by the sea, sweat glistening on her cheeks, she finally seemed healthy, l'Abeille said to Louise, at least to us, we weren't thinking then of the AIDS epidemic that was coming, we were just happy, happy with life, our projects, how sweet those days were, l'Abeille said, when we let ourselves live, we didn't know what was coming, maybe we were too young to fathom that kind of bad luck, we always said to ourselves, tomorrow, tomorrow is another day, tomorrow, we'll be serious tomorrow, we'll grow up, take stock, maybe I was like that too, l'Abeille said to Louise, nonchalant, just chasing pleasure, taking comfort in that, you have a body, Christie, Marie-Christine, don't forget it. In those days, in l'Abeille's smoky living room, it was neither day or night, l'Abeille smoked so much that Doudouline told her to be careful, the smoke is a halo around you, Abeille, you'll catch on fire, I don't smoke, it's not good for an actress' voice, Doudouline said, she always spoke as if she were onstage, you almost even smoke while you're sleeping, Doudouline said to l'Abeille, cigarettes were sacred for l'Abeille, Louise thought, it was true, even though Rosemonde didn't like it, and although most of the girls smoked too, from morning to night, l'Abeille, couldn't get up in the morning and not reach for the thin pack of smokes, it was as if she coaxed it to her with her eyes, girls, l'Abeille would say, to smoke is to live twice over, as if the smell of smoke were gold dust in their dilapidated house. It seemed to l'Abeille that the cigarette smoke gave off a light, a dim light, more like a fog, the fragrant smoke growing thick around her. There was smoking and there was love, l'Abeille said, even if love was in short supply, l'Abeille, a little envious, said to the Doudouline–Polydor twosome, we won't always be as graceful as we are now in the gymnastics of love, not as supple in our embraces, you girls won't always be this flexible, as worthy of aesthetic contemplation, no, like everyone else, we're going to get old, we're going to get old and die, right now I'm too plump, Doudouline cut her off, an actress has to be slim, the Great Sophie says it's the chocolates, l'Abeille said, the chocolates, the wine, we're already changing, l'Abeille said, in no time at all, think about it, like everybody else we're going to grow old and die, so it's better to enjoy life, to love now, and we have to remember that we're living today, not tomorrow, today. Polydor and Doudouline listened impatiently to l'Abeille going on about how fleeting life is, their days were too full, with Doudouline's rehearsals and Polydor working in the bookstore during the day and going to school at night, as Doudouline pompously told l'Abeille, we only meet in the evening by candlelight, in the bathtub, and even then, it's to rehearse, Polydor goes through my lines with me, is that any kind of life, Doudouline asked, dramatic, the bathtub was near the kitchen, it was separated from the living room by a curtain, it was a clawfoot tub, an antique, with four faded plaster feet, Doudouline would slide into the bathtub like a mermaid into the foaming waves, script in hand, while Polydor sat on a bench near the tub and started reading: if you love me more I will be outraged, Polydor read, I will be outraged if you love me more, Doudouline repeated mechanically, who was dozing with her eyes open, half asleep by the candlelight in the warm water, no, you're wrong, or are you asleep, Polydor said, from the top, if you love me more, I will be outraged, we have to start all over again, Doudouline said, her voice sleepy, just think, my mother refusing all those roles because she said she was too young, even Phaedra, what vanity, dear Mother, I'd like to play a modern version, you know, with electronic music, a new Phaedra, Doudouline was so relaxed, she closed her eyes, and Polydor would wake her up, try to inspire her a little, yes, Polydor said to Doudouline, wake up, I've got an idea, you know how I always get ideas after my evening cognac coffee, listen, Doudouline, you, the daughter of the Great Sophie, why don't you write a musical about us, about Gérard, about us, the girls in the group, it would be brilliant, it would be a blast, Gérard, us, you, our story, like a fable, with drama, comedy, tears, singing, lamentation, electronic music so loud it would literally bring down the house, why haven't you ever thought about that, Doudouline, and Doudouline started, alarmed, what about Mama, a musical about us, the girls, our group of friends, can you imagine, a musical written by her lesbian daughter, poor Mama would be so shocked she would die, Doudouline cried, getting out of the bathtub, waiting for the ritual of Polydor handing over the bathrobe, you're nuts, my dear, Mama's proud of me, but she would never get over that. We should have done this a long time ago, Polydor said, she was getting carried away, a long time, and only you can do it, Doudouline, or would you rather hide, stay underground, stay invisible out of loyalty to Sophie, right, secret and invisible, that's how you want to live with me, without ever letting me take your hand in the street, let alone kiss me, Louise could hear Polydor's

words echoing through the house, it was a time of revolt and gentle
fury, she said, but Mama is letting me come onstage with her,
Doudouline protested, that's already a gift, I wasn't expecting that,
you have to take it slow, Polydor, revolutions don't happen in a day,
never mind a sexual revolution, calm down, my Polydor, come to
bed, we'll talk about it later, I admit that it's an attractive thought,
it's a good idea, Doudouline added, thoughtful. What happens to me
if you forget? René asked Louise, feeling Olga's authoritarian gaze
on him, it was grating to be watched like that, confined to a room, a
bed, what tie should I choose to go with your silk shirt, you're going
to look so elegant, René, Louise said, the one with the naked girl on
a swing, René said, he suddenly felt energetic, he was ready to go,
he rarely felt like this anymore, it was too bad Louise seemed so far
away as she helped him dress, no, the pink tie, Louise said, even
though that was the one you wore to go out with Nathalie, you
might as well reconcile the past with the present, that's how we
evolve, Louise told René, she thought again of Johnie, now she was
Dr. Vanessa, a flash of lightning in the white sky, the white walls, the
white houses, when Johnie was looking for her sister in Greece,
alone, she could hear the sound of her footsteps in the quiet city,
Johnie saying over and over again, maybe she's here, behind that
tree, maybe she's here, behind that wooden door, did I hear her
breathing, her voice calling me, Johnie, Johnie, hello, how are you,
it's too bright, isn't it, I can't see you, I'm blinded, Louise was
thinking too of a phrase that haunted Doudouline, Sophie had once
said to her, it's such a surprise when a mother gives birth to a child
that isn't hers, or at least not the one she expected, was the Great
Sophie talking about her, was Doudouline a changeling, the Great
Sophie deftly waved away the tinge of unkindness in her words by
pointing out that Doudouline was one in a million, that was what
was charming about her, and she had almost been born on a theater
stage, which would have been deadly for her mother's career but it
was special, too, the Great Sophie's hope for her daughter was that

she would one day have a husband, you can't live without a man, you see, my child, no, you always need them, first of all they fix whatever's broken in a house, it's simple, without a man in her life, Doudouline, who had been named Anne-Sophie when she was born, did she remember that, she would be very unhappy, the love or the so-called love Doudouline felt for Polydor was an infatuation, nothing more, it would pass like a cold, the Great Sophie said. Doudouline thought of her mother, of the supposed husband Doudouline would never have, did her mother hate her that much, and Doudouline hushed her anger in the soapy water of the bath, all the girls knew that the bathtub, which was separated from the kitchen by a curtain, was the place for meditation and disillusionment, Polydor preferred the bathtub empty, she would jump in it fully dressed, boots and all, the hood of her navy-blue coat still on her head, knowing that Doudouline would come by and chide her because she'd had a bit too much to drink at the bar that night. Back then, those were the days in l'Abeille's smoky living room, it was never really either day or night, the girls came home late, Polydor hoped that what she had with Doudouline would last, Doudouline, whom her mother called Anne-Sophie but for Polydor she was Doudouline, a wonderfully carnal girl, she loved pleasure of every kind, in those days, Polydor slept fully clothed in the bathtub, Louise thought as she dressed René. Why does the end of desire exist, René wondered, as Louise's fingers adjusted the pink tie over the silk shirt, why did Nathalie stop wanting me, I was the same, except that I'd spent money on her, for the two of us, let's be honest, I'd spent the last of my inheritance, why didn't Nathalie find me attractive anymore, that was why she said she was leaving me, she didn't want me anymore, how is that possible when the day before she was moaning with passion in my arms, how do you explain that, the end of desire, desire can't cease to exist, René thought, it's the soul of life, we desire when we are born, and when we die we desire a little less. We desire, we desire because we want to be loved by our parents, we desire because we love, we desire, we desire, and then nothing. How do you explain the end of desire, René asked Louise, Louise hesitated, then said, firmly, it happens suddenly, you don't feel anything anymore, it dries up, desire goes cold, it goes missing, little by little. That's terrible, what you're saying is a terrible thing, René said, and it is a state of despair I've never experienced. And how do you get over it, René asked, by desiring someone else, Louise said soberly, it's as unoriginal as that, turn around so I can lift the collar of your shirt, a tie has to be tied perfectly, that's what you always said, René, perfection. René thought of his activism, was that the end of a desire too, from now on she would only be fighting from her bed, she remembered the day she had taken the girls to see the mayor, a solemn, purposeful visit, they were so young, Gérard the second and Polydor, Doudouline hadn't wanted to come with them, she said her mother would be embarrassed, those girls blushing with shyness though they were anything but, René thought, we were only going to ask for what was legitimately our right, the right to marriage, equal pay for women, we were begging for scraps, with my antelope by my side, she was bolder than the others, my Louise, the mayor came toward us in that reception room, the room where people came to ask for things, supplicants for justice, it was a beautiful winter day and he spoke courteously, his secretary was standing next to him, formal and stiff, what can I do for you on this beautiful sunny day, through the window you can see the snowy branches shining in the sun, what do you want, sir, I have only an hour to spare, I have business in town, so I told him, for two decades we have been waiting for justice, Mr. Mayor, for my companions and myself, and those girls, standing up for their rights for the first time, Gérard the second was so young, and Polydor, still blushing, oh, Louise, my faithful Louise, proud on my arm, yes, the right to marriage, Louise had said, the right to equal pay, Louise said, he called me sir and didn't understand what I, as a man, was doing there talking about the marriage of men or women, it was unheard of for him, he asked me several times to explain, he congratulated me for defending these ladies, I'm also defending the right of men to marry and adopt children, I told the oblivious man before me, and suddenly the mayor turned to his secretary, even though it's only noon, let's get some cocktails, yes, that will relax everyone on this fine winter day, I'm afraid the two girls are underage, the secretary said, no, no, the mayor said, do as I say, I couldn't deal with this bureaucratic bullshit anymore and I went up to the mayor, I think I made an impression with my attire, Mr. Mayor, I said, with all due respect, remember, you might be too young, but you must read the papers, surely you know a little about the history of our customs, you're an educated man, we don't usually elect just anybody, remember that in this very city where you were elected a few years ago, not so long ago, homosexuals, men or women, who met in a café or a bar, whether here in your beautiful city or in New York or Chicago, those people were put in jail, they were fired from their jobs, Mr. Mayor, remember, that wasn't so long ago, it's still fresh in my memory, I said to him, and I remember evil, tyranny, oppression in every form, sir, the mayor interrupted me, you've said enough, I understand, say no more, here, they're serving cocktails, to your health, the mayor said, and don't forget to sign the guestbook, you can add a comment, sir, believe me, I won't forget you, I'll be contacting my lawyer friends, they're not used to requests like this, but we'll see, I'll explain everything, you have to live in the era you're in, don't you think, and with that, the meeting was over, my driver is waiting, I'm expected in town, good day to you and to the girls, sir, don't hesitate to come back to see us, you're always welcome here, that was the end of the visit to the mayor's office, René thought, and no laws had changed, because the mayor had a business lunch in town. Our protests and actions were often for nothing, absurd. Nobody wanted to hear us. Louise thought of Doudouline, who one morning got up singing, her mezzo-soprano ringing out, yes, there would be a musical, a rock opera or a baroque canticle for several voices, because as Polydor says, I'm going to do it, I'm going to write this, yes, yes, while she was tying René's pink tie over the white silk shirt, Louise thought of how enchanting it was in l'Abeille's living room when Doudouline got up and sang, the beginning will go like this, she sang, with Gérard prowling the winter streets after doing coke, it's a pitiful image but we'll soften it with the music, a tender rock ballad, the background will be green, nighttime, you'll feel the presence of the woods close by, of something savage lurking, we need music like Janis Joplin, do you hear me, girls, Gérard is a listless character, sickly, a ghost dragging herself around in the icy air, shivering, and the voice, listen to me, it will yearn for the peak of fever and vertigo, the girls listened to Doudouline's voice weaving across the cracks in the ceiling and rising up to the gray sky, with sparrows fluttering above the snowdrifts, flying, singing, wasn't it sublime, when a day started like that in l'Abeille's living room, breathing in the cooling ashes of all their cigarettes, with the succor of Doudouline's vibrant, soaring voice, it had to end well, Doudouline would see her friend Mimi today, she'd play Doudouline's sketched-out storyline on the piano, she would turn Doudouline's words and her voice into music, everything seemed transparent on those mornings for girls who hated mornings, the bland, raw light. Polydor asked Doudouline not to forget anything, Gérard had loved Johnie, two beanpoles in l'Abeille's living room, Johnie said, no, it was coke that Gérard loved more than everything, nothing but coke, there had been one night of folly, only one, Johnie said, cool and short, Johnie had been able to feel Gérard's curls on her cheeks, her long legs against her own, and Gérard had whispered in Johnie's ear, sometimes, yes, I'm afraid to love, you're different, during that too-short night, Gérard had told Johnie about a moment of terror one night, alone, recounting in bits and pieces how she'd sat in the middle of the deserted street wondering who she was, where she lived, if she really existed, the cars rolling by had shaken her and she got up and walked to l'Abeille's, though how she had gotten there she didn't remember, yes, Gérard was afraid of love's restrictions, Johnie said, and I knew as I kissed her that I couldn't be careful enough, she would run away, I couldn't protect her and I knew it, Johnie said, I didn't want a painful affair, maybe I didn't support Gérard enough because of that, maybe that set her back on the deviant path of her destiny, the coke, the heroin, I knew it would kill her in the end, Johnie said, I didn't want a love that was unhealthy, no, Johnie said, and Gérard wouldn't listen to me, she didn't listen to anyone, I knew she was hanging out with a shady crowd, I knew that, Johnie said, I knew it would all end badly, Polydor asked Doudouline, how can you translate Gérard's story into music when it's not a story, and how we all live secretly in a house falling down, Doudouline, how can you produce your rock opera, your punk music with girls like us whose story nobody knows? There are no secrets when you want to sing about beauty, the beauty of girls, the beauty of love, Doudouline said, though what will the Great Sophie say, my poor mother, who's still hoping to find me a husband? What will she say, Doudouline thought. I love her so dearly but I'll be able to stand my ground, yes, Doudouline told the girls, I'll know how to face her, poor Mama, what I wish for her is a young lover who can open her mind so she can understand that in life you don't choose, there is only being and suffering. But Mama says she's too mature now for a lover. That even charming, distinguished maturity doesn't interest them. There would be a duet, two women, Doudouline said, it would be heavenly, a scene of the night Johnie and Gérard spent together, but modestly, oh, and so sweet it will be palpable, Doudouline said, Johnie's protective instincts, and Gérard absolutely incandescent. I can hear the melody, the voices joining together, an incantation exhaled into the universe, Doudouline said, with the scent of spring flowers floating up to the blue summer sky, I felt so alive, revived, that's what it's like when you're in the middle of creating, she said. But in those days when there was neither day nor night, in l'Abeille's smoky living room, Gérard the second, who was looking more and more like our first Gérard, Louise thought, wearing her jeans with suspenders, that same mismatched look, though her hair wasn't naturally curly like Gérard's had been, but Gérard the second curled it with cold water, she used the same blush on her cheeks and the same pink on her lips as the apricot shade of Gérard's face turned when she blushed or felt intimidated, which was rare, Gérard the second could get into such a brittle mood, it seemed like a challenge to Doudouline's elation, waking up to her musical project, which would eventually be produced, though much later, Gérard the second drank her morning coffee with Rosemonde on her lap, her eyes half closed, and then all of a sudden she was launching into it, hey, girls, hey, Doudouline, are you going to write about how we kiss, how we hold each other, are you going to talk about the chaste tenderness, or almost, between Gérard and Johnie, one night, and there she is, off to party, on drugs, are you going to say how it was for us who waited for her, so often until dawn, I was so worried that Gérard would go to jail, the shame that would have brought us, and her, Gérard, and her parents, they adored her, I've been thinking about all of that, yes, Gérard the second said, are you going to say that we still live in hiding, Doudouline, and even at night in the bars, it's all a secret, will you say that it's gone on too long, we love and we live like everyone else, Doudouline said, how can you be so pragmatic about this, so down to earth, Gérard the second who had been named Thérèse, we're like everybody else in the world, it's just that we love the night, that's what makes us different from others, how can you talk about hiding when I'm onstage with my mother every night, you're exaggerating, Gérard the second, and don't you go getting as pessimistic as the first Gérard, that would be a disaster. But Gérard the second started up again even more zealously, since you turned off the TV, since Gérard disappeared, she would be so pissed at you, you don't even know how many people are dying in Vietnam, the accounting of war, all those deaths, on both sides,

Johnie says we'll know in ten years, fifteen, you don't know, it's unforgivable, besides living in a house that's like a cave, full of secrets, there are wars going on, is that how you want to live, girls, is this how you want to live, under the cover of silence and secrecy, is it? Polydor's voice rose, people are divided, they're not sure, people don't want war, no one wants to invade Asia, they don't accept it and neither do we, Polydor said, Gérard was bleeding inside, sometimes I think that's what killed her, it's the end, believe me, it kills you, all these wars, I mean, that's what ended up killing our Gérard. Listen, Gérard, Doudouline was saying, as if Gérard the second had insulted her, if we're hiding, it's because no one wants us out there, you understand? We're ostracized, they don't accept us, is that clear, Gérard? We live in secret because we can't do anything else, not even Lali can tell her doctor colleagues who she is. Or Louise with her university professors, they already hate her because she's smarter than they are. What if they knew? We live in the night, Doudouline said, her voice lilting, as lyrical as ever, you see, Gérard, because the night is our refuge, it's safe for us, unless the police come down on us in the bars, guns blazing, but that's not how it goes, the bar manager is in with the mafia, she manages to save the girls from violence, which would be completely counter-productive anyway, especially since none of us knows how to use a gun. Louise reminded the girls that it was René who had introduced them all to pacifism, to protests, down in the street against the war, against wars, this one will end dishonorably, Johnie predicted calmly, Johnie who hated excess in all things, who spurned the other girls' arguments, you have to be cool and know how to control the chaos of your own emotions, she said, it will end in disgrace, Johnie predicted, but another war will follow that will bring devastation, the death toll will be unbelievable, I see it in the stars, there will be flood of fire over the city of Baghdad and children will wake in the night to the rumble of shelling and thousands will starve to death in refugee camps, distressed, Johnie refused to say anything more, she was holding back tears, yes, a flood of fire, she whispered, the girls listened to her in fear, we will be in the streets, we will protest for peace, Polydor said, we only go out to protest, Polydor repeated, you see, Gérard the second, we do have courage, we're brave, what are you talking about when you say that we're hiding, I'll say it again, Gérard the second said, think of Louise and Lali who have to live a lie, they can never say a word about their personal life, Lali, who's so devoted to her patients, we can't always live like this, girls, no, we can't, we are part of the resistance, Polydor said, the law is going to change, you'll see, girls. Louise thought of René, who had never hesitated, he was always on the front lines, would always be. Are you done pampering me yet, am I dressed yet, René said, careful, I could get used to this, I'm just an old shut-in, Louise, I'm forgotten here despite the precious care of my dear Olga, I'm going to tell you the truth, Louise, I miss my people, I miss you girls, it's hard, my feet and my legs hurt, my eyes see everything double, even though I can hear great music perfectly, those voices, every day I ask myself, am I already in heaven, are trans people welcomed into heaven with such kindness, if not, send me back to earth, tell me, Louise, where's Lali, is she coming to the party, she lives only for her young oblivious AIDS patients now, she once lived on love alone, she used to have so many lovers on the go, she was always in a rush, she was breathless for sex, especially fast sex, Lali has broken many hearts, Louise answered René, although we loved her dearly, you and Lali, you acted like boys, two boys scheming together, Louise said, that's life, René said, we can't all be as delicate as you, Lali and I had plenty of hard times, Lali was always brave, she would walk down the street holding her girlfriend's hand, if she were meeting a lover at the airport, she would hug her, kiss her, she wasn't afraid of anything except her colleagues at the hospital, no, nothing really frightened her, she was exemplary, my Lali, René said wistfully, she could still see Lali's stoic figure in the bar, Lali's old, disillusioned soul in that young, androgynous body, Lali was so mysterious in her coldness, I miss Lali, René sighed, and you too sometimes, Louise, when you forget to come and read to me, old age is no fun at all, it must have been invented by the devil. Louise listened to René's unsteady lament, despite all that ailed him René complained very little, Louise thought, Louise thought of Doudouline, of what Johnie had predicted in her prophetic wisdom while they smoked a morning cigarette in l'Abeille's living room, yes, we'll get to see your musical, the story of Gérard and all of us, but that will be later, much later, in the meantime, get to work, Doudouline, don't waste your time hanging out in bars every night, why wait, Doudouline replied, men make art that talks about them, their lives, the hardships they have to endure, why are we always a step behind them, always late, Doudouline asked, Johnie replied that Sappho was still misunderstood today, after centuries, and Doudouline had to admit that the world was behind, it was never ready to let go of cruelty, Doudouline's somewhat scandalous production would be staged in the Great Sophie's theater and it would be a success, but she had to admit the world wasn't ready for that kind of provocation, only so-called normal people had the right to be in love, only those who were unequivocal about their sexual orientation had the right to passion, think of Romeo and Juliet, that was legitimate, that was approved, but if Doudouline wrote about a couple like Gérard and Johnie rather than Romeo and Juliet it was shameful, it was better not to talk about it, let alone sing about it on a stage, but Johnie also saw in the stars that social and political change was coming, the world would be a better place, a more just place for Doudouline, the girls listened to Johnie's calm voice, knowing that Johnie would be leaving soon to study abroad, in Paris or Vienna, what an odd destiny, she was different, her parents afforded her every freedom, she was going to go and get all sophisticated while the girls would still be hanging out all day and late into the night in l'Abeille's living room, Louise thought, Johnie told Louise she was going to study Jung, she wanted to work on the study of dreams in psychology, she believed in the positive side of neurosis too, and it was as if she were still stubbornly looking for Émilie, for what had caused Émilie's neurosis, what made her run away in Greece, if Émilie had always been neurotic or disturbed, even as a child, no one had ever noticed, the pain of living, deeply rooted as it may be, can be concealed so easily and the person seems fine, it happened all the time, Émilie had been a playful child, affectionate with her parents, and no one really knew a thing about her until the day she ran away, Johnie said, maybe that's how it is for many people. We don't know anything about anyone. Johnie told Louise that our dreams were realities, they were often more real than our actual lives, Johnie confided to Louise that she talked to her sister in her dreams, sometimes Émilie came to her, she would sit at the foot of the bed and ask whether Johnie wanted Émilie to come get her, and Johnie would say, no, I don't want to, and her sister would touch her shoulder with her hand and say, little sister, you know, this is only the beginning of your struggle, you mustn't overlook that the earth is in pain, but a more beautiful world is always growing within, it's forever starting over again, that was my quest, Émilie said, and then she was gone, she was watching Johnie from the bedroom ceiling, see you soon, my treasure, my little flame, she said, and Johnie saw that blinding light again, like when she had been searching the white streets, among the white houses, the sea whitened by the strident sun, when she was searching for her sister in Greece, and everywhere else. For a long time Johnie thought that they should have had a funeral for her sister, her remains returned to the family, with dignity, in her jeans, the flowered blouse she'd been wearing that day, but she realized how pointless that would be, her sister was deathless, her sister had never left. That was what she had realized, Johnie told Louise, Émilie was still alive. They didn't know where she was, but she was alive. Maybe her parents believed that too, they had left everything in her room untouched as if she were about to return from a trip. One night a girl showed up at l'Abeille's house, Alexis, her real name was Catherine, we called Christie l'Abeille, the Bee, because she looked after her hive, she was the queen bee, the queen of the hive, Louise thought, she wrangled all her buzzing bees around her, l'Abeille introduced Alexis to the group and said, take care of her, I found her near a bar but they wouldn't let her in, look at her, she's only sixteen, she got kicked out of her parents' house, so no illegal stuff, they kicked her out, I don't know why, her father is a judge, her brother is in prison for homicide, she writes poetry and all she wants is a table to write on, I'll give her my room and I can sleep on the couch with Rosemonde, Alexis looked dejected, she wore her blue and green hair in braids down over her face, her eyes, when you could see them, were a liquid blue, not as dark as l'Abeille's, that evening she was holding a suitcase she never seemed to part with, as l'Abeille said, Alexis lived only for poetry, she could recite Rimbaud, Lautréamont, and Verlaine by heart, she carried her suitcase everywhere, it held all her poetry, she'd been writing since she was eleven, according to her parents, who had kicked her out of the house, what she wrote was blasphemous, they were deeply Catholic and all she was to them was a soul headed for damnation. Take good care of this little prodigy, l'Abeille said, for now she's still asexual, she doesn't prefer boys or girls, that's more restful for writing, let her write in peace, is there any more innocent desire than that, eh, and yet there's such a cost for those who write, isn't there, in life, think about it, girls, those who die because they write, in Russia, in China, abominable political leaders kill poets and poetry. How can you want to kill poetry, l'Abeille asked. Alexis wrote night and day without paying much attention to the girls. It was her passion, her nourishment, Louise thought. Only l'Abeille seemed to be her friend. Alexis' pimply face gradually cleared up, along with her eczema, she was covered with it and had flares now and again, the pain wore at her as she wrote though she resisted it stoically, sometimes she looked gently at l'Abeille, saying, thank you, thank you, that was all, she confided very little. Be careful not to carry the sorrows of others, l'Abeille said, Alexis, it's not your fault if your father, the judge, is a monster, it's not your fault if your brother is in jail for homicide, one day you'll tell me about yourself, for a long time I felt guilty, l'Abeille confessed, for Gemma, my little Gemma who was crushed in the street, for my mother Elena who was so beautiful, but Louise told me it wasn't my fault, it was God in his malevolence, Louise told me, it wasn't me who brought this on. It was a malignant God, Louise told me. But God doesn't exist, Alexis replied weakly, she was shy, almost feral under the mask of her hair and the pimples, that's why my parents kicked me out, they read poems where I'd written that God doesn't exist, that it's a joke to take advantage of our misery. God is a farce, a burlesque comedy, that's what I wrote, Alexis said. What violence, though you look like a bruised angel, l'Abeille said, she was pleased to be able to awaken in Alexis a healthy violence that could heal her, maybe, I like that you're so rebellious, we're going to get along well, you and I. L'Abeille and Alexis talked like that late at night, Louise thought, l'Abeille never stopped smoking though Alexis didn't smoke, she didn't take or do any drugs, anything. The smoke in the house didn't seem to bother her, she told l'Abeille over and over that God was the greatest lie imaginable, it was a sham. She knew that her brother represented evil and that she represented good, but she hadn't chosen goodness just as he hadn't chosen evil, there was nothing to uphold our thoughts except to stave off emptiness, it was all forced upon us at birth, good, evil, all the trials of humanity. Her brother had been tainted by those empty thoughts and it had driven him to murder, he felt nothing that day, he'd been driving his first car, it was his first day driving it, and he drove into a little girl riding her tricycle, he had annihilated her, he said in court, because he despised all human beings, what he had done was payback against an innocent little girl, his lawyer advised him to plead not guilty but he had refused, Alexis also believed that because their father, the judge, had sentenced men and women to hanging twenty years before, Alexis and her brother would pay for his crimes. Their line was cursed, wasn't it? What about me, René asked Louise, with a smile as mischievous as ever, you remember, my antelope, when I slapped you, on the beach by the Atlantic, Lali had a few days off, which was rare, we'd come up with a contest to see who could drink the most beer, I drank sixteen, and Lali drank seventeen, I lost control that day and I still regret it, you were lying on the beach a bit too close to your cute friend l'Abeille, I hope you regret it for the rest of your life, René, because it's a shameful thing to slap a woman, Louise, listen, I was out of line, how can I put it, it was out of my control, I can see still your face and hers, you were about to kiss, we were talking, Louise said, yet again you were acting like a shitty man, jealous, a brute, Louise said, it's a disgrace, it's shameful, wasn't it a sign that I loved you, lovers get jealous so easily, they're possessive, you know that, don't hold it against me. Louise listened to René, remembering the slap, wondering why she had since forgiven him. It was just a little slap, René said, I didn't even touch your nose, that long nose, from the side you look like Cleopatra, no, I remember, it was a very light slap, a slightly strong caress, that's all. René's gaze grew dark, he missed those days, the anger and the jealousy, his treacherous heart, those days were gone for good, making out on the beach, sun on their skin, in the winter the simmering passion, the wildness of intoxication, it was true what Louise said, it often ended in anger, and why was that, my dear René, I'll tell you, it's because you were a hard drinker, a mean drunk, to put it crassly, you had such a short fuse when you were drinking, or else you turned into a dirty old man and we just had to get out of the way, Louise said, smiling affectionately at René, René sighed in his beautiful party clothes, it's all in the past, it was already in the past then, but tonight we're looking to the future, Louise said, what jacket do you like best for going out, the tweed one would suit you, René could feel Olga's gaze on him, scrutinizing him, why does she look at me like that, René thought, does she think I'm ridiculous, she'll see that I'm alive, that I can get out of my bed, sitting up is painful but I have be patient, these legs used to run around all over the place, how can I move them gracefully again, I have to please Louise, I have to reassure her when there's nothing remotely reassuring, the saddest thing is not to be able to fight anymore, but who knows, you never know, one more time, why not, René thought, outside the first leaves of spring were stirring in the wind, the birds were starting to sing, maybe Countess would come out of winter, soon we'll hear her scratching at the door, as Louise dressed René she thought of Alexis, her arrival had upset the order in the house, in that smoky living room at l'Abeille's, Doudouline had said reproachfully, hey, Christie, you can't give your bed to someone you don't know, l'Abeille, the girl is underage, we can't have underage girls under our roof, you were all underage when we started squatting here, l'Abeille replied, except for Johnie, we were orphans, we had no home and no parents, that's how it started for us, in friendship, in trust, not me, Doudouline said, her voice as theatrical as ever, not me, I was still living with my darling mother, you were living in her dressing room, l'Abeille said, following her around, she'd had enough, she was so busy with theater, then you met Polydor and your mother said, enough, my treasure, go live somewhere else, that's how the gang grew, in welcome, in trust, yes, might you be biased against Alexis because she's not like us? She's sad, Doudouline said, she's too sad, she's bringing down our happy group, we had Gérard, she laughed a lot and we didn't even know she was sad, Doudouline said, but Alexis' sadness is heavy, Doudouline said, there's no room for prejudice, l'Abeille said, I'll protect Alexis, she will not leave this house until she decides to, let her write in peace, do you share your mother's intolerance, Doudouline, l'Abeille asked, Doudouline looked bewildered, what's wrong with a poet writing day and night, as if it were the seventeenth century, with a quill and ink, what do you have against Alexis, Doudouline? She has to look after her eczema, it's all over her hands, on her arms, it's not pretty, it's hard for others to take too, she has to look after herself, l'Abeille turned her back on Doudouline and went out into the yard, she didn't want to hear any more, soon they wouldn't have to wear boots, the night sky would be full of stars, the days were getting longer, l'Abeille would protect Alexis, Doudouline's most serious accusation was that they couldn't have the daughter of a bourgeois family, a judge's daughter, in the house, aren't we supposed to stand against the bourgeoisie, Doudouline had said, l'Abeille stomped around in the wet earth with her boots, prejudice, all of it was prejudice, it's disgusting, I'm going to tell her, Doudouline, it's shameful. But, Louise thought, one day soon Doudouline would read Alexis' poems on a theater stage, she would read with tears flowing down her cheeks. The mood in the house was heavy, Alexis sat writing at the table, it was more like a small school desk that l'Abeille had lent her, she was so diligent, her face hidden by her hair, Alexis was writing and writing, Doudouline had scrawled the title of her musical on the blackboard in the kitchen, there were several possible titles she found inspiring, Doudouline wrote a list in white chalk, *Gérard in the Night*, *Gérard and*, *Gérard and Friends*, *Gérard Gérard Where are You*, *Gérard my Gérard*, *Gérard*, *Wild is the Night*, *Gérard and Her Night*, *Gérard's Night*, *Gérard on Fire*, *Gérard oh Gérard*, *The End of a Spark*, *Gérard Come Back Gérard*, l'Abeille was using color now on wide canvases, several layers of a snowy desert piling up under a shady, motionless sky and the rapture of orange on the flat snow, what was that sun, the sun of life or a statue of a dying sun, the lines and signs and black dots were gone for good, no more, l'Abeille said, the almost scarlet orange before which l'Abeille had felt so reluctant was triumphant, Louise was finishing her essay on women and cancer, Louise had had a dream that seemed premonitory, she was swimming in the gray water of a lake surrounded by sand hills, the sky was gray, a landscape without birds or trees, and in the distance a screen shone in all the grayness and a doctor was talking to the screen, and as she swam closer to the screen, hovering between the sky and the water, it seemed to Louise that she could hear the words of her own healing from the doctor, and the woman was saying, yes, a confirmation that she was healed, Louise swam closer to one of the hills, it was shaped like a breast and in the dream Louise saw all the lost breasts of the women who'd had cancer, the dune was a sacrificial symbol of all the tests and immolations, Louise felt strangely relaxed as she swam in the lake, she was able to swim to shore and the shore was a sanctuary, a place to rest. In l'Abeille's living room, which was still filled with smoke and the smell of cold ashes, Alexis wrote at her school desk, but she went out for a few hours in the afternoon to write, even more alone, in the big university library. There she seemed to be studying, she read, she translated poetry from Greek and Latin just as she had learned at school, the private school she'd hated, and when she came home, her tired face framed by her braids, the suitcase of poems in her hand, she never parted with it, l'Abeille would serve her one of her soups, saying, Alexis, don't forget that your body exists. We only have one life and it's a short one, so you have to eat, Alexis. L'Abeille was constantly astonished by Alexis, her words, did l'Abeille know that Paul Verlaine had only lived fifty-one years, he had died of pulmonary congestion, he who had sung of the freedom to live, did l'Abeille know, fifty-one years was too short a time for a poet, any time was too short, Alexis said, and why did they call him decadent, people always tried to classify things, it was reductive and narrow, he was neither decadent nor a symbolist, Alexis said, he was only a poet forced to stick to a short deadline of fifty-one years, a poet misunderstood by the moderns, so sober in his crystalline clarity, his simplicity, you might say, without literary pretensions. What would come later in Alexis' destiny was utterly unimaginable for the girls, Johnie had predicted, according to the stars, that Alexis would follow a different path than the one she seemed to have chosen, all they could see in her was the quest for pure poetry, but her desires and aspirations would run aground on her destiny, for the moment she was an inspired child whose poems were being published secretly in avant-garde magazines, and wasn't that all any of us knew of Alexis? But little by little Alexis became less feral with the girls in the group, although she still didn't let anyone read her work, Doudouline tried to tame her by asking her to recite a poem, Alexis, touched by the request, recited flatly, *from the black, opaque well of nothingness from which I sprang*, and then she suddenly fell silent, as if she were about to cry, too sad, Doudouline said, much too sad, Doudouline immediately launched into more frivolous topics, Alexis' veil of hair fascinated her, will you let me do your hair, Doudouline said, you'll look great, you know, that's what I first learned in the theater with Mama, how to do my hair, how to do the actresses' hair, in their dressing rooms, it's an art, you know, and see, if you parted your wild, wild hair in the middle, you'd look like a Botticelli, yes, *The Birth of Venus*, with your mystical air, your Renaissance head, yes, every night in the theater I did their hair, these actresses who were playing these huge parts, and Mama said to me, that's how you'll develop, Alexis was listening to Doudouline's dramatic voice, which seemed to please her, no, she wouldn't let her touch her hair but as she listened to Doudouline she remembered evenings spent since childhood with her parents at the theater and in concert halls, they went to all the fanciest places with their children, didn't they, they were the most educated, the best educated, weren't they? How was that possible when Polydor had worked in a factory from the age of fifteen and had never gone to concerts or the theater? Alexis and her brother Louis were driven to their private school by a chauffeur while other children walked to school through deep snow, through cold and storms. That was what it meant to be born differently, to be born of privilege, Alexis thought, that was what was wrong, it was evil. Apart from concerts and theaters, Alexis and her brother Louis saw little of their parents, they had a governess. Alexis thought and she listened, she couldn't tell the girls that her brother had been sent back to a higher security prison, far away, in Calgary, because he was inciting riots, his case as a prisoner was getting worse, he's a criminal, Alexis thought, why is my brother a criminal, Alexis always remembered him as the little boy he once had been, in his rich-kid uniform, early on the adults' dress code was imposed on those little boys in their stiff white shirts and red ties, they looked like little men at barely eleven. In that stiffness, Louis could imagine he was like his father, puffing out his chest. Alexis thought that she shouldn't have existed in the world, she didn't deserve it. And suddenly the eczema was blooming everywhere like weeds on her arms, her hands, her hands especially, it was unbearable and so painful, so itchy, she closed her eyes, she wrote at her desk, there was worse misery than what she went through every day, Alexis thought, yes, and she wrote the rest of the poem, *from the black, opaque well of nothingness from which I sprang, from the black spring*, it's a beautiful day outside, come outside, girls, l'Abeille said, it's finally spring, l'Abeille had a letter from Manfred, he would be back a few days before summer to celebrate his wedding and the baptism of his first child under the lilacs, they might even have two, why not celebrate, right, both at the same time, he had written to l'Abeille, a wedding, a baptism, a new wife and a new baby, that's perfection, I have already told you about my musician wife, Yang, and I am finishing my concert tour in China, my dear l'Abeille, you of the lively beehive, and then I will go to India, how beautiful and immense our universe is, music will always be our joy, our happiness, sending you kisses, my dear little first wife, your Manfred, and René suddenly said to Louise, you know, the worst thing in life is to be in the hands of others, I hate being dependent, René said, when you dress me for a party, it's a pleasure, I chose Olga because she's a distraction from my dark thoughts, you have to know how to belong to yourself, people are only waiting for a moment of weakness to grab you, it's human nature, unfortunately, I always told the women I loved, resist those who want to possess you, be free, Louise looked at Olga, was she really that entertaining, all she talked about was selling off all the furniture in the house, about making a profit, was that what René found distracting, she was too earnest, she loved too easily, did René understand that she was being taken advantage of, never really accepted as her own gender, he would forever be an outcast, whether he liked it or not, Olga only provided a false sense of relief, was it even true that she was Russian, that was dubious, Louise thought, René was cheering himself up with illusions, with lies, everything was a lie, even his masculinity in a female body, Louise thought. Louise remembered again the dream where she had swum in the peaceful lake toward that giant image of a computer suspended between the sky and the lake and the doctor speaking to her, showing her the way to recovery, the words were spoken but silent, was the doctor the same Haitian doctor who had treated Louise, and the presence of the computer in the dream was the poetic prophecy that Louise would soon own a computer, which would be the most majestic gift she had ever received, she longed for a global vision of the world to come to her, for everyone to have access to that, to all of it, computers would mark a collective awakening, Louise thought, which might even encourage acts of kindness. Would the world become more enlightened, would it be a better place, Louise wondered, or would it only become more corrupt? René thought it would have been a great pleasure to see all his mistresses and conquests again, even in a dream, or in real life, that would be more delectable still, nothing obscene, only pleasure, these women, single or married, their whims and fancies, are you really a man, René, how mysterious you are, can you make love to me differently than men do, or both at the same time, how much pleasure can you bring me, René, and how different will it be, René, it's a pity, René thought, that all those bodies had vanished, not a single gesture could be picked up again, all those women had probably gotten married, René thought, mating with men like all the others, the hoped-for eroticism had been disappointed then forgotten, René was nothing more than a youthful mistake, not even a memory of the senses bewitched, the flesh was dead, there was only family, children, only existence in its most primal bloom remained, René thought. Louise thought of l'Abeille's smoky living room as Johnie read her sister's diary, yes, it was incredible. No one knew that Émilie was into hallucinogenic drugs, that was during the era of advanced experiments with psychedelic drugs, Timothy Leary, the doctor and writer, Émilie had written how much she admired the psychologist, noting in her diary that she agreed with the poet Ginsberg's opinion that Leary, the professor, had led to a rebirth in the American consciousness, several of Émilie's poems were written in a loose, looping handwriting while she was high on drugs, one of the poems was an affirmation, *I am HOPE, I am myself in all my beauty, my splendor*, she wrote too that a friend of hers, a young American, had jumped from the sixteenth floor of a hotel to avoid being sent to war, so he had said to Émilie, I won't hurt anybody, Emily had written in her diary, my friend left on the wings of angels, on his head a single drop of blood, that day he was wearing an immaculate white shirt, he is gone to where he wanted to be, my friend, and there, the words were written down, they were still there, I will leave that way too, without warning, without a word, but upon reflection, Johnie said, hadn't she been more tempted by the journey, the flight, the escape into the unknown, hadn't she, Johnie said, so she'd known the flood of distorted images people talked about, the colors that were almost like lethal radiation, the edge of nothingness when everything goes dark, color and hope, Johnie said, my sister did all that and I had no idea, I will be me in all my splendor, don't stop me, she had written, I will climb to heights like the top of Mexican temples, I will go, I will exist, Johnie read the pages of her notebooks, her eyes glistening with tears, but the tears wouldn't come, the soldier friend would have been her fiancé, Émilie had written a few days before her friend's suicide, why the decision to die when he could have gone into exile as a conscientious objector, why, Émilie wondered, they

loved each other, they would be the archaeologists of a boundless
future, why that decision, the ultimate choice, on a sunny morning,
the ritual of the white shirt, the tight white jeans, he had planned
every detail, flying into the sky, the untroubled blue, eyes open, had
Émilie wanted to follow him, to risk everything for love, it was a
huge enigma in a tiny human story, Johnie said, and the young man
had written to Émilie, listen, I'm a pacifist, you know that, Émilie,
my pacifist comrades are setting themselves on fire in front of the
Pentagon, they burned themselves alive, I'm on their side against all
war, my dearest Émilie, you will have the memory of holy smoke
rising to heaven, I hold you in my heart and I will always love you,
where I'm going I will be near you always, always telling you, my
love, whatever happens, love life, love life, Johnie was reading
Émilie's notebooks, people were horrified by the kids immolating
themselves, Émilie had written, but only they knew that their
sacrifice was not in vain, they set themselves alight just like the
monks before their temples, the same whorl of flames, they knew
that self-immolation was altruistic, not suicidal, altruistic, they
would never have to bear karma's ordeals after their nuptials with
death, Émilie had read so much and written so much, Johnie said, it
was a senseless monologue with herself, where was she going like
that, what storm or cyclone would blow her away? René sulked to
Louise, when I was in the nursing home, I could hear the nurses
laughing, I wondered if they were laughing at me, you see that guy
who's a woman, isn't that funny, we sure do see crazy things around
here, they would come up to me, René said, it was so humiliating,
they would say, has monsieur taken his medicine, or else, good
morning grandma, how are you this morning, grandma, let's see
how your urine is doing there, your blood pressure's too high,
grandma, come on, what's the matter, why are you so moody, I was
humiliated among all those women, René said to Louise, and I was
subjected to the same fate, I was no longer René, with a worldly,
seductive past, no, I was just a rejected woman, disgraced, negligible

dust, I had to go home otherwise they would have robbed me of all my dignity, all my pride, I would have died of neglect, of a lack of consideration, oh, Louise, promise me that you'll never leave me in such dirty hands again, you're with us, you're with me, Louise said, what shoes do you like best, the ones you bought for way too much money in Italy or the other ones, here, it's almost warm enough for sandals, René, the swallows and the blue jays are coming back to your garden, surely Countess can hear them, René said, she can hear everything, I can almost see her black, velvety ears rising up to taste these intoxicating sounds, she's peering out of her winter den slowly, gradually, blinking in the sunlight, she stretches, she steps into her feline body again, she breathes in the smell of the still-cold spring, and she says to herself, no, not yet, I'll wait for the real heat, it's still too cold for a pilgrim cat like me, I can't bear the cold, that's what she's thinking, my Countess, René said, she's tentative, she doesn't like the warmth of the leaves because it's too damp for her paws, the cottony pads of her feet, she knows I'm waiting for her, then René turned melancholy, when I was an activist, we were every age, every race and color, we were protesting against every country, but how united we were against police violence, we didn't know, I was so young then, we didn't know we would be defeated, beaten, we were insolent, indignant, we had no fear, the fear would come after, when we were lying in the street, dragged by our feet toward the screaming police cruisers, leaves clinging to our hair, and the garbage in the streets, what beautiful couples I saw, valiant girls who would be arrested that same night, incarcerated, what abuse awaited them, and I saw veterans of the resistance, former activists who were treated so badly, seeing all that, I thought to myself, does humanity have a future, does humanity have a future, I didn't believe in God or in humankind, why did they beat us when we were protesting peacefully, some of us were saying, we have to save the world and how else can we do it except through civil disobedience, passively, just not being on their side anymore, it was like a hymn rising to the sky, our voices rose up together, our cries, our complaints, I said to myself, this is the most beautiful meeting for peace, this is the end of intolerance, oh, the naïve faith of youth, those ideals that would soon be thwarted, defeated, it's enough to fill an old heart with bitterness, with regret, no, René, you have nothing to regret, Louise said, every experience is a good thing, I'm telling you, young women and young men are getting married today and that's thanks to you, let them all get married, René said joyfully, let them love each other, what's wrong with loving, isn't that the only salvation against hatred, Louise listened to René, to his irrepressible song unchanged by time, he would have been down in the streets tomorrow against the new, soft war as loudly as he once had been with his brothers and sisters in arms, Louise remembered another dream, from early on in her cancer diagnosis, she was alone in a forest where a table with a white tablecloth awaited, as if for a meal at which she would be the only guest, and on the table there was a plate, an oily black color, then the moon shone through the bristling trees and the plate turned white, during the dream Louise remembered thinking, this must be a sign that I'm going to beat this, the blackness of the plate and what it means, its prescience will be overturned by a bright light, she had recounted the dream to Johnie, who had replied with such compassion, what you're going through, your hair falling out, you're so gaunt, it's a curse, like it is for all cancer patients, we know what an ugly disease it is, how depraved, it slays the healthy, but the light will come and you will emerge from the woods of those who are dead and buried, bravely, Louise, you will get through it, it was winter and Louise went swimming in the public swimming pools, steam rising off the water, she skied on the mountain, she walked for hours, she kept her body away from anything unhealthy, she didn't see René and she would have liked to see no one at all, the treatments wore her down so completely, but in l'Abeille's living room she had people all around her, resplendent with life, and they slowly brought her back to life,

Alexis who wrote all day, the scratching of her pen on the white page, the buzz of the girls' conversations, l'Abeille's thoughtful care, it brightened her days despite the winter and the cold, in her fear she called them her suspended days, how could a person be condemned, how could she live like this, she was only twenty, how could she live through such a physical condemnation at twenty years of age, where was she headed, her soul and her body were disfigured, René sent her a message, through the delirium of carrying on elsewhere, my darling, my antelope, I love you even more, l'Abeille laid cold compresses on her forehead, you could be the love of my life, she said, the two lovebirds Doudouline and Polydor, and Gérard the second who was once named Thérèse, all of them were there, supporting her, loving her even though she wasn't well enough to respond to their kindness, their tenderness, the body seemed to fade away alone, Louise's body seemed to be slipping toward the ramparts without her consent, falling, she was out of breath and her heart was either pounding or else it seemed so slow, she didn't know anymore, it felt like her body wasn't hers anymore, it wasn't her living in that body but an ignominious, gnawing presence, cruel and sly, it was depressing, and she was so defenseless, facing unknown dangers, the girls came and went with their skis, their skates, they smoked the way they had always smoked, constantly, they went out to the bars at night, they chatted on the carpet with Rosemonde purring and meowing among them, they talked about love and philosophy until dawn, everything that seemed so normal and familiar for the girls was neither for Louise, who asked herself, how is it possible to love life less, how do you do that, they're alive and I'm not anymore, my life is a minefield and I've set one off, I'm different, I'm shaken, nothing is normal anymore, even the cheerful sound of the girls' laughter choked Louise, I had to stop laughing, I had to stop loving and choosing, everything had to be mute with terror, as if Louise's body had been found among the ruins of a bombed-out city and the silence of the explosion had to be respected, the silence of defeat, but Louise knew that her body had experienced wonderful things, sometimes in René's arms, more rarely, or with the girls when she was swimming in the Atlantic, with l'Abeille or Gérard, Johnie or Polydor, their crazy laughter, their conversations, they talked about their hopes for the future, all of them were in a revolution of existence, their thinking would change the world, humanize it, there would finally be justice, the end of indifference and intolerance, hatred, good-bye, what were the weapons of their revolution, Louise wondered, beautiful, sensual bodies, that was it, they were stems of love that would not bend, Louise thought, a wind might sweep over them but they were tenacious, feverish, though so young and inexperienced, suitable reason would eventually transform them, and the maturity that no one wanted and which they didn't want either, they would fold into the cult of a more ordered life, finally respectable, lawful, to survive you have to fall in and fit in, Louise thought. At the first whiff of spring, the girls would take their bicycles out of the sheds and garages, Johnie unhooked hers from the big nail on her brick wall, and they would ride along the river under the soaring gulls, the sky was no longer dark and threatening snow and lightning, it was a capricious spring sky, inconstant, but it was nice out and warmer, Louise thought, she wouldn't go out with the others, she stayed in l'Abeille's living room, languishing, tired of being tired, thinking of Gérard, *Gérard oh Gérard* Doudouline wanted to call her musical, she was already dictating the music to her pianist Mimi, singing to her at her mother's theater, the Great Sophie was being indulgent with her daughter, you can practice your singing here but be careful, don't crack any walls or windows with that voice of yours, and don't bother my actors either, they're studying their parts in their dressing rooms, my darling, my dear Anne-Sophie, Doudouline, Mama, Doudouline repeated, my name is not Anne-Sophie, there is only one Sophie in this theater and that's you, I'm holding on to my humble name, it's Doudouline, no, no, the Great Sophie said, that's all childishness, and your attachment to Polydor, it's just a distorted friendship, it'll pass when you meet a man, the love of your life, Mimi, the pianist, who was banging away at her piano, said to Doudouline, but *Gérard oh Gérard* isn't a musical, Doudouline, it's a drama, it's the story of our time, spring and life were exploding, Louise thought, triumphant, without her, what was it that Gérard used to say to Johnie when she was stoned? We thought she was ranting, but that wasn't it, Louise thought, she was going on about rivers of blood, too much blood as children grew up and went to school, went to university, while the great mourning of the assassinations pursued us all, she said, John Kennedy and soon, in the light of June, Robert Kennedy, and before that, in the weaker spring light, in April 1968, on a hotel balcony in Memphis, that crime, the assassination of the Reverend Martin Luther King, it was too much, Gérard had said, no one could take that much blood in such a short time, a few years, a few hours, and she saw that it would only go on the same, all that grief had seeped into her flesh, Gérard said, she smelled blood and carrion, the children's games had been flipped upside down, horrible images had seeped into their skin, they saw a pink dress spotted with blood, red blooms redder still falling from the dress, a man turned his head away somberly, he let it drop back onto the headrest in his car or onto his wife's shoulder, what was it, what had they seen, what was it they had caught a glimpse of, they had to rest their heads because the skull was wide open, an open wound under the sun, you could hear screams, gasps, what was going on, that was the kind of thing Gérard had been talking about, Louise thought, the great Black leader could speak no more, you could tell from the wounds by his mouth, he could no longer speak, had a bullet gone through his throat, what was the matter, why was he suddenly choking on a word, on a message no one would hear, he wouldn't have time, there had been a mistake, Louise thought, Gérard hadn't been delirious, searing visions strung together seemingly devoid of meaning, Gérard had the courage to say what she saw and felt, her visions of crimes and murders were all too real, Louise thought. It was an uneasy time for Louise, a strange, unrecognizable season, with her body slipping away from her, Alexis was going to visit her brother in prison, she was taking the train, her suitcase full of handwritten poems, the eczema blossoming on her face, her arms, her hands, the itching was intolerable, her face was barely visible behind her hair, Louise remembered the zigzag of loose braids, and there was her brother, she knew he was guilty of murder, he had killed a five-year-old child, there he was welcoming her with open arms in the prison visiting room, saying, oh my darling little sister, you're the only one I love in the whole world, but you shouldn't worry about me, I don't like it that you suffer because of me, while Louis was talking to his sister, gently caressing her face, Alexis was thinking, is this him, my beloved brother, who's accused of murder? Alexis brought him the books he wanted to read, I love reading, he said, I started a riot just as something to do, I'm so bored, the boredom is killing me, the bastards want to ship me off to a higher security prison, Louis was reading Nietzsche avidly, devotedly, he called the philosopher his master, Louis explained to Alexis the will to nothingness, Nietzsche was a giant, and the philosopher's realization that God was dead, at last, Louis said, an innovative philosopher, an artist of truth, he had searched for gold in the human heart, the envious, pretentious heart of men, neither good nor bad, mostly just mediocre, of which envy is undoubtedly the most sinister defect, Louis said, referring again to Nietzsche, finally knowing how to say that God is dead, Louis said, and following your instincts immoderately, however treacherous or wicked, what's the point of living according to social norms, Louis asked, you have to break down those expectations, you have to see what lies beyond, that's the strength of a superior mind, the philosopher said it well, didn't he, Alexis, do you remember you used to come to my room and I would lend you my books, Mom said you were too small, that you shouldn't be exposed to things like that, I was a child reading grown-up books, she wanted to keep us mired in Christian hypocrisy, because with Christians everything is hypocritical, they wanted to stop us reading forbidden books while Dad was sending men and women to the gallows, they were wrong about everything, Alexis, you and I knew, and Alexis would leave the visits upset and rush back to her little school desk, to her writing, but at the same time the philosopher's words rang true to her, Nietzsche, her brother's teacher, it seemed right that he condemned the hypocrisy of Christians, and their parents, and above all their father's astounding hypocrisy, yes, Alexis thought, my brother is right, but Nietzsche wasn't the brutal man her brother described, he was frail, as misunderstood as Verlaine had been, and he'd never recovered from his frequent mental breakdowns, maybe like Verlaine too, Alexis thought, he was still as misunderstood today as he had been then, maybe he had never been forgiven for his great cry, *God is dead*, because nobody wanted to hear it, Alexis thought. Alexis confided in l'Abeille, that spring, she was going to the university library more often, and she had made a friend, Dave, an English student, he loved Kant, and she liked talking with him, unlike her brother Louis, Dave believed in a spirited idealism according to which the soul could aspire to transcendence, an active spirituality, he believed in all that was good and pure, Alexis said, like Alexis, he was estranged from his wealthy family, he said they were snobbish and pompous and egocentric, and he had only one dream, he wanted to go live in Ireland and have a sheep farm, he wanted to raise them for wool, never meat, no, he was a vegetarian, one day, not now, of course, Dave would have liked to marry Alexis, take her along with him on his adventure, wasn't it wonderful, he said, to dream like that, Alexis had been moved by his voice, this big, protective boy, the young man's broad hand on her shoulder, but she told him no, she could never leave her brother again, it was her duty to visit him in prison, and Dave had replied, oh but I can wait, I'm sure we would be happy there. Polydor teased Alexis, hey,

Alexis, you're always talking about male philosophers and poets, women are great poets and great philosophers too, how can you not know that, and Alexis replied humbly, I am not as advanced as you are, Polydor, any time the girls said anything Alexis seemed so ambivalent that it was like she might not even have the strength to answer. Polydor brushed off Alexis' reluctance, I have books from the bookstore where I work, I'll lend them to you, you'll see, it'll be a whole new world for you, you'll see, Alexis, Alexis tilted her head, her heavy hair, I'm a woman who writes, she said to Polydor, ever since I was born I've thought of nothing but writing but I don't like any of what I write, none of it makes me happy. Polydor looked at Alexis, defenseless, poor little bird, a wren tumbled out of its nest, my God, what's going to happen to her? It was hard to know, Alexis was such a secretive girl, Polydor thought. Alexis would get disturbing letters from her brother, he wrote to her that the staff respected him in prison because his father was a judge but the other prisoners were humiliated, beaten and chained, they were poor, they were nothing, just numbers on a uniform, and Louis told them to revolt, he started riots, rise up, he said, defend your honor, fling your urine and feces at the walls, you'll never be free otherwise, they treat you with violence so treat them the same, Alexis wrote to her brother that he should quell his vengeful wrath, she no longer knew how to write to him, how to talk to him, until one day he told her, little sister, don't be angry with me for not telling you earlier but one day soon I won't be here anymore, our parents know already, I'm dying of leukemia, it's been so fast, good-bye dear angel, good-bye, I hope I didn't come into the world only to make you miserable, though it might seem like it sometimes, sometimes I believe that I have to die because I bear the sins of my father, but that's only about me, good-bye, my sweet sister, the news was painful and Alexis locked herself up in l'Abeille's room, two chairs stacked up against the door, the girls were watchful and worried, l'Abeille slipped notes under the door, hello Alexis, are you hungry, are you thirsty, I'm here, we're all here, you know we're here for you, Alexis read the messages, thinking of her brother sneaking notes between the bars of his prisoner friends' cells, revolt, don't let yourselves be punished, soon she wouldn't have a brother anymore, she thought, the image of him would shatter, he had been invincible, he seemed so strong, she could hear Dave's voice. They were leaving the university library together, walking together in the warm spring wind, a farm, some sheep, Ireland, the sea, he was saying, his voice was warm in Alexis' ear, the beauty of the world will be ours, I can see it already, I can see the lambs, the sheep, they're ambling down the hills and into the valleys and the evening light is so beautiful coming off the sea, Alexis would have no parents, no brother, heaven seemed to have no end of woe in store for her, or it was the crime her brother Louis had committed that had poisoned her slowly, it had caught his body in the deathly snarl of leukemia, another ordeal from an implacable God, a distant God, no, more than distant, he was absent, he was dead, hadn't that been said often enough, Alexis thought, on the other side of the barricaded door of l'Abeille's room, the girls were calling her, Doudouline was singing a song from her musical, *Gérard oh Gérard*, her voice tinged with a Schubertian nostalgia that moved Alexis in her reclusion, sitting on l'Abeille's bed, she saw her brother again, as a child she used to push him in his carriage and he would shout, Mama, Mama, later the two of them played tennis together in the garden, it was as big as a park, he was all dressed in white in the light of the too-short summers and she saw him dancing around on the other side of the net, a lock of dark hair over his forehead, he was sweating and laughing, the maid came out of the sunroom under the pergola with the climbing grapevines and said, it's snack time, kids, come on, don't go in the house, you'll disturb your parents, it grew cooler under the trees and Alexis shivered in her white tank top, Dad had court that day, it was the day of important legal decisions, the day of death sentences, he'd had a big lunch and lots of coffee, and Alexis and Louis' mother had said to her husband,

don't forget, a bit of empathy, never forget, even though he never
listened, and the children were playing outside, they couldn't let
him see them on those days, decision days, days of fatal
determination, and Louis said to his sister, his tennis racket in the
air, little sister, have you ever thought how much it must hurt, that
knot around your neck, do you think about that sometimes, I never
stop thinking about it, hanging a thief because he's a thief, is that a
good decision, no, it's dishonest, Louis said, one day our father will
pay for it, while she was singing, Doudouline could see Gérard
running across the beach along the Atlantic, she could breathe in
her smell of salt and water, she could see her flat breasts under the
bikini top, it had been a good time for Gérard, they mustn't forget a
single detail, not her curly eyelashes, her long legs in the sun, the
laughter and joy, Doudouline thought as she sang, in Doudouline's
song Gérard seemed so solid, so real all of a sudden, out running on
the beach at dawn, Alexis listened to Doudouline's melodious voice,
a voice that invited conciliation, she was thinking that she couldn't
tear herself away from her brother, wouldn't it be like ripping out a
piece of her own flesh, but maybe the time had come, maybe by
moving away for good and carrying him only in her memory, without
all the heaviness, with grace, and she left the room, suddenly free,
the green moors of Connemara are so lovely, she would say to
l'Abeille, the cattle in the fields resting in the rain, the stone parapet
along the sea, she would marry Dave, she had been too open, too
naïve, and she was pregnant with his child, they would have a farm
and raise lambs and sheep, the hills would be full of sheep, it was as
if she had the key to one of her poems, it was coming apart, all those
poems tied up together with string in her suitcase, when she left it
would be with that suitcase banging at her hip, Doudouline
exclaimed that she would do Alexis' hair for the wedding, she was
obsessed with Alexis' heavy hair, yes, you're going to look like *The
Birth of Venus* Alexis, Louise remembered Gérard running at dawn
on the beach by the Atlantic, those summers of splendor, under the

caressing, billowing light, when she was still living with her parents, Gérard, she was called Géraldine then but soon she would become Gérard, she wanted a male name, she had fallen in love with a woman named Mercedes, her first love, she didn't talk about her much, that was before she sank into drugs and the despair of addiction, it was a season of purity, of health, she had pushed it all from her mind in her new addiction to cocaine, heroin, Mercedes had tried to protect her, the memory of Mercedes was fragmented, shattered, although Gérard had loved her so much, Mercedes had been the first blaze of the senses for her, her first time trusting someone, her first time sleeping against a woman's shoulder, Mercedes was ten years older than Gérard, the oldest of a family of seven children, and she was more or less the head of the household, the father was abusive to his wife and children, he was an alcoholic and Mercedes was afraid he would rape her younger sisters, Esperanza and Paciencia, Mercedes was a social worker and a sociologist, she had loved Gérard with a love that was as maternal as it was sensual, and in the worst of Gérard's violence and delusions, she had told her, stop looking for your mother, that it would only cause her pain and disappointment, she had been adopted by parents who were as kind as they were generous, Mercedes said, true Christians, like her Spanish mother she was a believer and she thought it was scandalous that people suffered so much in the world, she took in addicted kids on cold nights and brought them to the hospital, though she only managed to save a few, she warned Gérard about drugs and about how Gérard seemed to get drawn into fantasy, it worried her about Gérard, I will always pray for you, little soul, Mercedes said, as if she could sense Gérard's slow slide into a night from which there is no escape, and maybe, Louise thought, Mercedes was still praying for Gérard's little lost soul, Gérard rejected Mercedes, her premonitions and prophecies, she's too religious for me, she's not a lover, she's a saint, she told herself, how can she love someone like me, your mother abandoned you at the orphanage, it's better to forget her, Mercedes said, but Gérard felt a hollow, dizzying emptiness, she had to see her mother again, she kept thinking of those other babies left in the cribs at the orphanage, my skin is dark even in winter, maybe they were my brothers, she thought, and in her mind they were all one family and Gérard was tormented no longer, they had to find each other, but where were they, where was her mother, how wretched she must have been when she decided their fate, sometimes it's better to forget, Mercedes said, my dear Gérard, it's better to forget, where would we be if we were all paralyzed by misfortune, we wouldn't be able to grow or to love, Mercedes felt the sudden distance between them, Gérard started saying strange things, she said that sensuality could be tiresome, which seemed an affront to Mercedes, who cherished sensuality, she said that love could never last, that all passion was vain, Mercedes' beloved child was pulling away, she was leaving her, obviously they would always be friends, Gérard said, they would stay close, but Gérard, who'd had such contempt for the kids who took drugs every night, needles dangling out of their arms, getting high in hovels or behind dumpsters, Gérard, who'd been so sanctimonious, gave in to those dangerous, deadly games, Mercedes told Louise later, we have to understand what Gérard is going through, it's a solitary drama, Mercedes was all mercy and forgiveness with Gérard, who had behaved so badly with her, Louise thought, I was afraid, Mercedes explained, I could see the impending catastrophe, perhaps it was my fault, I couldn't save her, I couldn't rescue her, it was so painful for me, Mercedes said with that same compassion, that quality or fault that was a form of moral rectitude, of neutral, almost detached goodness. Mercedes could see Gérard in her dreams, she saw the burning walls crumbling around her, she saw her frozen, unable to get up while everyone else was already outside in the winter night, she could hear their footsteps on the fire escape, she was lying on the floor, her feet and legs were useless because she was so high, towering waves of smoke were descending upon her, smothering her, Mercedes woke up gulping for breath, her heart pounding, my God, she thought, the flames didn't get to her, she didn't have time to suffer, it was the smoke, it was all that smoke that killed her, my lost little soul, why did you run away from me, why didn't I keep you close to me? Gérard, an only child, left Mercedes in agony, Louise thought, Mercedes, who even felt sorry for her father, the drunk, he was a man consumed by nostalgia, by regret for having left his country, he was an exile, Mercedes said, Mercedes' grandparents and parents had fled, taking very little, the shirts on their backs, Mercedes said, they ran from war and fascism, poor immigrants hustled from country to country hoping to find peace. Gérard had had a good first love, happy and serene, Louise thought, and she had clumsily destroyed it, Mercedes told the girls that Gérard's absence was only the illusion of departure, in the fierce faith she shared with her mother, a faith that seemed unshakeable or stubborn but which for her was radiant, you could see it in her face, Louise thought, Mercedes was sure she would find Gérard again in another life, a life free from hardship, an eternal, heavenly life, as if Mercedes had glimpsed in Gérard and all her wayward ways the possibility of an ascent to heaven, she saw her like a little martyr. In those days, in l'Abeille's smoky living room, when Lali came back late from her nighttime peregrinations and it was too late to drive out to her house far in the country, she would stay over, she would lie down on l'Abeille's couch and sleep soundly until the alarm rang for her shift in emergency, and then she would get up and head straight for the kitchen sink, bypassing the bathtub by the kitchen, wake up by splashing water over herself, and shiver into her military coat as she headed outside, into the world as cold as the icy trees along the street. She said to Louise, tell René, tell my brother that I will go see him when he has fewer mistresses, you put up with too much for him, Louise, he has to change, you know that, Louise, you know you're his true love, as she opened the door onto a world hemmed in icicles, Lali's words didn't reassure Louise, not at all, it was as if Lali had confirmed that Louise was in love with the most sybaritic man, the most unworthy, and that she should be ashamed of her feelings, her love offered up in sheer waste. Yes, it was a waste, Louise thought, such an abundance of lost love. L'Abeille went back to her room, to her bed, feeling the lack of Alexis, there was a hollow in the mattress where she had slept, you will be my child's godmother, Alexis had told her when she left, l'Abeille breathed in her smell, the fragrance of her hair, when she slipped under the blanket at night, Alexis had been writing the beginnings of a poem that l'Abeille found in an envelope on the pillow, or maybe some mysterious message, *my dear Abeille, may our generation be sincere, without rancor and without fear, for tomorrow our duty will be to save those who come after*, like all of Alexis' messages and poems, l'Abeille thought, it was a surprising and disturbing incantation, it was like having a leprechaun or a fairy in the house, l'Abeille thought, poets are like no one else, and l'Abeille imagined Alexis writing diligently at her desk by the fireplace, or when she went to the library, holding her suitcase of poems, poets are an enigma, l'Abeille thought, honey for our bitter days and sunshine in the night, but then l'Abeille remembered that Alexis had told her that Dave was a charming man, and she took up his philosophy of a world that could be transformed by nature, but that she had no feelings for him, was it her brother's bad luck that had withered her like this, she didn't know, but she felt like the man she was going to marry would always be a stranger to her, and she to him. What would become of Alexis in the vastness of Ireland, l'Abeille wondered. Louise told l'Abeille that Alexis' youth and innocence would stand her in good stead, she was carrying a tragedy that wasn't hers and escaping to Ireland would allow her to finally heal. Manfred was away on a concert tour in India that spring and l'Abeille wrote to him that her heart and especially her head were drunk on the scent of the lilacs in the yard and that it was time to look for a great love, Manfred told her that his first baby had been born, he said there would be many more, all of them musicians like Bach's famous children and it would be so beautiful, making music in the evening with the whole family, he was overjoyed, he wrote, and soon he would come celebrate both his marriage to his musician fiancée and the birth of his first child in the yard under the unfurling purple of the lilac bush, what happiness, my dear Christie, dear l'Abeille, I owe you so much, thrumming with life, l'Abeille started going out every night, out to the bars. The night was glowing with love for her, while the girls danced against each other in the whirling music. Spring was the season of desire, while summer was often the season of disappointed desire, l'Abeille said. Later, she would remember how she had met Geneviève, and for a long time, it seemed like she was living a slow passion without really knowing if it was passion at all because what she felt first for Geneviève was admiration, Geneviève was not only a brilliant student, she was already a practicing architect. In a quieter part of the bar, where you could still hear what the music actually sounded like, Louise said that she wanted to build herself a house, she wanted to break up with René once and for all, be independent, she didn't want to see him anymore, and Geneviève showed her some drawings, plans for a small house, think of yourself first, forget about your friends, you have to be independent, you have to stand on your own, Geneviève said, I'll help you, l'Abeille was taken with Geneviève's green-blue eyes under her thick glasses, her short hair so neatly groomed, the blond highlights, that sophistication she had, though she knew she was pretty, l'Abeille thought, she was loyal and professional in her advice to Louise. You understand, Geneviève, Louise said, I could finish my thesis in peace, without constantly being disturbed by René's infidelities, I could be healthy and normal, I would have a quiet, domestic life, a dog, a cat, I could live like everybody else, you know, Louise said, I could find myself, I know girls who are good carpenters, we can all work together, Louise said, invigorated now, if passion can be as toxic as cancer, you have to run away from it, right, Louise said to Geneviève, yes, absolutely, Geneviève answered, quite aware that Louise would never leave René. It was an unbreakable bond, she later said. L'Abeille found it alarming that, as much as she was drawn to Geneviève, she felt no real desire for her. It must be the winter, l'Abeille thought, the cold had invaded her and settled in. Winter, snow, cold, the still-painful memory of Johnie leaving to go study in Paris and Vienna on scholarship. L'Abeille's living room was being deserted. Even Alexis would probably forget about l'Abeille out there with her sheep on the green hills of Ireland. L'Abeille was devastated, the girls were dropping away from the tree of friendship and affection rooted around her, even Louise wouldn't be coming back to huddle in l'Abeille's living room. She would just be lying around her cottage, with a little stove to keep the house warm in winter, a dog to cuddle in her lap, and a yellow-eyed cat to erase the memory of her once-beloved Rosemonde. Of course, Polydor and Doudouline and Gérard the second would still be there, buttering their toast in the morning, Polydor and Gérard the second drinking coffee with cognac in the evening, at night, but Louise would be gone, how could l'Abeille bear the sadness of not seeing her anymore? I really want to see your paintings, Geneviève whispered in l'Abeille's ear, I've been told they're very beautiful, your friend Louise told me, and the other girls too, l'Abeille feigned modesty, or maybe it was self-doubt, the extent of how much she didn't want Geneviève struck her like a cold wind in the face, it's because of Gérard, and because of Johnie, that bourgeois girl who can afford to study abroad, no, don't say that, I love Johnie, soon her name won't be Johnie, she'll be Dr. Vanessa Laflamme, an expert in complex neuroses, because she believes neuroses and hallucinations can lead to art, but that's not true, l'Abeille thought. No, I really want to see your paintings, especially the latest, the one that was inspired by Gérard, Louise told me it's striking, Geneviève said to l'Abeille, who was lost in thought. Suddenly l'Abeille was afraid of Geneviève, she couldn't love her, wouldn't love her, that night at the bar had been a mistake, l'Abeille was faithful only to the girls in the group, the house, their past with Gérard, everything that bound them so strongly in her smoky living room, the ramshackle house where Manfred was welcome too, and Alexis, an oasis for poets and artists where Doudouline was composing her musical inspired by Gérard, *Gérard oh Gérard*, and this girl, Geneviève, she already had a career, she was an architect, l'Abeille wouldn't let her turn her life upside down, already Geneviève's authority was weighing on her, we'll do this and that, come see my brand-new office, I want to hang that magnificent painting of yours on the wall, and, Louise remembered, l'Abeille was especially wary of depending on Geneviève's money, of any benefit that would demean her. While l'Abeille was in the throes of doubt and hesitation, telling herself, it's my fault, I shouldn't have gone to the bar on a full moon, you know what happens to me when the moon is full, I'm a horny raving mess, I shouldn't have gone out, Polydor and Gérard the second, wearing the first Gérard's suspenders, were going to plant flowers on Gérard's grave on the mountain, Gérard the second was the gardener for the flowered meadow where the red cardinal came to land, a volley of sparrows flew around too, and blue jays, Polydor and Gérard the second left gifts every day on what by now had become a garden beneath which Gérard lay sleeping, Gérard the second said, and Doudouline came to sing and Alexis laid a poem by the grave, oh, dear Gérard, the infinite is with you and all the waves of the oceans and the seas, may your fragile boat find safe passage, Gérard, that luminous and occasionally rainy spring, Gérard had visitors every day. Mercedes came to pray on her knees, which would have annoyed the rebellious Gérard, Polydor said, but the earth needs sunshine, and a few prayers from a pious lover would do Gérard no harm, Polydor said, her rest among the flowers and the grass would be untroubled. A few times, Polydor had seen a veiled Black woman standing near Gérard's grave, her head bowed, praying. Was that her, Polydor wondered, was that Gérard's mother, how sad that they would meet again so late, how sad. Louise no longer dreamed of belonging to René, she dreamed of owning a cottage by the river, of belonging to herself. So that's how you forget me, René said suddenly in the half-light of his luxurious apartment, the snow falling in large flakes behind the window, yes, here I am, crammed into the fancy clothes I used to wear, you can see I'm no longer the ladies' man I once was, my Louise, what do you think? Louise smiled without answering, then they heard Olga, her splenetic accent, Madame is handsome like he was before, even if I didn't know her then, there was bad time, she went on, the Berlin Wall fell down, girls with greasy blond hair, all young, like they came out of caves, begging men for food, strong and powerful men, that's what attracted them to their misery, they wanted to marry them because they were starving, they were dying with loneliness, and the men said to them rudely, hey girls, you are all whores who try to swindle our male officials, that is what you all are, and they would climb on the men's laps to be seen, admired, contemplated, what a sad picture, Olga said, their misery, rags on their backs, their dirty hair, they were so hungry and no one had pity for them, Olga said, no, no one had pity. René listened to Olga, this was maybe the first time she was talking about herself, her life, whether what she was saying was true or not, René respected and pitied the poor creatures Olga was describing so vividly, starving little rats peeking out from cracks in a stone wall, from dark caves where they had been cowering for so long, beaten down by hunger, by abandonment, rejection, an army of girls who are hungry, hungry for men and bread, hungry to death, Olga said, what happened to them, René asked kindly, what happened to your friends, oh, they are not my friends, Madame René, Olga said, there was a lot of talk about them, about how savage and cold they were when they attacked a man like choosing a prey. That was what it was, like hunting prey. They had to survive, Madame René, they worked hard to survive. Many died of tuberculosis, no one took care of them, others died of syphilis, it is great evil, Olga said, women and children are always first to suffer, Olga said, she clasped her hands together as if in prayer, and I pray for them, yes, I pray for them, Olga said. René's heart sank thinking of the girls Olga was describing, she could have done more, fought longer, gone to prison like those other protesters who got dragged away by their feet by the police, choking on tear gas, a whole lifetime wasn't enough to express all the indignation, the anger. She'd had too much fun, she was just a playboy, a slacker, a stupid romantic, and now who was he, an impotent man in fine clothes, a man without a mistress, Louise seemed to be reading his mind, she guessed at his disappointment, listen, René, she told her old friend, you've done everything right, Louise said, as well as you could have, and surely in his wisdom God will beckon you to a paradise where all the women you've loved will be waiting, and many others too, all I want is to find my animals, my pets, René said, Venus and all the others, nothing more, I don't want to be disturbed by any women. Don't make fun of me, my giraffe, you know I can be mean. Olga was whispering again, lamenting, Madame René, I'm telling you, it was very ugly sight, when Berlin Wall fell, those ratty blonds who wanted to eat men, men and their money, to feed on them or bite them, they bit their hands when they pleaded, and the men scorned them, they laughed and made fun and shouted, whores, whores. Of course, they were high officials, they did not let themselves be devoured by those girls, rather they insulted them. Women should be pitied, Olga said again, and René answered, men too, my dear Olga, men too, we must pity them. But Monsieur René, Olga sighed, you are not a man, you cannot understand, you are only a woman like me, Monsieur René, when you were in the hospital, the nurses told you enough, we women should all be pitied, you know that. As Louise combed René's hair, parting it like Lali's, that discreet masculiniz-ation, René and Lali looked so much alike, they had the same haircut, Louise remembered l'Abeille's smoky living room, and

Geneviève, l'Abeille's new lover, though l'Abeille was slow to reciprocate, she was trying to adapt, like Lali Geneviève had to get up early in the morning to go to the office while l'Abeille's world was nocturnal, roaming all night from one bar to the next, coming home to chat until morning with Gérard the second and Polydor over spiked coffee, and Geneviève, worn out by all the excess, would cry out, listen, Christie, my Abeille, I can't take it anymore, I have to be more disciplined than this, how can you live like this, you girls, you never sleep, how do you do it, and Geneviève got in her car and went home, l'Abeille had never seen such a beautiful car, a white convertible, soon Geneviève would peel back the top to let in the blue sky, the wind, the rain, what auspicious rides, l'Abeille thought, she felt melancholy all of a sudden, she loved being in love but that joy was dampened, her hive wasn't as full as it had once been, yes, she thought, they're all leaving, the house is going to be empty, her magnificent, buzzing hive, one by one the girls were taking flight, Louise to build her house, Lali because she had more hours at the hospital, and Geneviève seemed to live at the office rather than her own apartment, she worked so hard, she was obsessed with her career, and with keeping up her environmental mission in the projects she chose, l'Abeille's hive was deserted, it felt like her mother's departure long ago, interrupting summer vacation or the holidays at Christmas at her grandparents' where l'Abeille's idyllic childhood had unfolded happily. Her grandfather had wanted to be an actor but they had inherited a farm and the big family gathered around him in the house, a family hive where they sang, where l'Abeille's mother's sisters, musicians all, they could play every instrument, oh, the happiness of summertime, winters of joy, of jubilation when l'Abeille, the cousins, and their mothers all got up at daybreak with the chickens, there were roosters and hens, l'Abeille thought, a chicken running around free followed l'Abeille everywhere, it slept out in the fields in the afternoons among the cows, how good it must have been, that sleep, and how fragrant the air, even in the morning, when her grandmother came to wake them, get up, children, I've got blueberry pancakes for you, the uncles drank a little too much but that was the way it was, the grandfather had built a large wooden library with beams where mice and squirrels scurried in the dawn light, rivers and streams flowed nearby, it was a magical place, l'Abeille thought, and that was why she needed her house to be a hive, even if the girls were just squatting, she needed the company, the buzz of voices in the evening, at night, l'Abeille felt conflicted, divided, Louise thought, when she heard from Alexis, from her farm in Ireland, Alexis was having a difficult pregnancy, she should never have left l'Abeille's living room, the desk by the fireplace, she no longer had the strength to write, the nausea was so bad, no, she should never have left l'Abeille's room, her monastic life, her writing, she saw her belly getting bigger while she was wasting away, her husband came home late from the pub, he had been a delicate and attentive lover and now he was rough when they made love, I lost everything when my brother died, Alexis wrote to l'Abeille, everything, but the most painful thing for me, she wrote, is what I'm going through here every day with my husband, he's not the same anymore, in our garden I saw a calf tied to a stake, it was only a few months old and couldn't understand what my husband was about to do, it was tugging on the rope, playing, it was prancing and jumping around, I ran to Dave, shouting, you can't take him to the slaughterhouse, you can't do that, you said all animals would be safe here, but he replied that his parents had screwed him out of his money because he refused to marry the rich wife they'd chosen for him, for their social class, and we had no choice, our animals had to be sold at market, no, we had no choice, he said, and I felt such hatred rise up in me, I hated this man, this killer, he fooled me, my dear Abeille, I'm sorry to be writing you such sad, unhappy things, I loved that little calf like I love my unborn child, I watched it grow up with me, and what's going to happen to the other animals on our farm, when I met Dave he was a vegetarian, and here he is leading our animals to slaughter every day, no, Abeille, I should never have left you all, my girls, I'm horrified as my belly grows, I'm going to give birth to a traitor's child, I'm ashamed and afraid for the baby, dear Abeille, my friend, I do feel some sense of peace when I come down the hill in the evening, where sheep graze freely, the ewes and the lambs, under the sweep of birds I can watch the sea as the sun sets, and there, close to the benevolent waters, I might get back to the illumination of writing, the grandeur of the words when they are given to poets, it's as if I'm ravished by the magnificence of the landscape, from the top of the rocks drunken boys leap into the rumbling waves of a sea that's changing every second, they laugh and shout, I can hear their bodies falling and then they bounce off the waves, they feel invincible and maybe they're right, they climb higher and higher on the rocks in the purpling sun as it paces toward night, and from the peak of these gigantic rocks they dive straight into the waves, other evenings, I grab my husband's Jeep and I leave, I run away, I drive for a long time along the coast, by the sea, the wind and the rain do me good, I don't want to stay at home anymore, I don't want it, the monotony of marriage, I don't want to be a couple anymore, a woman just withering away, and here I am enormously pregnant, what can I do, do you know, Abeille, you understand everything about other people's moods, do you know how depressed I am, I'm taking something for it, how dark my mind is, my body, they gave me medication, but I have to be careful because of the baby, because in spite of everything this little one might save me from my thoughts, I'm so sad, and I'm thinking of my brother, no one could save him, he must have been in such pain, so much remorse, even though he never even admitted it to himself, it was remorse that sank into him and killed him, just like he had killed, and he couldn't hold out anymore, his flesh was rotten through, that's the only way I can think of to explain how quickly he went, he disappeared in a few weeks, l'Abeille read Alexis' letter and it pained her, though what a delight all of a sudden it was to be with Geneviève, she went over to her place at night, Geneviève often worked late, drawing at her work table, there has to be sun and air suffusing the houses I want to build, yes, even the winter sun can warm a house designed like a greenhouse, it's a renewal, you have to let nature permeate the houses, what do you think, l'Abeille, you're taking Louise away from me, l'Abeille would have liked to say, yes, you're about to steal my Louise, even though René still possessed her, our terrible René, she used to come visit me fairly often, I was her friend, her confidante, and now she's going to live alone with a dog, a cat, without me, but this is what it's like to expand your hive, the colony has to be open, I'll get used to it, l'Abeille thought, if Geneviève was going to be kissing and stroking her all night long, methodical and slow, maybe l'Abeille could get over it, who knows, little by little, she thought. At that time, Louise thought, Doudouline and her musicians had borrowed the Great Sophie's stage to dance and sing and work out the artistic details of Doudouline's musical, *Gérard oh Gérard*, the Great Sophie had agreed to let them use the theater on one condition, she told Doudouline, that Doudouline would marry a man, the Great Sophie told everyone that she had found a husband for Doudouline, listen, daughter, he's a good-looking man, an actor, just how you like them, with broad shoulders, he's a tenor, he has a kind of conquering manliness about him, are you listening to me, my daughter, we have to put an end to your abstruse relationship with Polydor, she's a girl, might I remind you, not a boy, I'm tired of seeing you two hugging and walking hand in hand like you're engaged, it's just not done, you need a man, a real man, and I want you to get married as soon as possible, Doudouline, listening to her mother, shrugged her shoulders, Mama, dear, you know I would only marry Polydor, Doudouline told her mother, oh, what a disgrace this is for a mother, the Great Sophie complained, she was always on, always onstage, she never stopped acting, her voice rose, you know full well that I have a heart condition, Anne-Sophie, my daughter, I'm going to die from this, do you want your mother to die? You're positively glowing with health, Doudouline said placidly, Mama dear, what are you even talking about, you will be polite and well-behaved and you will be Polydor's mother-in-law, regardless of what you think, Mama dear. Sophie mopped up great crocodile tears, times are changing too fast, she said, I'll never get used to it, my daughter wants to be another girl's wife, progress is going too fast, if I don't have a heart condition yet, I'm going to, this is too much pain for a mother to bear. And these people you're seeing, Doudouline, the Great Sophie went on stubbornly, this Lali, René, what are they exactly, what sex are they, are they men or are they women? It's all very well when you're a teenager, but when you start to grow up, really, you don't know what to think anymore. Lali is an androgynous girl, Mama, and René a man in a woman's body, is that clear enough, Mama dear? When will you leave me alone, Mama dear? Never, the Great Sophie answered firmly, never, because for a mother it is a matter of honor that her daughter gets married, she has to be normal. On her first computer, up on the screen Louise was getting messages from Johnie at her student residence in Paris, green and white letters on a black background, Johnie was studying constantly, she wasn't interested in love, she had to be cool and reserved, she wrote, although she admired the courage of the boygirls, the trans kids who only went out at night, walking briskly to private clubs and secret bars, it was all very secretive and closed, at that time women's homosexuality felt clandestine, Johnie wrote, it was illicit, but those girls were so brave, she admired them, at night she watched them from a café that closed late, they were so well dressed in their suits, distinct and solitary, they walked along the Seine toward whatever haven of furtive sexuality awaited, who was waiting for them there, Johnie wondered, soon I'll be Dr. Vanessa and I won't be the same, Johnie wrote to Louise, I might have to lie in my professional life, too, like so many others. No, you won't lie, Louise wrote to her, no, you'll always be our Johnie, we should never lie about who we are, Louise wrote. I blend in with a group of students, I've become impersonal, Johnie wrote to Louise, that's what I want, cool, unapproachable, no one knows who I am, I'm just a stranger blending in among other strangers. I'm going to a lot of museums, I'm thinking a lot about mental illness in painters, neurosis produces hallucinatory effects in their work, Johnie wrote, my sister Émilie might not have had a chance to express it, maybe she was one of those artists whose creativity turned self-destructive instead, and maybe the same thing was true for the others too, Johnie wrote to Louise, I'm thinking of Van Gogh cutting off his ear, ranting under a sky dark with black birds persecuting him, but through the abolition of the self they created living works beyond the mark of insanity, without the revelation that Rubens was painting for him, Van Gogh would never have realized that he was a painter, that he would create more than two thousand works, no, he wanted to be a preacher, a mad preacher, there was already that religious imbalance coming out in him, he was in and out of institutions, giving in to delusions and sudden rushes of lucidity alike, and painting all the while, with the roughness and refinement that became his trademark, we never talk about all those lost hours for those who are called insane, at the end of a hallway or behind bars, was he painting, was he still drawing during those dement-ed days and nights, Louise read Johnie's messages and she imagined her solitude, the distance she felt and kept even when she was with friends or lovers, even the girls in the group knew so little about it, she had loved Gérard with a protective, vigilant, almost chaste love, their long limbs entangled at night, they often liked to sleep together, Johnie said to Louise, nothing more, quiet and restful, before Gérard was taken by the drugs, before the plummet and flight, she couldn't just have an easy relationship, Johnie said, or was it that her need for distance was stronger than any carnal desire for kisses and caresses, Johnie did not understand how her sister Émilie had always felt so drawn to men, how she had given herself to them and to such unremitting pleasure, every time and everywhere, Johnie had witnessed Émilie's dizzying sensuality constantly during their vacation stay in Greece, the last time her sister had been with her, little sister, her little flame wasn't lit brightly enough, pestering Johnie to love the bodies of men, I don't like anyone's body yet, Johnie replied, saving herself from any depravity, she was so cool, Émilie was so over-stimulated, so sexually charged that she blew everything out of proportion, annoyed, Émilie would ask Johnie, then to whom will you belong? To no one, Johnie said, or else the person I love will have to be able to elicit such ardent desire, but would that kind of desire ever happen? And Louise saw Johnie's profile, distant and beautiful in its detachment, its noble youth, Johnie alone in a café watching the parade of androgynous girls at night, or walking in the street with them, not too far from them, in the rain, it was a light rain, gray sky, perhaps one of them would remind her of Émilie, her departure, in the night, the way they held their neck, or the impudence in their eyes, and then the procession of bodies would drift away in a pink mist, it was as if Johnie had dreamed those nights already back in her hometown when the girls all went out cheerfully to the bars, the clubs, they were less secretive, though the Great Sophie would say to Doudouline, on my honor, I will not be climbing any of those stairs that lead to those places where people smoke and drink until three in the morning, where young girls from good families like you, Doudouline, waltz around with each other, no, I'll never understand, the Great Sophie told Doudouline, who was insulted that her mother would dare speak to her like that, she sounded so disappointed and so critical. Mama dear, I'd rather you said nothing to me at all than spout nonsense, Mama dear, I'd rather you just shut up, Doudouline said. Johnie wrote to Louise that she had finished reading her sister's diaries, they are disturbing notebooks, a pitiful mess, yes, but she had a rich literary imagination, Émilie painstakingly recorded each of her experiences, she'd been born into a narrowminded middle-class

NIGHTS TOO SHORT TO DANCE

background, Johnie wrote to Louise, and she wanted to discover a different and diverse humanity, she was searching for a new humanism, when she wanted to learn Russian, she took the train with Russian students, she slept with them on uncomfortable bunks and shared their vodka and their samovar when the ancient train stopped at a station, it was as cold as Siberia, she was eager to behold the beauty of the universe, she wrote, she drew that beauty from everywhere, rejecting ease and wisdom and solace. We don't know how she survived, her parents couldn't reach her anymore to send her money, we had no idea how lonely and destitute she was as she drifted from one country to another, alone, she had no support, Johnie wrote to Louise. Louise thought of her airy little house filled with sunshine by the river, in summer there would be a green lawn in front of the house, a dog playing outside and a cat in the window, Louise was teaching in the evenings after her own classes, soon she would be self-sufficient, she didn't want the cancer to come back, just living could be exhausting, especially because she was still seeing René, often late at night, in what René arrogantly called his spare time, how could she get out of that relationship, how could she end it, Louise thought, was the bond that unbreakable, Johnie had told Louise that l'Abeille should watch out for Alexis, there was a planetary transit that would be detrimental to Alexis, harmful planets could do a great deal of damage, Johnie's astrological research would prove all of this soon, Johnie wrote to Louise, how exhausting it was to live in a world in which conflict and war and riots raged, where people were assassinated in the middle of the street, the hostility was relentless, Johnie wrote to Louise, the fact is, wherever we are, we are in a constant state of war. René heard the muffled tug of the brush through his hair as Louise parted it, you and Lali, Louise mocked, you and Lali are so finicky, the way you part your hair, you and your ties, you just can't go unnoticed, can you, René, yet Lali likes being unobtrusive, while you're far less discreet, René, René couldn't hear Louise's voice anymore, only the sound of his hair being parted, pulled close to the skull, she suddenly felt the full weight of her physical vulnerability, the weakness in her arms and legs, even if Louise had helped her slip on her most elegant Italian shoes, she wondered if she would have the courage to get up and walk, such a simple thing even yesterday, René didn't want Louise to know what he was feeling, no, nothing, any admission of failure would be demeaning, René wouldn't tell her about the nightmare he'd had, and besides, old people talked too much, they rambled, there was no need to be any more like an old person than was absolutely necessary, René thought, at least in his appearance René made an effort to seem young, like the old René, the indestructible René, even if that was a bit of an act, had the bad dream been an omen, a warning of impending doom, or was it a sign of René's periodically postponed surrender? People called it passing on, but where did you go, by what winding road, people said that someone had crossed over, but toward what, toward whom, where was that invisible footbridge to the other side, René's nightmares, the bad dreams she'd been having for some time now, were they images or fragments of a passing that was already underway, she would wake with a start from a deep sleep, was it afternoon or was it night, she couldn't open her eyes, there was like a dark, molten metal stuck to her eyelids, René could only compare it to Dalí's melted watches, was this the end of days, and finally she would lift the black plates to find herself at home, in her bed or in an armchair, among her things, but there was no one, not Olga or Louise, she opened her eyes into terrifying silence and at that moment René thought he was only a man after all, weighed down and plagued by nightmares, René thought that the melting plates might be a symbol of the tomb closing over his eyes, his whole body, soon he would just cease to exist, what is it, Louise asked, René, what is it, nothing, René said, you really think that the girls will come to this party for an old man, they always thought I was a very bad husband, you know we all love you, Louise said impatiently, you're our René, though it's a good thing there's only one of you, Louise said, smiling, even Lali is going to come from her province far away, but she might be a little late, Mercedes is coming too if she can leave her mother alone, because now she's taking care of her mother and her sisters in their big house, her whole life has been devoted to others, she never recovered from Gérard's death but she likes Gérard the second too, she says it's like the first Gérard has come back except healthy, she's still working outside all summer and winter to keep up the plot at the cemetery, a second Gérard, bursting with health, with life. You're all still young, René said jealously, at my age, no one gets to be reborn like your second Gérard among the plants and flowers, whether in the graveyard where the first Gérard lies or working to make the landscape more beautiful, no, you just slip away, but René didn't say that, at my age, you have to settle down, she said gently. What Johnie wasn't telling Louise was as much as she seemed detached, Johnie could be overcome, she had flashes of something that felt like the shock of love. In a lecture hall at a German university, among other top students, Johnie, who was going by Vanessa, she was the student Vanessa Laflamme, she was reading her paper on the chaos of mental illness, about obsessive neurotics like Van Gogh thinking about cutting off his ear or about the flock of crows over the fields, *did the thought of cutting off his ear overpower everything, something akin to artistic redemption,* Johnie wrote, *Van Gogh's wounded self-portrait with his ear covered by a white bandage, as if he had resurrected the ear under the bandage by the miracle of his art, didn't the miracle of art reconcile the man and his madness,* while she was reading the article, hiding her apprehension, she was afraid that there might be some minor confrontation with the students before her, Johnie caught a student staring at her, Heinrich, Heinrich had a friend or a lover standing not far from her, Johnie hated any notion of possession and she immediately felt the other woman watching her, Heinrich's gold-flecked eyes were riveted on hers, the whole lecture hall looked like a golden cloud, like Lali's golden gaze, the sunshine that was

Lali, how she looked in the winter, the pink in her cheeks, her short hair crowned with what looked like crumbs of gold in the snow, Heinrich would tell Johnie how much she had loved hearing her paper, was it the lilt of Johnie's voice that had enchanted her, she was walking beside her, touching her hand, her shoulder, her sullen friend trailing behind, Johnie was about to catch the first bus or train to Paris, but she had known, during that joyful flash, how open she might have been in a foreign land, how available, Heinrich's free spirit, the ardor in her eyes confirmed for Johnie the pleasant peace of love shared far away, exuberant and passionate and unattached. Johnie knew she would never think of Heinrich in that lecture hall with any regret, blazing there like the sun for an instant, she would come back often to Heinrich's face, as if Heinrich had held out a hand to her, and she said to herself throughout her studies, love is everywhere, it runs through the whole world. That look of Heinrich's, the unexpected smile in a university lecture hall, Johnie thought, maybe it came from somewhere beyond the earth like a rainbow after a storm low in the sky, who knows, maybe her sister was coming to her from beyond the earth, was it Émilie saying, yes, little flame, love is everywhere and it's up to you to grab it and warm yourself with it, my little fireless flame. In l'Abeille's smoky living room, the nights were still long, dragged on by endless discussions, Geneviève went into l'Abeille's studio, yawning, admiring l'Abeille's paintings, she wanted to buy them all, it's so beautiful, a flood of light, my office is new, my walls are still empty and white, I need these paintings, some of them are so white and majestic, like a desert of snow and then there's a beam of purple on the horizon, Geneviève was moved, she repeated what Louise had said, yes, Christie, Marie-Christine, since that's your real name, you will be the painter of our generation, but l'Abeille, rather than being pleased, listened to Geneviève's praise in uneasy silence, she drew, first her black ink drawings, her sketchbooks were overflowing with them, she'd made thousands, all of them shut tight, hermetic puzzles of which she alone knew the solution, but l'Abeille had never thought that her drawings and her paintings were worth anything, never mind trying to sell them, their foundation, their raw soil was so rooted in her history, like her own heart or her liver. You'll see, one of these drawings will end up in a museum one day, Geneviève said, she sounded so certain, they're fascinatingly complex, and l'Abeille thought, these drawings I've been making since childhood, my paintings that are haunted by the capricious ghost of Gérard, who comes and goes, never quite ready to leave, as if she were prowling around me, in my studio, no, these are my only possessions, I don't have anything else. I can't sell what has been lent to me, because talent is borrowed, isn't it, from the divine, from the stars? As Geneviève slowly woke up, telling herself that it was almost time to return to the office, she kept saying, yes, it would look gorgeous on my wall, a flood of light. L'Abeille thought of Alexis, her suitcase of poems, never in her purity and wildness would Alexis have allowed her poems to be bought or sold, yet she too had been writing for a long time, the suitcase was getting heavier and heavier. Johnie has already predicted that one of your drawings will end up in a museum, Geneviève said, you have to believe in the prophecy of the stars, Geneviève said, taking off her thick glasses to look at l'Abeille with love in her eyes, I'm so tired, she sighed suddenly, you girls, it worries me that you all sleep so little. You have to sleep to be healthy. How can you be disciplined if you don't sleep? The comb dragged a straight line along René's skull, making a faint noise, after the nightmare, René thought, I saw a pale yellow color, didn't I, almost diaphanous, sometimes women wore light yellow dresses like that in the summer, that color, that transparent, evanescent yellow, you could feel their trembling flesh under the undulating yellow, often in the sun, out walking, a fleeting embrace quickly consented, they would say to me, but René, who are you, a great charmer, aren't you, you lavish such praise on women that they can't resist you, I promise to meet you at the hotel at five o'clock, for cocktails, before my husband comes home for dinner, but believe me, René, I'm only flirting, that's all this is, I'm a reasonable woman, and I'm faithful to a husband who isn't, he likes them young, he neglects me, that's why I'm coming to see you, anyway, René, you're quite the player, I don't know what comes over you, but you're attractive in your own way, René remembered the confessions of women conquered, after cocktails in chic hotels there was nothing left to do but go up to the room, but René suspended those delectable moments, what mattered to him then in his dreamy convictions was above all to make people believe in love, make them believe that love existed in all its forms, as if she or he was a merchant of hope, by providing dreams and desire like that she enhanced his precarious masculinity, although he was aware that the masculinity offered up to women like a talisman was a dream too. But life was too short not to dream, René thought. Were they still dreaming, those poor old men dying on the wards on gurneys pushed through the dark halls of the hospital, no, they weren't dreaming anymore, René thought, she remembered a woman, you could still see how beautiful she'd been, saying to him, my bones are cracking, I'm stunted and scrawny, I'm like those chickens hauled off to the slaughterhouse, aren't I, see, nothing remains in these bones of what I once was, this flabby chest, the indecency of dying, sir, it's a taboo subject, isn't it, the color yellow, René thought, the color of women's dresses in summer, those halcyon days, that yellow washed away the ugliness of the wards, where even the memory of beauty was wiped out. In the hospice, René had heard a nurse say to him, her file in hand, we have here proof that you are not a man, isn't your real name Germaine Cécile, Madame, you are on the women's ward here, not the men's. Germaine or Cécile, insulted, René had immediately called Louise on his cellphone, asking her to come to his rescue, he never wanted to see this place again. If there was a hell, this was it, he told Louise. René was or had been an activist forever tied to a huge community of transgender activists, whether they were in

Russia or China, he continued to fight with them for their rights, while they, in China, in Russia, were fighting for their lives. As they were being beaten and molested by prison guards, they repeated bravely, the fight for our rights is worth it. The fight against cruelty was still in its infancy for them. An elegant Chinese dressmaker had to hide to meet his clients, his beauty and the silken quality of the clothes he wore attracted the attention of the enemy, the censors, those vulgar men he rode alongside on his bicycle or when he walked through the alleys, the toxic air poisoning the cities, his hair loose around his shoulders, he knew he was being noticed and judged in his long black coat, the cut he had designed himself, he had to run away, forever, go into exile, but even exile was forbidden, René thought, he had friends with him in hiding too but sometimes that seemed like so little, such misery, his friends were threatened with prison and punishment too. And yet, René thought, they all said that the fight was worth it. Was it true, was that much injustice unavoidable, did youth have to be sacrificed? Careful with that comb, Louise, René told her, I was just thinking that you have beautiful hair, René, really, you'll never grow old, it's how you wink, I think, I've seen you do it a thousand times, you wink your left eye, sometimes it looks like you're still a boy, a kid, Louise said, putting her hand on René's head. You can still bring me such comfort, René said, by what blessing of heaven did I ever come across you, my antelope, I brushed you off, I told myself that you were too tall for me, we wouldn't have made a good couple, but I was so wrong, so vain, I was pure vanity back then, René said, a man's vanity is bottomless. As you know. René seemed preoccupied, you know, Louise, I had a friend in China, I think about him often, I wonder what happened to him, is he free, is he in jail, was he murdered, or ambushed when he got up one morning, there are murderers who like to surprise their mark, you don't feel them coming up behind you, that's what he was most scared of, that he would be murdered without warning. In those prisons, there's a hole in the dirt floor for the blood to flow out. The blood of the dead caught off guard. Louise broke into René's sad thoughts, you need a little makeup, Louise said, you're too pale, it's just the winter, René said, nothing is whiter than snow and cold, but he was thinking about the Chinese friend's makeup, by putting on makeup he was already risking punishment. The Chinese friend couldn't wear makeup or dress up as his imagination decreed, no, he wasn't allowed to do anything, René's heart clenched with sadness, it was like when he couldn't sleep at night, he was afraid his heart would stop beating. All of a sudden, he would stop hearing his heartbeat, or it felt like a heap of stones were crushing his chest. The suffocation lightened a bit when Olga opened the bedroom window, listen to the wind, Monsieur René, it's cold here like in Moscow. Think of people who have no home to warm up and sleep at night, Olga lectured, they have to sleep in metro stations and in the street under trees, just like in Moscow, they are found in the morning and they are dead. Have you thought about that, Monsieur René, you have everything, even Louis XV and Louis XVI chairs, wouldn't it be a good idea to sell them at last? Shut up, René cried, stop thinking only of making money, Olga, money is the most degrading thing there is, aren't you ashamed? My dear chairs, my cherished armchairs, they're the last thing I own from my wealthy years with Nathalie. You'll welcome the girls from your most beautiful armchair like you used to when you received your mistresses, the grandeur of the past, Louise said with ironic conviction. In those days I had the power of kings, René said, laughing at himself. You should tell Olga, my dear Louise, that the chairs are fake, they're worthless, even the fabric is worn. I bought them on sale. You know that Louise XV or Louise XVI can't live here, but the illusion that lulls the hearts of men is sweet indeed, what do you think, Louise was half listening to René, she was thinking about Alexis, the boundless Irish landscape where she was lost, they were tiny, they were only miniature little beings, Alexis, her husband Dave, the baby in Alexis' belly, it seemed like no one could rescue Alexis from her bad luck, not even the unborn child, and certainly not l'Abeille, she was so far away. Louise wondered if the birth of Alexis' child would replace another, fading, life, no, no life was replaceable, no death could be justified, or at least not by the renewal of birth, as René said, each person in departure vanished into eternal darkness, though sometimes she might have told Louise that death didn't exist, it was a myth to frighten men, we are born alive, he said, to undergo physical decay, perhaps, but everything that lived could only be forever moving from one life to another in a chain of all the human forces moving toward the pinnacle of immortality, we are mountaineers climbing all the mountains toward a treasure we'll reach eventually. Above all, let's not imagine anything dramatic, René said, while Louise dabbed powder on her nose and cheeks. Yet wasn't it disturbing to imagine Alexis driving in her Jeep, the fetus asleep in her belly or already awake and wondering why her mother was driving so fast and where were they going, up and down the slopes, the hills overlooking the sea with its high, tumultuous gray waves crashing against the rocks, the cry of the seagulls, Alexis telling her son, don't be afraid, little one, Mama knows how to drive in a storm, haven't I always lived in a storm, my angel, sometimes she talked about her brother Louis to the baby, are you the thread that will continue his life, for him that thread has been cut, snipped by the great master of nothingness, as she spoke to her son she thought of the poems she would write, she wrote her poems, nervous and gentle, she would be there for him, she said, even if his parents had been disinherited, Dave and I are orphans now, and from now on, with you, we will live only on what our farm can yield. Alexis went out alone in the rain at night, she walked barefoot in the sea, her hair like a bouquet of flowers snapping and stretching in the wind, her belly was swelling slowly, she thought of her brother, she had seen him the last time she visited at the maximum security prison, she wanted to kiss him through the bars, she talked to him on the phone, she was separated from him, Louis, she said, Louis, and suddenly she was silent, respectful of the unchanging, stubborn, obstinate suffering that emanated from him, see you soon, she said, I'll be back, yes, I'll be back very soon. When she came back, he would no longer be there, his body would be covered with a black sheet. They would say to her, you're too late. But he was just a murderer, you know, why do you love him so much? And she would say, he was also my brother. Why didn't people talk much about what women went through after giving birth, Alexis asked l'Abeille, it was probably the most extreme event they had ever gone through. Families rejoiced at the birth of a child without thinking of the mother's pain after giving birth, the sudden emptiness of the body, flayed, defeated, and often despised by the father. How laughable that such deep desolation was referred to in the medical profession as the baby blues, it was full-blown depression and it put women's lives in danger. L'Abeille didn't like it that Alexis was so sad, was it a bad omen, she should have been happy, Alexis, wrote l'Abeille, you'll see, everything will change for the better as soon as Louis-Jean is born, that was what Alexis wanted to name her child, Louis-Jean, for John, beloved disciple of Christ, Jean, in the name of love, l'Abeille wrote to Alexis, who was irritated that Jesus had been brought up, don't you know, Christie, my friend, l'Abeille, how much I hate all religion, l'Abeille was waiting for Louis-Jean to be born as if she were the mother-to-be herself, as if she held in her fingers the hope of beauty's perpetuation on earth, like a blade of grass waving in the wind. What are you thinking about, Louise asked René, who nodded impatiently but didn't answer, René was back in those long, endless summers in her apartment among her beautiful armchairs, suddenly her animals were everywhere, when Nathalie wasn't around anymore, running around with some man or other, what a savage, ferocious time, René thought, I was alone, the girls had gone to Cape Cod, I was abandoned, I looked around and found I wasn't young and charming anymore, I told myself that's why Nathalie left me, I gave her everything, even what I didn't have for myself, the illusion of power intoxicated me, and now I wasn't hungry or thirty, I could hear the neighbors laughing in their swimming pool, what wicked merriment, they all seemed to be laughing at me, but those families and the whole neighborhood didn't care about me and my afflictions, it was summer, I wondered what was worse, what was more cruel, losing my old dog Saturn, or that Nathalie left without saying good-bye, I channeled all my pain onto my dog, Nathalie was going to dissolve in the fog of her own lies, she liked men, she said, was René a man, the ambiguity was too strong, it was better to have a manly, virile man, wasn't it, with everything that entailed, Nathalie said, René could still hear her melodious voice, the monologue of deception and lies, no, René had wept for Saturn, Saturn had real heart, you could see it when she looked at you, and it hurt so much when she knew she was condemned, Saturn, my dog, it was so painful, I can still see her big wet eyes, she wasn't even pleading, she was resigned, like any beast when execution is near, she had some treats, eating out of René's hand, my dear dog, René thought, Nathalie's false image faded quickly, while Saturn's unalterable gaze still pierced René's soul, it stirred up enormous grief that nothing could quell, because she'd had to accept that Saturn would die. That kind of momentous decision was always the wrong one, because the animal couldn't defend itself from a verdict that cut it off so brutally from the human world. Everything was a mistake, René thought, when it came to how we acted with animals. René had loved Saturn so much, definitely more than Nathalie. Among the other dogs and cats, Saturn had shared René's pillow, his bed, his rich man's chairs, Saturn had been his queen, while Nathalie, René realized too late, Nathalie had a servile soul. The animals destined for the slaughterhouse, all the animals that were wounded or killed, from the innocent lamb to the noble horse, all of them, René thought, had a right to a better paradise than humans, the human race deserved nothing, purgatory maybe, which would be impossibly boring, and who wanted to be bored for all of eternity, the void would be just as boring, whereas animals would be praised and cuddled in a heaven for all the beasts of the earth, the birds too, they were already angels flying above us, tiny angels, even the voracious eagle pouncing on its prey, even the lion attacking the zebra, whatever couldn't be achieved among humans would be decided among the beasts, a pact of peace, a never-ending pacifist decree, and meanwhile humans would never stop killing each other, even in hell. Up there somewhere in the white clouds, Saturn sat in perfect dignity, just thinking of her, of her open eyes, her pure, beseeching eyes, and René would start to sob. She felt nothing of the kind when she thought of Nathalie, as he told himself over and over, that treacherous woman inspires only rage, yes, only that, rage. But during those despondent summers while the neighbors shouted and splashed happily in their pools, René felt so unwanted because Nathalie didn't love her anymore that she started looking for any pretext to disparage her body. Even her bathtub, now that she was poor, René considered that bathtub to be ridiculously luxurious, the bathtub Nathalie had coveted, it'll be like bathing in a pond inside the house, René, it'll be so nice for two people, even the bathtub seemed to heave René out of its foamy, lavender-scented waters. Only the scorching heat of those endless summers, with all the windows open, could induce René to take a bath. And what he found was that he was decomposing from the lack of desire, he'd lost a tooth here, a toenail there, the slow alteration of a body that had been beautiful, and above all it had been useful, imperious in its swiftly satisfied desires. That little yellow fleck floating on the fragrant waters, what was that, it was a nail, where had it come from, René felt himself incredibly, suddenly mortal. Without Nathalie, he wasn't the same anymore, this was the merciless beginning of his decline. He might as well die, he thought, because if we die in advance at least it's over and done with. René thought of Louise, when she went on a trip, far away and inaccessible, when he needed so much for her to be close to him, caressing his hair, reassuring him, her words as kind as they were irritating. He loved Louise but he was so bad at loving her. He got out of the bathtub and shook himself off, not only am I poor, but Nathalie, by detaching herself from me, has made an old man of me. Wrapped up in his dressing gown, another luxurious object he'd bought to please Nathalie, he went to his bed as if he'd been struck with a sudden fever, an irremediable ache, although none of that was true, he thought, it was only the effect of his complacency, a poor man mistreated by a cruel woman. The neighbors were still shouting in the pool, long live summer, friends, long live summer, it's a shame it's so short but long live summer, friends. Shut up, all of you, René thought, all those young people, they were so loud, I don't want to hear you anymore, shut up, all of you. You enrage me, everything enrages me, because that's all I feel, raw rage, a time will come when you will lose your teeth too, your hair, your toenails painted every color of the rainbow. What's going on, Louise asked, you're being very dark, René, I was thinking of those miserable summers when you weren't around, the girls weren't here and especially you, I missed you so much then. But René said nothing, his thoughts wandered, solitary. Then suddenly she revived, you know, Louise, last night I dreamed that Lali had come to live near here, a few streets away, she told me she was tired of these kids with AIDS who refused to use condoms, the carelessness was staggering, why did she work so hard if they wouldn't listen? We know, René said, youth are like that, the young listen to no one. But Lali didn't like the accumulation of preventable, early deaths. She should have retired, but she said that doctors couldn't, they always had to be on duty. Lali simply refuses to grow old, Louise said flatly, and she's right. Well, in my dream, René said, cheery now, Lali came to live in my neighborhood and she told me, I'll be your family doctor, that's what she told me, and when I woke up Olga said she had heard me singing. I was singing like I used to, at the piano, mumbling sweet nothings to the women sitting next to me, I was singing songs from another time, and they all said to me, sing it again, René, it's so romantic, you know, Louise, you can waste a whole life at the piano, in flattery and romance, and those hours of my existence taken up with dreams flowed like water, one drop at a time. That's how everyone lives their life, Louise said, you weren't wrong. Besides, I can assure you that Lali's going to come back from her far-away city, she'll be close to you one day. Like all of us, like all the girls, you know we'll always be close to you. I don't believe it, René said, who wants to see a penniless, grumpy, cantankerous old man, in the past, at one time it would have been understandable and even acceptable, but now, oh, now, René said, anyway, I like it when Lali comes to me in my dreams, little brother, René sighed, where did the time go?

PART THREE

Grief, Rebirth

René heard Louise popping the champagne in the kitchen, the most festive sound. Here come the girls, Louise exclaimed, I can hear them coming up the stairs, and then they were in the entrance of René's lavish living room, Olga flanking them with a look of distrust on her face, as if she were saying, what are they doing here, it's my house, Madame René's and my house, this is disturbing our peace, here are Doudouline and Polydor, Louise said proudly, they got married, that's thanks in part to your activism, René, you were already fighting for our right to marriage way back, at the mayor's office, and later on in New York, in San Francisco, René, you were the consummate activist, this is all thanks to you too, my dear, these strange women, Olga thought, why are they here, Olga was irked that Madame René was walking, she never got out of bed, and now Louise was holding her up by the arm, leading her to the Louis XV chair, or was it Louis XVI, a majestic armchair where Louise had sat René as if she were royalty, she was dressed to the nines in her old clothes, the Italian shoes, Olga didn't recognize her anymore, it was unbearable to see Madame René like this, Olga thought, her patient, Olga's patient had been at death's door and now she was so alive, that mocking glint in her eyes. And here's Gérard the second, our florist and landscaper, Louise said, directing the girls to the spacious couch. René looked at each one, she felt a bit better all of a sudden, at least they're easy to be around, René thought, they all still look so young, it's nice to see. I can't forget that I'm old enough to be their father, or their grandfather even, though Louise did my hair and dressed me up, I must still seem like an old man to them. But René could tell that the girls were looking at him affectionately, with sympathy, almost tenderness. My beautiful Gérard is a landscaper, she was always the one who went to tend to Gérard's grave, summer and winter alike, red roses, you look like her, René said, but healthier, with your rosy cheeks, you must spend lots of time outside. I like it, Gérard the second said confidently, you have to spread beauty everywhere, you can't let ugliness win. You know that too, Gérard said, you love art, you love everything that's beautiful. What about you, René asked Doudouline and Polydor, what have you been doing all this time, I hear about you sometimes, on TV or in the papers, Doudouline and her musical, *Gérard oh Gérard*, and you, Polydor, you're running a bookstore, right, where people can come warm up in the winter with an Irish coffee if they want, I called it Pen and Drink, we get lots of people coming in. They're probably there for the cognac, René said, people never read enough. They don't read, she repeated, as if to quash Polydor's pride at owning a bookstore. It was a profession René envied, she was jealous of every one of these girls who'd done something with their lives other than dream them away. Doudouline and Polydor were holding hands as if they were intimidated by René, his experience with women from every social class was spectacular, no one had had as many lovers as René, Doudouline looked at Polydor, her blue eyes protective, they were married, finally married, she thought, but the most moving thing about their wedding had been her mother. The Great Sophie had converted, like Saint Paul, who had been an inveterate sinner, they said, she had wanted to be there, in l'Abeille's garden in the summer, honoring the brides, the mother of the bride standing up for her daughter Doudouline, Anne-Sophie, even though there was no wedding gown, she couldn't believe the girls would get married in jeans, Polydor's jeans even had holes in the knees, at least their pants were clean, but except for the flowers in their hair, they looked like they got married every day, it was an ordinary ceremony, there wasn't much of a ceremony at all, except the kiss, which the Great Sophie had gotten on video, on her phone. She even told them to kiss again, I want to take another photo for your father, Doudouline, you know how much your father adores you, he always said you're the best thing about our family, as if I didn't even exist. The Great Sophie had turned out to be a repentant mother, she even cried, begging Doudouline for forgiveness, I didn't understand but now I understand everything, love is love after all, and everybody deserves to be in love, be happy, my children, I'm your loving mama. Everybody needs one. Although, Doudouline, you must admit that you gave me a lot of trouble from the time you hit puberty, your father and I were at the theater every night, working, and during the day too, we had nannies looking after you, you and your brother always had nannies, both of you were always falling in love with your nannies, even though you were barely old enough to know what love was. It was because they spoiled you, they would hold you on their lap, they pampered you. Yes, Mama, it's all true, Doudouline replied, we didn't dare tell you but we were in love with our nannies. When we were older, we looked them up again, one of them was directing an experimental theater company, she was my first love. The Great Sophie replied curtly, you were only sixteen, weren't you ashamed to fall in love with a woman whose theater was in direct competition with me, she was almost as old as I was, you were so precocious, Anne-Sophie, your brother too, though he's married to a woman at least, your brother is a set designer, it's so inspiring, your father taught him everything he knows, you were an early bloomer, it was shocking, it always bothered me, so I'm happy that you're finally stable and married to Polydor, you're not breaking any more laws like you were with your nannies. Love at sixteen isn't legal, especially with a woman who was my competition, believe me, Doudouline, I was going crazy. But I've calmed down, you have my blessing, my dear girls. On the day Doudouline and Polydor were married in l'Abeille's backyard, the Great Sophie rushed into Doudouline's arms and then she hugged Polydor, a new state of joy and reconciliation. People can change at any age, she said, and to tell the truth, she had never believed that Doudouline was really marriageable, not to a man. So, Polydor was the best solution in special circumstances, she added. Mama finally likes the way I am, Doudouline thought, flicking her hair, it wasn't wheat-blond anymore, like it used to be, no, now she went to a proper hairdresser. It was awful to be almost sixty years old. How could this have happened, but René had said it himself, think about it, girls, I knew you when you were barely twenty, you were little girls, and you'll be sixty one day too, life will take you elsewhere, into the realm of your fragile, prowling mortality, never mind seventy or eighty, let's get to ninety, ninety-three, for me René, you'll have to stand up like men, I'm telling you, because society condemns us to decay, the world just gets rid of us. We're not men like you are, René, Polydor said. So learn to listen to your own strength, René said, rather than to the voice of your detractors. René's commanding voice echoed through the room. Olga thought of the girls' winter coats she had to put away in the hall, and the boots dripping with snow and water on her freshly washed floor. She longed to be alone with Madame René, she wanted her dependent again, she would have liked her to be even weaker, not only unable to get up and walk but forever immobile up against her pillows, all she wanted to do was play her the great music of the morning. But everything had changed, Madame René was doing too well, it was as if she were young again and holding court with her disciples. She was no longer Olga's master, she belonged to all those girls now, total strangers to Olga. Through the living room window she could see it was still snowing, like in Moscow. It would never stop snowing. Doudouline, in a burst of warm admiration, praised her mother, just think of my mama, the Great Sophie, she runs her theater, she puts on new plays by young playwrights, she's always innovating, she travels with her shows, her actors, her technicians, oh, Mama, my divine mama, she'll never grow old because she's an artist, and like so many other artists, she's a rock. Plus, she's a woman, Polydor added, her voice hoarse from smoking. We don't talk enough about the intellectual and physical power of women, Polydor said, or else men have always denied it. I know men, René said, I was with them a lot in my piano bar while their wives flirted with me, feeding me their tasty, provocative words, I know them well, men are often weak and jealous of their wives. That's why religion forces faithfulness, to avoid upsetting those poor men, they're so fragile, I understand them, I'm like them, René said. No, come on, Louise interrupted, and, listen, girls, l'Abeille is coming, I can hear her footsteps on the stairs, don't rush her, especially not you, René, like you used to, it annoyed you that we were friends, you jealous old man, be gentle with l'Abeille, she's coming alone, she's just lost Geneviève, the woman she loved, they'd gotten married just a few months ago, the joy of the wedding and then her brutal death from cancer. Polydor, Doudouline whispered, I've been telling you forever not to smoke, you'll make me a widow one day if you keep smoking, didn't you see how our dear Geneviève ended up, don't you see, Polydor had gone outside once for a cigarette, she was upset, she took Doudouline's hand and laid it in her lap. Smoking is not allowed here, Olga said officiously. There's no sense blowing virtue all out of proportion, René said, a little cigarette now and then never hurt anyone, Olga spoke even louder, Madame René, you are suffering because you have smoked so much, more than you should, I say. That's how it was in the bars, while I was singing, people offered me either those flavored cigarettes or whisky and I took both, René said, there's no reason to die over it. In any case, it's never normal for a life to end, there's never enough outrage. Poor Geneviève, René sighed, I liked her, she knew how to build ecological houses, she loved the trees and birdsong, the light of the sky. She was a really good architect, an artist, and think about it, girls, she took you all out of your crumbling houses, moldy and run-down, and designed sunny homes for each of you, even the cottage in the countryside that she shared with l'Abeille, and with you. It was time for your squatting years to come to an end, more than the cigarettes and the whisky it was the damp in those walls that was going to kill you. It's true, Polydor said sadly, we loved her so much, l'Abeille cheated sometimes, l'Abeille and her irrepressible need to know everything, to experience everything, Polydor said, she ended up with Gabriela in Mexico during an exhibition of her drawings in San Miguel, and Geneviève waited for her for three years, Polydor was unsparing. That's how it is, unfortunately, René said, we always cheat a little, there's no other way, we live in a world of desire and attraction, René said, but Polydor was adamant, I think you should be faithful to the one you love. As Polydor spoke, she thought again of the prostitute who had taken her into her car after her night of perdition, after leaving the bar, she'd never told Doudouline about that night, it felt too close to cheating, emotional infidelity, the prostitute could have been the mother Gérard had dreamed of, Polydor remembered the warmth of the fur coat, beneath which the dignified woman wore no clothes, a pair of silk panties and black garters maybe, that's all, the car smelled like cheap perfume but Polydor was so grateful to escape getting raped by the vagrants half asleep in their dirty coats against the bank wall, at least the building shielded them from the cold, the snow. Get in my car, she'd said, you lost little girl, those men are drunk and they're going to get you, I'm waiting for a man myself, to make my night, but the cold is keeping them away, where do you live, I'll drive you home, it's late you know, it's almost dawn. As for me, I won't be getting a man, not at this hour, they've gone home to their mistresses and wives. What were you doing with those degenerates against the wall, you're falling-down drunk, are you trying to sleep it off, be careful, there are dangerous people in this town, especially when they're high on coke, they're not afraid of anything. Polydor took Doudouline's hand again and squeezed it tighter, who was she to judge anyone. Be gentle with l'Abeille, Louise repeated, she's going through a tough time, she lost Geneviève, and Alexis too, a little while after her son was born, Alexis, a tragic accident, Alexis had been taking too many drugs, for the depression, all the medication her doctor had prescribed, it was careless, it's a shame, our little Alexis. At the bottom of the stairs, l'Abeille was putting one foot slowly on one step, then the next. She'd been out of breath since Geneviève's death, as if Geneviève's last breath in the hospital bed had caught her own. She wasn't sleeping, she couldn't breathe. Life would be hell from now on, it already was, there had been the elation of the wedding, the celebration, and then pneumonia, and that unspeakable thing, death. Louise had described it so well in her essay on women and cancer, despicable and cruel, it struck so many women, breast cancer or lung cancer, it devoured them, any kind of cancer, it was gangrene, it was taking so many young lives like Geneviève's, still in the full bloom of youth. They had been wild enough in their youth, the late nights, the bars, the booze flowing freely, all those places where they would dance together night after night, when l'Abeille would say to Geneviève, why do you have to work so much, can't you sleep late one morning, rest, lie around a little like me, no, Geneviève burned the candle at both ends, she worked too hard, she had never been lazy a day in her life. L'Abeille could hear the hum of the girls' chatter as she leaned against the railing, lost and drained all of a sudden. What would become of her among the girls when she was so unhappy, now she would always be alone, even at the cottage, which she imagined she would have to sell. Those memories of Geneviève swimming in the lake haunted her, below the forbidding, almost black profile of the mountains. As for Alexis, the pain was beginning to settle, it had been a long time ago, Louis-Jean had grown up in Ireland with his father, he didn't know how his mother had died, they didn't talk much about Alexis in the house, on the farm in Ireland. L'Abeille remembered when Alexis had first come to the house that night, her suitcase of poems in hand. Our friends are sometimes our children too, l'Abeille thought, and I lost Alexis as if she had been my chosen child. Never again would l'Abeille be able to smile or laugh like she used to with the girls, it was as if Geneviève had made solace impossible when she said good-bye to her, don't forget, if you are happy, I will be with you. Louise came down the stairs to bring her into the living room. It will do you good to see the girls, Louise said, giving l'Abeille a hug, you know how much we all love you, Christie. To spite Olga, l'Abeille refused to take off her cowboy boots and the pleather jacket she wore over a thick white wool sweater, Olga, that look she had, like she thought she was the lady of the house, as far as l'Abeille was concerned she was nothing more than an impostor in René's house. The girls saw l'Abeille come into René's living room as if she had been walking into her own living room all those years ago, she was still dressed the same way, the same pageboy cut with bangs, her eyes twinkling under her hair. Don't let the grief show, she thought, I have to smile at them, this is part of life, from life to nothing at all. Her heart was tight, but l'Abeille hugged each one of the girls and René with the same intensity, and she sat at Doudouline's feet as if they were sitting in her living room all those years earlier. Doudouline put her hand on l'Abeille's head, I read Alexis' poem, the one about the black well of nothingness, I read it onstage at Mama's theater, and I couldn't stop crying. A single tear rolled down Doudouline's cheek. Alexis should be here with us, Polydor said, it's so easy, isn't it, we just discard depressed women after their children are born, we give them pills, it's as if they were birthing machines, it's a traumatic experience, it's so unfair, Polydor said. We miss her a lot, even more now that we're all together, Doudouline said. She would have loved to be with us. Dave wrote to me that Alexis used to go up to the cliffs in his Jeep with her son, it was so close to the ocean that he would get scared and bring them home, mother and child, l'Abeille said, the psychiatrist wasn't monitoring Alexis, he gave her drugs to calm her down but they were too strong, and dangerous, I know all about it, Dave would write to me, l'Abeille said, he said it himself, a young mother died from a lack of medical oversight. That's what it was. Gérard the second was listening, Doudouline and Polydor were married, Gérard the second thought that even if it was a bit late in life, she would like to have a companion, you go to bed at night and there she is, you get up in the morning and she's still there, her presence warms up the air, it's always cold in winter, even in the house. Gérard the second thought of Mercedes, she'd been Gérard's first love, she'd loved her imperfectly, badly, Gérard had been so troubled, in thrall to the drugs. Gérard had made the wrong choice, Mercedes was the kindest woman Gérard had ever known, and she was the most compassionate about Gérard's addiction. Whatever happened to Mercedes, Gérard the second wondered, her office was always open, as a sociologist she was always available, she even worked at night, taking in her pitiful teenagers, giving them clean needles and driving them back to rehab, the sign in her car said *emergency twenty-four hours*. Smoking a cigarette outside, breathing in the outside air, Gérard the second imagined what a garden might look like here in René's yard after the snow melted. Wouldn't it be lovely to plant some white lilacs and purple lilacs here and there, even a vegetable garden, with tomatoes, carrots, and herbs. René should be eating better, Gérard the second thought. L'Abeille sat at Doudouline's knee on the oriental rug, another passion of René's, as if she were back in the smoky living room in the house they were squatting, losing Geneviève, she thought, losing the one you love was like having your hand cut off, or an arm, like your bereaved body had lost a limb. If you hadn't gone through that you didn't know what it was like. L'Abeille thought back to Sundays with Geneviève, their sumptuous Sunday dinners out in the country, in their cottage by the lake, Sunday was the only day when Geneviève didn't work, and the other girls often came out to see them, the smell of roast beef, l'Abeille loved to eat, she could still smell it, for Geneviève cooking for their friends was an occasion. The girls would walk down the path to the lake on those hot afternoons out in the country, an overgrown trail beneath the trees, they were bitten by mosquitoes and flies and it smelled like fir and the leaves crushed under their bare feet. They would dive into the lake, Geneviève could hear them laughing, or they would take the canoe out, head out on the water in the boat, so far out that Geneviève couldn't see them anymore from the terrace. It would have been pointless to tell them to be careful, that the currents could gather into waves, Geneviève knew they wouldn't listen. And the summers went on like that, in the light, ethereal heat of stunning, beautiful days under the intoxicating sun, until the birds swept through in the fall. None of them knew that Geneviève was sick because she didn't talk about it, although she did let on to l'Abeille that she was tired. Can someone so young be so tired, l'Abeille thought, while Geneviève locked herself up in her work and in her silence, unfolding blueprints on the kitchen table. In those days l'Abeille thought that she didn't want to be tamed by anyone, not by Geneviève, who dreamed of protecting her, of creating a haven for them, not by anyone, she said, l'Abeille was free, she was an artist, hadn't her mother warned her before she died so young, Christie, my child, don't be like me, you see how much I belong to your father, don't belong to anyone, your life must be your own and no one else's. During the dull, gray winters, although Geneviève loved her patiently, she didn't even ask l'Abeille to move in with her, what would you call that, l'Abeille wondered, it was a love that didn't close in on itself, a love as wide open as the earth, yet with all her escape fantasies, l'Abeille now saw, she could barely repress her selfishness. It was winter when l'Abeille decided to go to Mexico to study painting. Go, it'll be a learning opportunity for you, your search for new color, Geneviève told her, as if she could see l'Abeille's hidden desires, beyond the attraction of art there must have been someone waiting for l'Abeille, a woman, an art teacher, a drawing teacher, and the bewitching Mexican colors, so hot, torrid, would surely be magnified if l'Abeille, whose heart was willing, fell in love, Geneviève knew all this, or she sensed it, she told herself that the certainty she felt about their future together, as tame and domestic as l'Abeille didn't want, would lead her back to a home that didn't exist yet. Or at least it would lead back to Geneviève, who was stable, whether she liked it or not, Geneviève believed couples were stable. Gabriela, l'Abeille's teacher, showed her Frida Kahlo's use of color, her aesthetic frenzy, l'Abeille already loved Kahlo and at the same time she fell in love with Gabriela, she was a little wild, and why not, l'Abeille thought, in the thrill of the adventure. She was acting only on instinct, as her mother would have done if she'd had the right to freedom. L'Abeille had fled the monotonous whiteness of winter for a paradise of unbridled, eternal color. The world was pure color, luxuriant greens, pink doors, and beyond the door a garden bloomed and there was a meadow and hummingbirds that came to sip from the pond. With her hand on l'Abeille's shoulder, Gabriela told her that Kahlo had painted self-portraits, which were more portraits of her city than of herself, the pleasure of color everywhere was so dominant. Kahlo was delicate in her black jumper, her hair parted in the middle like a schoolgirl, the arc of her eyebrows meeting above her dark eyes as if she had borrowed an eagle's mask, those indomitable arched brows appeared in every self-portrait of Frida, the little girl painting took up the whole canvas, full of color and regal, Kahlo carved out a tall figure with her brushes, its head a bird's nest or a garden of white and purple daisies, spiders, snakes, a whole jungle could have been tucked away in there too, her head was filled with the color and movement of an infinite folk dance. Sitting in René's well-appointed living room, under the occasionally sullen gaze of the old man René, though he still had bedroom eyes, l'Abeille thought, it was surprising that l'Abeille felt such intense emotion when she remembered the colors of Mexico, and under all that color, Gabriela's head blurred into Kahlo's, her hair in curlers like pyramids of green ribbons, woven through with flowers, she forgot that she was mourning her dearest friend and lover, Geneviève. Nothing makes sense in our lives, she thought. Perhaps beneath our reasonable appearance we are all completely insane. Are you happy to be back, l'Abeille, René asked, back here with the girls, don't say anything, I know all about that, far-off flings, whether they're forgivable or not, we have to go through them, what would I have done if I hadn't found Louise, my little too-tall wife, when I got back, right? Louise was already running to the door to let Johnie in, Dr. Vanessa Laflamme, René laughed and said, I'm a dunce, that's how it is when you live on love, you don't bother taking the time to learn anything, and suddenly here you are, all of you like Louise with PhDs, or artists like l'Abeille, such mastery, what kind of an education was I supposed to get playing in a piano bar, right? That's how you learn to love, which is verboten, Polydor told René, you learn to sing and laugh when everything seems sad, even the women who went out with you, Polydor said, and where are they now, God only knows, René said, it was better not to know. Polydor thought René would never admit her disappointment or even the pain that kept her bedridden, so she kept teasing, turning the conversation to laughter, or else she was laconic, one eye closed in that mischievous wink. Johnie touched l'Abeille's shoulder with her long, gloved fingers, you know, we're right here with you, she whispered, Olga was watching Johnie, she didn't have the same bohemian look the other girls did, she seemed like she had a brain in her head, she was more distinguished, and she was impossibly tall, except l'Abeille, who was still tiny as ever, all these women were too big, Olga thought, she herself was of modest height, they almost looked like boys, the one they called Gérard the second, Olga thought, she was lost in the middle of the group, Olga was the same height as Madame René, a bit taller now in her Italian shoes, Madame René might look taller but it was an illusion, her antique chair was high, all of a sudden she was taking up a lot of space, Olga thought, she was used to seeing her lying in bed, Olga greeted Johnie, calling her Madame, she was still the same Johnie, l'Abeille thought, long lashes over those turquoise eyes, but her hair was neater now, she didn't have that straggly shoulder-length mop anymore, it was neat, though not quite even, and she had a patch of color that stood out on her forehead, sometimes purple or white or dark pink, and that sign of irregularity, that subtle rebellion, brought l'Abeille back to the Johnie she always had been, standing next to Gérard, the two girls about to go out in the evening, it was dark out and l'Abeille didn't want to go out with them because they were such a perfect pair, l'Abeille thought, standing against each other, two marble statues, the real blood in their veins imperceptible beneath their stony facade. Will your girlfriend be joining us, Gérard the second asked, Johnie was intimidated by all her friends around her, we don't live in the same country, Alizia and I, she's a poet, an essayist, a renowned feminist, she's quite exceptional, you'll see, we'll see each other next month when her students in San Diego are on Christmas break. Johnie's voice was barely audible but everyone was attentive, even Olga, who couldn't understand anything Johnie had said. Johnie dropped her eyes, she had wide eyelids, and l'Abeille noticed her eyelashes, they were like Gérard's, that was Johnie, loving but remote, l'Abeille thought, it was just like her to keep her romance hidden far away. Pressing her lips closed, Johnie thought of the mess her life was with those far-away loves. Of what she had wanted to learn from one to the next, the openness and innocence she had lost. The girls couldn't imagine how much Johnie had searched everywhere for her sister, all her schooling, her doctorate in psychology, all she had done to better understand Émilie, how she'd vanished, why she had run away so rashly. Johnie had to unravel the mystery of the curves and convolutions in Émilie's head, she thought all heads must contain equally fearsome labyrinths but they mostly remained at a larval stage, passive or inert, while Émilie had broken down the forbidden door. The living do not meander over to the other side of life. L'Abeille thought of the old Johnie, the one who would go out at night with Gérard, the snow glowing in the moonlight, Johnie didn't like to come home late because she was working so hard in school, but she went out anyway, mostly to keep an eye on Gérard, to keep her away from bad company, if Johnie stayed with Gérard, standing by her, vigilant and friendly, nothing bad would happen. L'Abeille remembered her long hours in the parks, too, watching for Gérard's shadow, she ran too fast, darting from tree to tree, toward her bait. She was like the shadow of a fairy or a hare, her footsteps sinking into the snow. What a wild time, l'Abeille thought, the Gérard years. A friend somewhere, a friend far away, that's wonderful, René said to Johnie, embracing in airports, you find her eyes in the crowd, it's a perpetual reunion, that's what makes the passion last, René said. Johnie listened, saying nothing. I don't have your astrological gifts, René said, but I predict that soon you'll be living near each other, maybe not in the same house, but in the same city, and that even when the passion has waned you'll stay together, because you're bound by the same intellectual instinct, the same need to know things, to explain, Johnie smiled cautiously at René's words, René had put her finger on what was so cerebral about her, unlike Louise's humanism or altruism, there was something aloof about her mind, like Alizia's, their research, their quest was benevolent but detached, Johnie, like Alizia, was afraid of intellectual mediocrity, of the idle lure of desire, Johnie regretted that the whole time she was in Europe she didn't even want to kiss a woman, she told herself she had no talent for the art of kissing and caresses, her long fingers, her mouth, how thin her lips were, as if by some unspeakable disdain everything conspired to keep her from the flesh of others, as if through all her previous lives she had already touched and penetrated those bodies. Yet she had tried to be gracious and humane, especially while she was living abroad, she had tried to love, to desire bodies she didn't want, in her parents' higher social class, she had known few women, apart from the girls in the group, from a different social background. Then, out of nowhere, she had gone out to cafés and bars in search of bodies she knew she couldn't love, pretending to be interested in the music playing in the nightclubs, because she was sure nothing about those lowly dalliances could compare with how dazzled she had been that day in the lecture hall, looking into Heinrich's face, her body, her sharp, dizzying intelligence, which had been immediately obvious. It was humiliating to remember those moments in some woman's shabby apartment, it was even more humiliating to have lived it, to have been in that bed, the woman, who was a manual worker, said to her, dear lady, what do you come to me for, love, yes, is it because you are bored, you know you could never live with me, my apartment is a closet, were you looking for pleasure, I don't even believe that, I can feel it, you could never love my world, the misery I come from and which sticks to us, even when we manage to get ahead, I could never trust you. I'm calling you a taxi and saying good-bye right now. Her words struck Johnie, she was right, Johnie's attempts to understand the riddle of status and class were merely intellectual curiosity, her heart wasn't in it and never would be. She had learned to be a good lover from various women, and women from various countries. Even that didn't come naturally. But Heinrich, her intelligence, the emails they exchanged about art and how quick Van Gogh had been to cut off his ear, the genius, they always came back to that, that was Johnie's real concern, but Heinrich was taken, so she had to give up. Sometimes Johnie would come across Heinrich's picture in a book and her heart stopped for a second, go on with your life, my friend, Heinrich's sparkling smile seemed to be saying, your life has only just begun, while as a young European I feel that I have already lived too long. Lali had never been able to escape her parents' past, sometimes her eyes flashed such uncontrollable anger, while in Heinrich's, Johnie thought, there was only an acknowledgment of misfortunes quickly forgotten to live joyfully. Johnie was happy to have met Alizia, whose soul was like her own, easily upset. L'Abeille thought of her father. After his wife's death he was unrecognizable, he broke his violin, he refused to go to work, he didn't want to play in the orchestra anymore, the grief he carried was so heavy it was toxic, it was poisoning him, he threatened to send his children to reform school, l'Abeille had taken a gun, the only gun in the house, which was mostly ornamental, there were no bullets in it, and said to her father, if you send us away I'll kill you. Her father turned pale, he was scared, l'Abeille remembered that feeling of impotent power, she loved her father, and she was scaring him. But it was no game, the possibility of being shipped off seemed unspeakably cruel to an innocent child, and for her father to threaten that, wasn't that the cruelest thing, though her father wasn't cruel, no doubt the words came directly from God, l'Abeille thought, she was thirteen then. As she sat at Doudouline's feet as if she were still in her smoky living room, l'Abeille's memories of those years mingled with Mexico's ravishing colors, the wooden doors painted pink and green, and suddenly she was back in the street and a heavily made-up woman walked past, holding a child's coffin under her arm. The coffin was empty, the woman was walking along the street with the pink doors, all those gardens behind the freshly painted doors, where was she going, l'Abeille thought, to what ceremony, with the little coffin under her arm? Tears ran down her cheeks, streaking her makeup, the woman was crying openly. It was hot, with no wind off the mountains, and l'Abeille had wanted to follow the woman, to comfort her, but she disappeared in the traffic, in an instant she was no longer there. L'Abeille pictured herself carrying Geneviève's coffin under her arm, crying out, help, help, and she heard Doudouline's voice as if it were coming down from heaven, Doudouline was singing *Gérard oh Gérard*, Polydor was singing with her, how beautiful, how bracing, René said, though then he seemed to close in on himself, sulking. Do you have a less sad song, René asked, I remember that song you used to sing, "Off the Wagon Today," we heard it on TV, it was one of the first songs you sang onstage, I laughed so hard when I heard it. One day I sang it in a bar where I was playing piano, except that the title of the song, René, Doudouline said, was "Off the Hook Today," René could still see a group of women coming toward him, it was so clear in his mind, they were coming up to the piano, drink in hand, suddenly the memory went black, like a candle had flickered out. You have to preserve your fondest memories, René said, Doudouline, your voice takes me back, although part of me wonders if any of it happened at all. René lapsed back into his gloom and Louise put a hand on his head, listen, René, we're here for the party, l'Abeille was withdrawn too, thinking of the colors in Mexico, the pink doors, the green gardens, everywhere a flood of colors like Gabriela had taught her. She was proud that her work was selling in Mexico, it was an honor. At night, Johnie still heard that tremulous voice, Gérard telling her about her outlandish adventures, why hadn't she shaken her, Gérard, wake up, aren't you even a little bit ashamed of how you're acting, Gérard, I wanted my free coke, she confided once to Johnie, I was broke and that night, I was hurting, I was freaking out, and I told them, there were two dealers, twenty-year-olds, I can pay with my body, one after the other, and they did what they wanted, but first I wanted the coke so I wouldn't feel anything, afterwards I saw the blood on my thighs, on my legs, and the smell of semen, I washed it all down the toilet in a bar, I thought I was going to pass out, and finally I was able to get up but all I could feel was the coke, nothing else, they ran away, one of them said, thank you, thank you beautiful girl, that was my first time, I'm a man now, thank you, beautiful girl, come back tomorrow at the same time if you want, they were just kids trying out sex, trying out my body, Gérard had told Johnie, it was night, whispering night, secrets tinged with horror, Johnie thought, why hadn't she said anything, given her hell, why hadn't she shaken Gérard and said, this is a disgrace, this is shit, how low are you going to go, Gérard, but Gérard was falling back asleep, dozing, the golden indifference of cocaine, an ecstatic coma, and up close, under the glare of the lamp, Johnie could see Gérard's nostrils twitching, her mouth gone slack. This is nice, I feel so good, Johnie, my Johnie, is it true that you got that scholarship to Europe, is it true you're going to leave, what am I going to do without you, who will I be, my Johnie, Johnie thought, was that a prelude to Émilie, or the sequel, Gérard, in all the cosmic nothingness, Gérard who was so far away from us suddenly. A whole generation would lose itself; we would be lost. In those days, Johnie remembered she was doing astrology, she would see clients at her office, it was the same now, but in a different profession, her bicycle still hung off the brick wall on its nail, it was several flights up and suddenly there she was, leaning over as if she were still a lanky teenager, she'd had a client once, a very pretty student who asked Johnie, do you see a future for me, she pulled the devil card, what future do you see for me, none, Johnie had wanted to tell her, though she said nothing, I see suicide by overdose or murder in the street, don't you dare tell me that, the girl said, I know why you're saying that, you've guessed everything about me, you already know everything, no, Johnie said, I'm not getting anything, really, yes, but that's the devil card, the student said, the devil. You're right, I'm not even in school anymore, I'm on the street, I'm working, there was no other way, you didn't dare say it but you guessed right, didn't you, and Johnie said, go back to school, you'll have a bright future, I promise. Don't you understand I have no other choice, the girl had shouted, Johnie saw her ten years later, on the street, she was waiting for someone, chain-smoking, she was no longer the exquisite young woman who'd come to see Johnie, her face was ravaged, so young, Johnie thought, God doesn't love us women, God hates us, she would have wept with pity but she had to forget that face, the trembling hand holding the cigarettes. Johnie was startled when Doudouline called out, Mama is on the stairs, I can hear her footsteps, I hear her charging up the stairs in her red stiletto boots, poor her, the street is a skating rink, and there was the Great Sophie in her red satin boots, perched up on her heels as if it were summer, Doudouline said, the scarf around her neck was fluffy, it looked like it was made of feathers, Doudouline looked at her mother as if she were onstage, Sophie was declaiming her lines, praising René, dear René, the Great Sophie said, you know, I have always held your activism in the highest regard, you were so brave in New York when they were throwing bricks at your head, when you were being dragged off to jail by your feet, oh, you did great things to defend my daughter's rights, Doudouline finally married Polydor, the woman she loves, whatever your sexual orientation is, I admire you, dear René, I'm a man with the heart of a woman, René said, or the opposite, a woman in search of her male body lost somewhere in nature, René smiled at the Great Sophie, complicit, welcome to the party, René told her, the Great Sophie thought René was growing old like a bachelor, though he wasn't quite withered yet, his male vanity kept him relatively intact, Sophie hadn't yet reached René's advanced age, she felt a certain superiority about it, it was a momentous age, though he might yet live to a hundred, she was still directing at eighty-eight, she still wrote, produced, traveled, artists and writers were an alien species, she thought, as Doudouline said, the Great Sophie was a planet wheeling through the sky, a comet, a sun flashing its beams everywhere, look at my mama, she never changes, isn't she adorable, but those red boots, Mama, stilettos, it's dangerous, you'll fall and break your neck, Mama dear, and you'll break your daughter's heart too, Mama dear. René, the Great Sophie went on, as you can see, I have repented and now I love my daughter, I no longer merely tolerate her like I used to, I love her. Her father convinced me to love her, let's love them as they are, he said, it's simpler that way. I chose simplicity, dear René, and even you, man or woman, I didn't understand before. Mama, that's enough, Doudouline said, you've said enough, Mama dear, any more would be tactless. Enough, Mama. But the Great Sophie wouldn't shut up, her exuberance, her red boots, the Great Sophie had invaded the room, her voice high, singing, cooing, we're at the theater, Doudouline rolled her eyes, and l'Abeille thought back again to the Mexican woman carrying a child's coffin under her arm, striding through traffic, an exalted figure among the cars, as if she were blind, l'Abeille ran behind her, she couldn't find her, it was so hot, Gabriela took her hand, let's go visit some painter friends of mine, she said, maybe they will let us use their house for the night, just like before, in the days of l'Abeille's smoky living room, l'Abeille was still squatting, one day in the home of millionaire artists and the next in the shack of a destitute painter, that was how Gabriela lived, she ran a gallery, those brazen bohemian days, under a scorching sky, without the cold or snow or windy nights when you came out of the bar, racked as much by the cold as by an icy solitude, the unbearable ache of those who find themselves alone after a drunken night. Her time with Gabriela was delirious and easy, sleeping in a hammock in a garden with a nightingale singing all night. She kept painting the pink doors, the rows of roses in gardens, she wrote to Geneviève, I'm coming back, I'm on my way home, I miss you, she remembered Geneviève's face when they had said good-bye at the airport, outside it was storming, Geneviève was wearing a fake fur hat, it looked like rabbit, it was a kind of cap with the flaps like ears hanging down over her cheeks, she couldn't stand still, she wanted to get the good-byes over with already, I'll be back before you know it, l'Abeille said, feeling guilty, you know that, Geneviève, you know me, Geneviève was quiet, she walked back to her car, the roof closed now for the winter, the sky full of swirling snow was relentless, l'Abeille thought, you know I love you, Geneviève, she murmured, you're the only one I love. But it was too late. Geneviève had fled into the storm, the car with the roof up, the implacable low sky. Doudouline's tinkling voice rang out, she was praising the Great Sophie, girls, I wanted to tell you,

Mama has won a best-actress award, and another for best director, it was true, the Great Sophie said humbly, she herself had just heard the news, the girls clapped, bravo Sophie, we're so proud of you, stop, she said, you're making me blush, there was a time when I was young when I could play Mademoiselle Julie, I was the very height of cruelty, I could tame a man, humiliate him, I knew the part was diabolical but without wanting to I cleaved to Julie's violent passion, I was so diligent in learning my part that I lost myself in her consuming chaos, and here I am now, so many years later, in the director's chair, working with a young Mademoiselle Julie, how strange it is, the Great Sophie sighed, the passage of time, isn't it, Sophie was lost in thought, Gérard the second slipped out of the living room door again, cigarette in hand, it's a pity you can't smoke inside anymore, she thought, you have to go out and freeze your fingers off, before you know it we won't even be allowed to smoke in the street, what a world, Gérard the second thought, the Great Sophie was serious all of a sudden, standing close to Polydor and Doudouline, she seemed to want to protect them, she was benevolence incarnate, she had an idea, Doudouline, let's stage *Gérard oh Gérard* again with a different ending, yes, without having her die for the cocaine, what about if we just see her gradually moving away into the mist, but Mama, that wouldn't be true, Doudouline said, it would be bogus theater, down in the street, leaning against the wall, Gérard the second was trying to light her cigarette in the snowstorm, it's not fair, Gérard thought, you can't ask smokers to stop smoking, you can't, a woman was getting out of a car covered in snow, a piece of paper on the window that read, *emergency twenty-four hours*, Mercedes ran toward Gérard the second, you're smoking again, she said, taking her cigarette and flicking it into the snow, how can you be smoking when Geneviève just died, Mercedes was usually so pleasant but she seemed angry and exhausted that night, she was working nights to try to save a few addicts, scraps of humanity, these kids were sleeping rough, they were out at night in the cold, between two garage doors, in the worst spots, the cigarette landed in the snow and Mercedes planted an apologetic kiss on Gérard lips, remember, Mercedes said, I had to identify Gérard's body, Gérard the second thought she might weep at the memory, remember, that wasn't even her lying there in the morgue, remember, Mercedes said, but I look at you, beautiful and solid, you're not gaunt like she was, and I tell myself that you're Gérard saved, she said, Mercedes was smiling now, Gérard the second saw her gleaming white teeth, it was like a miracle from your soul to hers, when you think of someone doing what you did every day, every day you went to lay flowers on her grave, such love, yes, Gérard came back to live again in you, she's back, I was wrong, she said, and why not, Mercedes asked urgently, I don't know how it works, the transfer of souls, Gérard the second said, whatever happens in heaven isn't happening here anymore, but I think Gérard wanted life, not death, maybe she gave me this life so she wouldn't feel sad anymore, so she'd have no regrets, Gérard the second said, let's go up to René's, it's warm in the living room, Mercedes said, curse this winter, I don't know how many bodies I'm going to find tomorrow, winter kills my victims, literally, starting with their feet and their hands, do people know that kids are dying of cold every single night, aren't we ashamed of ourselves, they're frozen to death, all they want is to satisfy a need, they need to shoot up. Let's go up, Gérard the second said, taking Mercedes' arm, she had a thick coat on, let's go see René, tonight René is a prince, Gérard said, he still gets into those moods like he used to, it's like nothing has changed, Mercedes was moved, as they went up the stairs she kissed Gérard the second on both cheeks, laughing now, life had finally brought them together, maybe it was true that the first Gérard was alive again, maybe there was a reason to hope, to believe, to love, in her serene sophistication, she'd always been a little different from the others, Johnie thought of the student, she was a delinquent, she'd come up to her office, the way she talked about sex, Johnie could hardly believe her ears, this pretty girl who seemed otherwise quite normal was saying how much she craved sex, she wanted to be with a man day and night, her body was wired that way, it was gratuitous, maybe that's why I'm on the street instead of in school, it's perfect for me, Johnie didn't dare ask her where she was living or if she had parents, she'd never heard anyone so young say such things, Johnie hardly ever felt the rush of sexual passion, she often told Alizia that she loved first with her brain, her mind, she was cerebral, and here was this girl telling her all about how much she loved sex, it all seemed a bit messy, she wanted to wrap herself up in a man, she wanted him to hold her, to keep her far from reality, from real life, what was real life anyway, Johnie thought, that girl needed a man, night and day, a life preserver, she needed him draped around her body, she said, I just like pleasure, you can spend forever just drowning in it if you want to, and who's to say we can't, it's up to each of us to decide for herself, it's my life, life is only worth what it can be worth, a moment of abandon, the body passing through strange hands, filled by strange bodies, she said, there was a patient Johnie sometimes saw, a seventeen-year-old man, repulsively arrogant, he was quite sick but he never stayed on the psych ward for very long, his arrogance was a wall Johnie kept crashing into, you had to have compassion for all of them, she felt sorry for both the men and women, but that arrogance or insolence in very young men lashed at her, so she did what she had so successfully done as an astrologer, the past was so long ago, Gérard was still alive, she would throw open the apartment windows, even in winter, to clear out all the wayward, wanton vibes, it was too bad that Alizia lived so far away, today would have been a beautiful day to go snowshoeing on the mountain, to forget all about the delusions and destruction of men, of women, everybody, the garden of their lives was so small, so very fragile, and whatever they could harvest from such a wasteland. There were people who never truly lived, who were always waiting for a better time, though there never was a better time. Johnie heard Doudouline's voice through the turmoil of her mind, Mama, Doudouline was saying, maybe what we need is a third act, Gérard comes back in a boat sailing across the waves by night, through the thin moonlight on the water, she used to go swimming far out into the ocean at night, we always knew she would come back, we could hear her laughing, that high, burbling laugh, Mama, if you let me use your theater again I can write a third act, Gérard's return, just happy ocean sounds and images, Gérard's return to the waters, Doudouline started singing *Gérard oh Gérard*, Gérard the second and Mercedes were tracking slush and snow into René's fancy living room, their boots and coats dripping, my living room, Olga said, my carpet, I just polished the kitchen floor, Madame René, they destroy my work, and René said, no, no, calm down, my dear Olga, do what we're doing, have some champagne, René had a glass in her hand, she looked over all of them like the lord of the manor, I have to tell them so that they never forget, girls, you have to fight, get out of the cozy nub of coupledom and head out to the streets, go, it'll be my sermon on the mount, they have to listen to me, René thought, I'm the head of an empty household, the man of the house reigning over nothing but my dreams, but they have to listen to me, I'm going to tell them everything, right now, what we have to do if we don't want to lose our rights, she gestured to Louise who poured some more champagne, sparkling nectar of ecstasy, they're still beautiful, they're happy, Johnie is wearing a bit of makeup, not much, she always looks put together no matter what, l'Abeille is hurting but she'll heal, she loves life too much, we live, we die, alas, dear Geneviève, we live, we die, and even me, even though I don't want to think about it, I'm wasting away, there's a little less of me today than there was yesterday, Olga turned to Louise, you know, I was born in Moscow like the poet Pushkin but not the same year or at the same time, and it snows all the time, like here, and Louise replied, Madame, it is a great honor to have been born in the city where Pushkin was born, I don't know, Olga said,

Madame, because we were so poor, they used to say about us in the village, are they going to eat their children, they are so poor, that was before we came to Moscow, before everything collapsed, hey, where's Lali, Polydor asked, you know Lali is always late, René said, she would even get to work late, when she worked in the emergency room, she couldn't drag herself away from l'Abeille's living room, she was so tired she almost fell asleep standing up, her lovers wore her out, that was it, the conquests of a hungry young wolf, René said, l'Abeille blushed thinking of Lali leaning over her on the couch under the blanket, l'Abeille pretending to be asleep with Rosemonde warm around her neck while Lali kissed her slowly, as if it was a game, but maybe that was all it was, a game, l'Abeille thought, l'Abeille walking with Gabriela in the streets of Mexico City after a cocktail party in a gallery for a young painter Gabriela had just discovered, lighthearted at the end of a long day, the sky was still pink, l'Abeille remembered, and thousands of people were pushing through the city, they thought they might get lost in the crowd, never to be found again, they were going to the university, Gabriela was explaining to an Indigenous woman, they could already hear the cheerful strains of music, and l'Abeille remembered that she had walked by a dead dog on the sidewalk that day, her feet almost touched it, why not bury it, l'Abeille had asked Gabriela, that poor dead dog on the pavement, and all those feet in their beautiful leather shoes are just walking over it, the indifference is so cruel, l'Abeille had said, and Gabriela replied, Mexico is the land of the dead as much as it is the land of the living, it's in our art, we express it in everything we do, let the dog rest, our feet aren't bothering him, he's asleep, he's gone back to the ancient lands like all the dead, to the country of wind and sand, l'Abeille had to run to keep up with Gabriela, land of the living, land of the dead, she thought, and they were tearing the dog's body apart with their feet, with their boots, crushing its belly, its furry ears, it was unfathomable and l'Abeille couldn't accept it, how many dogs, men, how many children were trampled like that every day, the Indigenous festival was a celebration of life, follow me, Gabriela said, come dance with my friends, come into the circle, l'Abeille was dizzy dancing with Gabriela, with others, dancers she didn't know, around and around, spinning around, as she danced she felt like her feet were keeping a morbid beat, stomping on the poor dog until there was nothing left on the sidewalk or in the street but a patch of fur, what you might see after a car drives by, the imprint of wings in the concrete, the wings and feathers of birds that flew too low. Now here was Lali, still wearing a long military coat and a cap as austere as the coat was, from the armchair René opened his arms, little brother, he shouted, my little brother from your far-away English-speaking town, how could a plane even take off in this weather? Louise told the girls to put their phones away, their noise and flicker was incessant, put them away, Louise said, it's not like we see René every day. And this might be the last time, René added, laughing, the bell was tolling. The girls laughed along with René, they had to laugh at death, death wasn't real, though they had wept at Geneviève's funeral a few weeks earlier. Doudouline was going to call Mimi soon, her pianist, she liked the idea of a third act for *Gérard oh Gérard*. Standing next to René like a soldier stiff under her cap, Lali announced that she was moving back, a few blocks away, René would have her own personal doctor a few days a week. You spoil me, you're spoiling me, little brother, René was euphoric. René drew Olga close, reassuring her with a wink, of course I'll still keep you, you won't leave me. Without you, Olga, I can't listen to my great morning music. It is true, Madame René, I think a lot about the joy of your awakening. And it is true, you cannot live without me, without the music I give you to listen. No, I can't live without you, Olga, René said, as lively as ever. What a couple needs, Johnie thought as she thumbed Alizia's picture on her phone, is reconstruction and creation, that's how we love each other best, but Johnie also loved her solitude, that was another source of creation, albeit more isolated, she was getting up early to learn the violin, to paint, even if all she managed was a square of light, she could paint for hours, to write her articles on art and mental illness, she was working on Goya's rage against an inquisitive society, the terror of the Church or any other institution, she was drafting and redrafting the paper, and she was reading Alizia's autobiographical book on feminist engagement, these days all Alizia was doing was running from one burning house to the next, California was burning, burning, when would Johnie see her again, Alizia wrote to Johnie that she had a specific mission in the city, saving the land, the burning land, the land that men were burning, it was criminal negligence, young people were suffering because of government apathy, in her classes at the university Alizia was awakening a whole generation of youth, who were already very much awake but they felt powerless in the face of the disasters brought about by climate change, the repeal of safeguard laws, the inertia of those in charge, that inertia, the abject inertia of the people in power who were ready to sacrifice the future, entire generations, for their own comfort. Johnie thought of the animals, deer and wolves running away among the burning trees, nature that had protected and fed them but they were protected no longer, they were being evicted from their homes, the birds, powerful birds of prey saw their feathers through embers raining down, the earth was burning, Alizia wrote to Johnie, the earth is burning. Johnie thought that if she got better at painting her square of light, that sunny opening cast down through the skylight, if she learned to play her violin, to read better, if she treated her patients better every morning, then in her own small way she would be working to save a world that was already condemned, more so with each passing day. Lali told the girls that she wanted to rest, and she especially wanted to be closer to René, to take care of her. Lali's smile seemed brighter, Louise thought, not as sad as before, her cheeks were round, though in other ways she was the same, flint and discipline, you are good, little brother, René shouted from the armchair, bring your dogs for a visit won't you, I miss Saturn so much, and Countess hasn't come back yet. When will I see Alizia again, Johnie wondered, the forest in flames before her eyes, people fleeing in their cars before being buried in ash, each and every one of them going into exile, while the trees bowed under the raging wildfires, stripped of leaves and flowers, skeletal, as if they had been drenched in black ink, in a new, scorched landscape. Alizia's face, her curly hair, seemed to pass through layers of clouds, like Heinrich's face once had when Johnie left her. Alizia was involved with her students, she followed her political commitment, but Johnie felt the distance between them stretching out, a long ribbon of absence, and it was getting harder for both of them. But she couldn't go down there when the world was burning, they couldn't come back to each other when the earth was so dry and thirsty for water. René was looking at Lali with such delight, what a gift if she does come back, what happiness. L'Abeille felt like she was cloaked in mourning, in a black veil, Alexis, Geneviève, the enormity of the loss was beyond words, it was too much pain, too much silence. Like in the days when she and the girls had been squatting in the house about to collapse, l'Abeille was still the den mother of a nest, straw and grass flaying out, even though Geneviève, the architect, had built houses for each one, or at least she had designed such an astonishing, luminous ecological project, even though the squatters' nest had been deserted. L'Abeille had several children, godchildren really, if Doudouline and Polydor were thinking of having children the Great Sophie would be elated, she would finally be a grandmother, l'Abeille had adopted Louis-Jean and Manfred's children from afar, one of them was blond like Manfred and the second looked like his mother, it was l'Abeille's dream to have them all nearby in the sunny home Geneviève had designed, they would all come to live in the pink-doored garden of her house one day although everyone else had left, even Geneviève. Louis-Jean had written to l'Abeille that he remembered everything, before he was born too, how his mother liked to drive for hours, they stopped at that rocky outcropping facing the sea. His mother would talk to him then, he could hear the roar of the waves. Should they stop there or keep going? Louis-Jean could hear the rush of her breathing and Alexis would say, no, let's go home instead, let's go home, quick, and they would go back along the slopes and down the hills, and Louis-Jean would go back to sleep. Louis-Jean remembered his mother writing poems, she took him out on horseback over the hills where the sheep and the lambs grazed beneath purple clouds in the evening, Louis-Jean's father was a farmer, Alexis wrote books but was slow to publish, whether out of modesty or to protect her solitude, he remembered her, he wrote to l'Abeille, when he was still in her belly and she sang to him, riding in the Jeep to the high hills, the rumbling of the pebbles, the gravel under the wheels, the fear of never being able to get back down again, yes, it was those moments of love and terror he remembered most. The Great Sophie thought about the huge meal she was going to make for the girls at her country house at Easter, or would she lend them her beach house in Florida, her generous heart poured out a thousand dreams in which she cherished her children, how could she organize her life, she wondered, her crazy schedule of rehearsing every day and never taking a vacation. A single life was too short, she didn't even dare think about getting old, how immodest that would be, how self-indulgent, you didn't get old, she wouldn't, there was no time for that. Actresses who talked only about their age were irritating. When you're active, she thought, there's nothing trivial, there's not a moment wasted. As she scratched up Olga's freshly polished floor with her red satin boots, she thought, you have to be all action and nothing else. René shows us how to be, how to act—with impatient dignity. Good for René. Johnie thought of the painting she'd made a few weeks earlier while she was in California with Alizia, it was an abstract of the two of them making love, only she knew the secret of the picture, only her and Alizia, the city was full of smoke, smoke seeping under the doors and into the windows. Who could have known that in the gray space in the canvas there were two people who loved each other, that gray section must have been the crawling smoke, through cracks in the doors and windows, mothers had to wake up their children, slumbering with their pets in the sovereign heat of the fire, we have to leave, we're going to the emergency shelter. In the stables, horses were afraid, you could hear them moaning. The smoke and its pungent blue-black ring thickened around the rabbits and the birds of prey and they all woke up to flee. Whoever didn't leave was going to die, the mother told her children. So they got up and got dressed, crying, the mother put them in the car and the father tried to get the horses, it was important not to die. Suddenly a red blade cut through the gray in the painting, a few drops of blood hanging there, was it about the fragility of the female body, too sensitive after love, especially during your period, Johnie thought, or when you get your period unexpectedly, or was that the painting's secret meaning, pleasure mingled with menstrual blood when you didn't want any of it, the pleasure startling the body, the release of excess, the painting was bothering Johnie, the unfinished scream of it, while smoke seeped in under the doors and the drops of blood staining the sheets, the unstoppable course of a disaster unfolding. She would have liked to kiss Alizia, Johnie thought in René's plush living room, that was what they were texting each other when Louise had said not to use their phones, those agile messengers of earthly love. Johnie thought of the three essays Louise had written on women and cancer, she thought of the students Louise taught in the evenings, of the few hours a week Louise went swimming at the pool, even in winter, that must be a satisfying life, successful, even. Mercedes was sitting next to Gérard the second, looking affectionately at her, this Gérard was alive and well, Mercedes was utterly selfless, she spent her nights at the rehab center with kids who would be back in the streets shooting up if they didn't listen to her, she was looking after her sisters Esperanza and Paciencia too, and their mother in their big house, so much adamant selflessness, did it make sense, Johnie thought, did we always have to set out to fight what was demeaning and un-salvageable in the universe, she wondered, could the world of drugs that Gérard had chosen ever be redeemed, could that be saved? Johnie had run away from Gérard's brush with death, she was still running away from Alizia, who was wise, she abhorred corruption and decadence, Gérard's arms had been covered with the constellations of her decline, Johnie thought, wasn't choosing to do coke or shoot up a sort of continuous decadence? That was how Johnie had lost Émilie, her sister had probably tumbled into LSD and lost her mind, she thought. You're being very quiet, Dr. Vanessa, it's full of doctors in here, all the girls, I'm surrounded by doctors, Louise, Johnie, Lali, I'm an ignorant old man, René said, I have no education but I can play the most sentimental tunes, yes, I think I still could, all I'm missing is a bit of strength in my fingers, I'll make a feast for Easter, the Great Sophie said, a big party in honor of my daughter Doudouline and her musical, Anne-Sophie, you won't forget, will you, I have an opening night, too, Mama, my dear Mama, Doudouline was distracted, her mother was an excellent cook, everyone loved coming over, children, actors, artists, Mama, it's too much for you, you always do too much, that's how it is, it's in my nature, the Great Sophie said, you'll come, and bring all the girls, won't you, René was calling to Lali like she used to, hey, little brother, do you still go out to bars at night? Lali had a mysterious, defiant smile but she didn't answer right away, René, you forget that I work nights in the emergency room, even if I'm back, always in the emergency room, it's my job. And love? René asked with that wink, eyes half closed, what about love? No, Lali said, only emergencies. No time for love. Lali had taken off her snowy hat, she held it in her hand, in the emergency room, Lali said, doctors work like soldiers. But René thought Lali's smile was slightly forced, enigmatic, she wasn't telling her everything, René could still see the hunter stalking the bars, grabbing a girl to dance, probably taking her home only to forget her afterwards, when her watch sounded, she would change quickly to go to the hospital, she barely had time to feed her dogs. Love had to be plucked like the ripe fruit off a tree, but Lali had no choice, she was an emergency-room physician, she thought, this was the grievous story of her life, she was quick to get what she wanted and moved on, since the family tragedy back in Europe that forced her to leave, the chimney that had collapsed, killing her younger brother, she had never stopped running, from one escape to the next. But now, here, her other brother was waiting for her, and for a long time René had seemed to be doing quite well. Even though Lali hadn't known the dire consequences of the war, the terrible sound of the shelling over the city, as her mother said, she had long carried the sounds that had broken her family, her brother's bloody face and head, she took that with her when she left the country and the whole wrecked continent. She would never forget him. When it fell, she thought, the chimney had collapsed on them all. Lali laughed and said that when she visited René later, she would teach him to walk again and even do yoga, you want to kill me, René cried, oh, little brother, be careful, I'm made of porcelain, not rubber, but, René admitted, a little exercise wouldn't do him any harm. You are lazy, Lali said, you have been lazing around in your bed for years, she said. That's not true, doctor, René said, don't you understand, brother, I'm an old man, suffering, I was a young man enjoying life, pleasing women or sitting at the piano, but that's all over, the pettiness of old age struck me down in one fell swoop. Which is not to say, brother, that it keeps me from enjoying life. You have to take it an hour at a time, I would say, one minute at a time. You have always been very lazy, Lali went on mercilessly. Olga looked at Lali with admiration and fear, Madame René would never be alone with her again, she thought, since she had so many friends. Lali saw Olga as a tragic figure, a familiar icon of prostitution, how many years did she have to sell herself before she met René and sought shelter in this house? Her field was obviously online sex work. But Lali thought she had to protect René too, because there would be a price to pay, René's possessions, the apartment, the piano, and what else? Lali felt that René was too trusting with Olga, she wasn't a suspicious kind of person, she wasn't used to it. René said to Lali, do you remember, Lali, one day, when we were coming back, it was almost dawn, I think I was driving the wrong way, you said to me, be careful, René, even when you're drunk you have to watch out for the police, they're everywhere at this time of night. You were right, René said, I felt so good at the wheel, like we were alone in the world, you and I, brother. The city was deserted, I was whistling some song, there we were under such a lovely summer sky, and what was there to be afraid of? Yes, you were very inebriated then, Lali said, I wondered what Louise was going to say when she saw you. Oh, Louise was running away from me in those days, she was holed up at l'Abeille's, studying. Johnie listened to René, thinking of the places she had visited with Alizia, the most beautiful in the world, would they all be destroyed by fire, that spot out by the Pacific where they camped, the forests, the woods they cycled through, their excursions out at sea, would everything go up in smoke? Alizia wrote to Johnie that she got up in the morning and went to bed in the evening in a blanket of smoke, the sky was crimson and blackened birds flew by, burned like the fields were burned, the trees, the forests, the charred trusses of stables as wild horses galloped across the plains, the long echo of their screams. This was the fate of men, Alizia wrote, men were destroying the world through their indifference, the climate crisis would be the next war, though we didn't know yet who the enemy was, what the battles would be. Alizia wrote to Johnie that she was afraid, she was so proud to have been born in the paradise of California, its endless promises of every evolution and revolution, a land ready for a new future, she wrote, and suddenly the doors of paradise slammed shut and they were trapped and burning, those verdant forests were an inferno, and all the splendor of the wildlife.

For generations to come children who weren't yet born would have only distress and deprivation, disillusioned at having lost their birthright because we destroyed it, death's hot wheeze passing over these lands engulfed and wiped out by fire. This would be the next war and we were going to lose, Alizia wrote to Johnie, the land we have betrayed with our trash will turn against us, the sea, all the seas and oceans will throw up cyclones and hurricanes will let loose for days and nights of terror, we'll have nowhere to go, we will have no houses, no home. Do you remember our campsite by the Pacific, Johnie wrote to Alizia, we went water-skiing, the bright blue sky, our heads almost touching as we read side by side in the tent, I was holding the flashlight, and when we went skiing in the Alps, what a happy memory, your face against mine in the night, and we would just laugh at how nice it was to share those moments, do you remember, Johnie asked Alizia, l'Abeille hadn't changed at all, that thick pageboy cut, she had the same hair, Johnie thought, while René seemed to have gotten more masculine, but more nuanced in his masculinity, l'Abeille used to say that René was a guy like any other, it wasn't a compliment, l'Abeille didn't like bullies and she said that René was a bully with Louise, now even l'Abeille would've had to admit that René had softened, he had become less rough and more elegant, even how he spoke, it was a different language, it wasn't just about physical possession, he finally loved Louise, he didn't just dominate her, maybe l'Abeille had always unconsciously worried that René would be violent with Louise, especially during that disastrous time when he was in love with Nathalie, l'Abeille thought. L'Abeille suddenly felt inconsolable in such a cheery gathering, the Great Sophie and Doudouline were laughing, yes, they were going to work together on *Gérard oh Gérard*, adding an extra act would make the musical brighter, yes, she was inconsolable, she thought, none of the girls could imagine what it would do to her to have to sell the cottage in the mountains, you couldn't keep what belonged to the realm of the dead, just driving back up there would steal her breath, she thought, everything would be ghostly, the canoe on the shore, the paddles, and the slim figure of Geneviève loping along the dock and jumping in the lake, arms wide open under the gray sky as if she were welcoming the clouds, she had been so certain that she was going to get better, it would have been better to have no hope at all, l'Abeille thought, but that's how she was, Geneviève never talked about the abomination that was eating away at her, maybe she was in denial, the canoe would be empty, the paddles abandoned in the sand, but Geneviève's pale silhouette would still be there and then all at once she would be gone, l'Abeille wouldn't see her anymore, as if the moon's first glimmering had swallowed her up. Johnie would write to Alizia tomorrow, she would ask her if she was making any progress with her autobiography, Johnie would never have written that candidly about herself and her coming out, but Alizia would say that she had never come out of anything, she had been the way she was since she was born, and openly recount every lover she'd had, from childhood, she has courage, Johnie thought, I couldn't do that, but I could write about how cavalier my sister was about any form of sexuality, or I could try to understand it, sex counted so little for her, it was so much more about refusing to follow the rules, a refusal of restraint, she lived against convention. These were things too personal to think about. Johnie carried a tiny faux-leather backpack, she wore an expensive scarf and fake leather gloves, she tried to be quietly attractive, while Alizia didn't care about clothes, though she looked after her mass of naturally curly hair, she wore the same jean jacket, and, in the summer, jean shorts when she was out on her bike. When they met at Johnie's place, Johnie, after seeing patients all week, would unhook the bike from the brick wall and they would go ride along the river together. What bliss, Johnie thought. The lake, taking the boat out at the end of the summer, it was so lovely, l'Abeille thought, when Geneviève finally allowed her work to be interrupted, when she agreed to have fun, which didn't happen

NIGHTS TOO SHORT TO DANCE

often, l'Abeille thought. Already those radiant walks by the water were gone, except the few crumbs of memory l'Abeille had left. Geneviève liked the good life, l'Abeille thought, she drove fast, that white convertible of hers, she liked good food, good wine, the cognac she used to drink in the evening with Polydor in the smoky living room at l'Abeille's, like Polydor, she smoked a lot, a bit of hash too, brown cigarettes with a damp tip and an ashy smell, and they passed it back and forth, wetting it with their lips. Geneviève knew how to forget and how to forgive, she took l'Abeille back from Mexico without question, or maybe her dear face was only a mask, l'Abeille thought, maybe she didn't admit what she really felt, there was no threat or anger, only the slightly strained silence of her welcome. As they drove away that day, she said, I made your favorite meal, you'll see. It's good to see you again, my darling. Slow down, l'Abeille said, God, you still drive so fast, that's how I drive, Christie, you know that, I'm impatient, Geneviève's voice comforted l'Abeille, it was the voice of someone she loved, she was finally home, would l'Abeille finally give in now to a quieter love, a love that was tamed, she wondered as she laid her hand on Geneviève's knee. Gérard was leaning against Mercedes' shoulder, it felt casual, easy, she thought, you get up in the morning and someone is there, someone you want to kiss, a beautiful face on the pillow just waiting for that kiss, you want to take her in your arms and she's there, she's yours. What more can you ask for? Mercedes already calls me her little Gérard, I'm sturdy, a gardener, in my own way I craft landscapes, in summer and winter alike. I am her little Gérard, a light in a dark sky. L'Abeille remembered telling Johnie one of her dreams, was it a dream or a nightmare, or a translucent truth, as dreams often are, in the dream l'Abeille saw Mozart in his grave, he'd been buried in a mass grave, it was right after she saw that woman in Mexico, the woman with lots of makeup crossing the street with a child's coffin, l'Abeille wanted to know what Mozart had felt in that grave, an anonymous, public grave, when he realized he would no longer be able to compose, yet still he heard the perfect musical echo of everything he had written, a whole life, what had he felt in that prison, between two boards, the only music was a smolder, or rather that music was still burning within him, consuming him, he was about to ask God for notebooks to write in so that he could compose when l'Abeille woke up, her heart pounding, what did my dream mean, l'Abeille asked Johnie, who explained that Mozart, entombed like that, represented l'Abeille's mother hearing all of her compositions at the moment of her death, especially her oratorio, she had only written the beginning, the overture, she could hear every note, but it was l'Abeille's dream, she was its unconscious author in sleep that translated her story as it went along, she was the continuation of her mother, the mother was dead and the living daughter was composing, creating, and Johnie said maybe the thought could bring l'Abeille some peace, serenity, even contentment. It was that pink strand in Johnie's shiny hair, a bit of wildness peeking through her otherwise orderly life, that brought l'Abeille back to the dream. The dream slipped into real life with the news of some professional success, when l'Abeille got up she had a message from Gabriela on her tablet, you sold another painting, one of your green doors in my gallery today, isn't that good news, I'll always be your friend, even so far away, and I wish you a financial freedom that few artists have, though they deserve it completely. But Gabriela's warm, lively message made l'Abeille sad, as if through Gabriela's electronic words she could smell the garden where she had slept against her in a hammock, and something else, the clean smell of her hair, as if she had come from her daily swim in the sea. Maybe they had drunk tequila, they were so thirsty in the parched midday sun, under a straw roof, before walking hand in hand to the gleaming water, which was as warm as the day. Seeing Lali getting up to whisper something in René's ear brought l'Abeille back to René's living room. Lali bent stiffly toward René, you can keep Olga, you old Romeo, you can't live without a woman, but I will give you your bath, I don't want this woman to interfere with your intimacy. Why, Lali, Olga takes care of me, Lali was stern, it's not her business, I will wash you like before when you didn't want to get out of your bed. For a woman then too, that Nathalie. René seemed to come back to life as he listened to Lali, hey, little brother, welcome to my house, I haven't seen you for so long. René didn't like her body anymore, it wasn't so long ago that she had a smooth stomach, a boyish torso, and now her body seemed deformed, she even used to love the parts she regretted weren't a man's, but that will be in another life, she thought, her belly, her vagina, her chest, everything was stiff or shriveled, she had to admit, the swell of time was mortifying, that was all, but René didn't like Olga witnessing her decrepitude, being delivered like that into Olga's hands, her invasive, impudent gaze, Madame is still beautiful, Olga said with that flustered devotion of hers, Monsieur, don't call me Madame, Olga, it's insulting me, I'm a man, you may imagine my metamorphosis as you wish. I, René, know that I am a man. And that I was born in a body that refuses to accompany me in that truth. I belong to a mendacious body, it has lied about what it is every day of my life. It would be a relaxing change to be taken care by Lali, washed and perfumed. Whenever she'd be able to come. It wouldn't be every day, since she was still working in emergency, René thought. Louise thought of Marie-France, one of the women she had interviewed for her book on women and cancer, she was a young mystic preparing to die because, she said, you had to learn to become a mystic if you were going to leave behind your whole life when you were just thirty, a husband, two young children, was there any other option, Marie-France said to Louise, yet Louise remembered that Marie-France seemed happy as she hoped for some divine consolation. Or was it merely the ultimate admission of resignation, since she had no other choice, she said. Louise was surprised that even when she had been very ill, almost on the brink of death, she had never felt that call. It was the opposite, she thought, she had only thought of her transcendent love with René, that was it, she'd thought, she would never get to feel that way again. And God stayed far away, in a cold cynical halo. It was rare for a cancer patient to experience mystical splendor, Louise thought. Sitting up taller in his antique armchair, René looked at the girls, one by one, one after the other, while the Great Sophie laid a benevolent hand on his head. I think René is going to make a speech, Polydor thought, looking at him, he's about to lecture us like in the old days, maybe I should go out for a smoke, but no, I'm fine here, I'm good, next to Mercedes. It's nice. Louise had also noticed René's suddenly pedantic expression, what's he going to tell us, what does he want to teach us, Louise wondered, and René's deep voice rang out in the room, outside the snow was heavy and at four in the afternoon the darkness was already spreading over the trees, dusk, the dark fabric of those long winter days, l'Abeille thought of her painting of the pink door, she had painted a hibiscus crown and a hummingbird, and behind the crown slept the dead dog that had been trodden and trampled, he can't feel anything, Gabriela had said, he's sleeping his forever sleep, the pink door brought l'Abeille back and she could smell the scent of Gabriela's brown skin, her eyebrows were thick like Kahlo's but her eyes sparkled, so black and clear under the arching brows, the thick, insurmountable eyebrows, her warm voice and the foreign tongue, what was left of summer in l'Abeille was there because of Gabriela, but she couldn't keep her warm now in her winter clothes, her sweater, in the apartment with René's voice so like a man's now. Friends, René said, there's a protest in Washington, in January, in a few days, I want you to continue the fight, I want you to go there for me because your rights are in danger, girls, you've got to stop just gazing at your own bellybuttons, caught up in your life and your lovers, the rights of millions of women, men, and children are at stake, you have to stand with all of them, rise up against the tremendous threat, the destroyer who's about to devastate humanity, whole countries and cities, and the rights of the poor, hard-won with blood and tears. I hate crowds, Johnie thought, but I promised Alizia I would be there, close to her, she isn't like me, she's been an activist since she was young, Johnie was reserved and refined, she couldn't imagine herself in a crowd screaming about rights, she was so uneasy at the mere thought of a crowd that it made her dizzy. Yet she had promised Alizia she would be there with her. Gérard wanted to leave René's place but she didn't, after all, maybe it was true what René said, they had to keep up the fight, and if she left who would plant flowers on graves? Who would water the flowers and the fruit in the greenhouse? I have my patients, Alizia has to understand that, they need me, Johnie thought. Listen to me, girls, René's voice was low, think of future generations, it's a women's march to call out the cowardice of that criminal, to challenge him, because the destroyer must stand down and be gone, René said, he will leave nothing but disaster in his wake, we have to speak up for women's rights, women like you, the girls here and all the others you support, we need immigration reforms, you know all this, Mercedes had been responsible for her sisters, Esperanza and Paciencia, and for her mother since the death of their alcoholic father, she went to see them every day in their big house, she took care of everything, she could never leave them, her mother wouldn't understand, especially for a political protest, Mercedes thought, even though René is right, this man could be the end of us, can we allow such a dictatorship, can we, no, his name stands for the end of the world, it's true, he could kills us all. René turned to Louise, you must be able to convince them to go to the march with you, Louise, you have to. What are we doing, Doudouline asked Polydor. We're starting again. René isn't wrong, the Great Sophie said, Johnie has had terrible visions in her dreams, we have to go to the march, I can take some of you with me in my car. But Mama, the rehearsals, Doudouline said, we can start a couple of days late, this is going to be the biggest women's march ever, the Great Sophie said, we'll be there, girls, the future is now or else we're dead, Sophie said. She had spoken. Everyone listened. The room was silent. Olga stood at the window, she had no idea what Madame René was talking about, the thunder of words struck her conscience, the end of the world, a cursed man, a dangerous demagogue, the abolition of rights, Olga's heart was torn by the intolerable words that called back the harshest wars and conflicts, and she looked out at the falling snow.

It was still snowing on the day of the women's march in Washington, a fine wet snow, René thought, or a drizzle, Lali walked René from the kitchen to the living room, holding her arm precisely and stiffly, you have to walk like this every day, Lali said, you have to get out of the bed, no more lazing around, oh no, and as René made the momentous effort to walk, one step after another, they watched the incredible, enormous march, women from all over the world, in the streets of Washington, protesting, some were wearing pink wool hats, others held signs, and maybe Alizia, Johnie's friend, was among them, was she there, shouting, destroy the destroyer, stand up for our rights, every one of the girls was there, somewhere, marching, l'Abeille had said she couldn't, she was in mourning and Sophie told her, I'll take you, little one, with Doudouline and Polydor, my secretary is getting plane tickets for the others, they were all there now, René thought, his eyes on the television set, the chain will not be broken, René thought with pride, my work will go on, look, Lali, isn't the march a success, but Lali wasn't looking at the TV, she was only thinking of René, holding her up with one arm, René who wasn't bedridden now, René was walking from the kitchen to the living room, René was alive again, with every step. Olga, who was at the window, suddenly cried out, Madame René, Countess is back. Countess strode in, shaking the snow from her fur, I told you she would come back, René said, letting in the little cat who had strayed into the snow, Olga, I told you Countess would be back.

Marie-Claire Blais was a giant of the French literary scene and a queer icon. She authored over thirty books which won her the Médicis Prize, the W.O. Mitchell Literary Prize, four Governor General's Literary Awards, and two Guggenheim Fellowships. Fans of Blais will recognize in *Nights Too Short to Dance* the community of queer characters she introduced in her celebrated novels *Les nuits de l'underground* (1978), English title *Nights in the Underground,* and *L'ange de la solitude* (1989), English title *The Angel of Solitude.* Marie-Claire Blais was born in Québec City. She spent much of her life in Key West, Florida, where she died in 2021.

Katia Grubisic is a writer, editor, and translator. Her work has appeared in Canadian and international publications. She has been a finalist for the Governor General's Literary Award for translation and the A.M. Klein Prize for Poetry, and her collection of poems *What If Red Ran Out* won the Gerald Lampert Award for best first book.